TIES THAT BIND

Emily Slate Mystery Thriller
Book 13

ALEX SIGMORE

Dark Woods Press

TIES THAT BIND: EMILY SLATE MYSTERY THRILLER BOOK 13

Copyright © 2023 by Alex Sigmore

1st Edition

ebook ISBN 978-1-957536-45-3

Print ISBN 978-1-957536-46-0

Prologue

JUST FOLLOW THE PLAN. That's what Shin said. *Follow the plan, and you'll have nothing to worry about.*

Except Xi has everything to worry about. He's the one who's here, not Shin. And he's the one who must make sure things go off without a hitch. If he does, then everything is golden. And if he doesn't…well, best not to think about that right now. The Dragons aren't known for their mercy.

After all, that was why he joined in the first place, wasn't it? To find a new purpose, to get out of that shit job paying minimum wage and finally start making some real money. Once this is over, he can get his mother the help she needs with her gout *and* make sure Jasmine isn't out screwing around with guys every night. He's told her over and over again that's a good way to get herself killed. But when she turns right around and tells him he's doing the same thing, he has a hard time arguing with her.

Xi pushes the thoughts from his mind and tries to focus on the task at hand. It's colder tonight than he'd expected, and all he has is his jacket to keep him warm, even though they're still in the van. He doesn't want to keep the engine running in case someone happens to come by. The van is just supposed to look like a car parked in the alleyway overnight. Unremarkable. That was Shin's word exactly.

If only people knew.

Though, given his fingertips going numb, Xi is starting to question that decision. He looks over at his passenger who seems no worse for wear. His arms are crossed, and his seat is back far enough that he's tucked off to the side, wedged between the seat and the side panel of the van. A hood is pulled up over his bald head, and to anyone else, he would look like he's fast asleep. Xi knows better. Haitao is like a tiger; he pounces when you least expect it. Even though he hasn't moved for the better part of half an hour, Xi knows Haitao is completely aware of everything going on around them.

Outside the van, the alley is dark, lit only by a single street-light which flickers on occasion. They'll be lucky if they get this job done before it goes out completely. Xi lets out a frustrated breath and pulls his phone from his pocket, checking the time. Three minutes to go.

"You need to calm down," Haitao says without opening his eyes. From the back of the van comes a chuckle, though it's short and cuts off abruptly when Xi turns in that direction. The third man, Yufei, is a small, high-strung son of a bitch, and Xi has never liked working with him. Shin might ignore it, but it's obvious to everyone else that Yufei is high most of the time. No one is that jittery by nature. Xi argued to keep him off this job—he's been nothing but a problem in the past. But he's Shin's second cousin or some bullshit, and that means he gets in on the jobs, no matter how incompetent he might be.

Though, there is an upside: if things go wrong, Xi will at least have a scapegoat. Even if Yufei doesn't do anything but sit in the back of the van the whole time, Xi can pin things on him if they go south. Haitao won't contradict him, and despite being related, Xi's word is more reliable than Yufei's in Shin's eyes.

At least, that's what Xi tells himself as he lets out another breath, watching the vapor disappear before his eyes. "I'll calm down once this is over. I don't like having this much product in one place. It's not a good idea."

"Are you callin' the shots?" Haitao asks.

Xi knows better than to answer the rhetorical question. Instead, he hunkers down and shoves his hands under his armpits, wishing he'd brought some gloves. He closes his eyes and can hear Yufei mumbling to himself in the back of the van, probably running his hands up and down the crates, just like he does back at the shop. Just another one of his "eccentricities" as Shin calls them.

Personally, it drives Xi nuts.

"*Raz-a-ma-taz, raz-a-ma*—"

"Shut *up!*" Xi yells before Yufei can get into his whole *raz* routine. First it starts with a few short verses, but by the end it always devolves into him singing fifty bars of some nonsense song at the top of his lungs.

"Give the kid a break," Haitao says, still not having opened his eyes.

"You want to listen to that shit, be my guest," Xi says. It may be colder outside the van, but if it will spare him from having to deal with Yufei any longer, it might be worth it.

As soon as he grabs for the handle, a pair of headlights appears at the other end of the alleyway.

"Well, look who's on time," Haitao says, sitting up and adjusting the passenger seat so it's no longer reclining. "And here I was thinking this would be a bust." Apparently his eyes hadn't been closed after all; he'd just made it look that way.

Xi stares at the headlights growing larger as the other car approaches. "Why did you think it would be a bust?"

"Too good to be true." Haitao clears his throat. Somewhere deep in there is a rattle, probably from all his years of smoking. And not just tobacco either. If it can be dried, rolled, and lit on fire, Haitao has smoked it. Xi estimates the man has maybe another five years if he's lucky. Then again, like Yufei, that's not Xi's problem. Especially not after tonight. Shin has promised him a stake and a place at the head table if all this goes according to plan. That's something neither Yufei nor Haitao will ever have. They're lackeys. Always have been, always will be.

"Shin made the deal. You don't think he'd be able to deliver?" Xi asks, deepening his voice and turning the question back on Haitao. If he's going to help run the Dragons, he'll need to command more authority. And that starts right now.

The larger man glares at him a moment before taking the handle and getting out of the car without answering him. So much for respect. No matter. In a few hours, this will all be over.

"You," Xi says, pointing to Yufei. "Stay there and shut up. You're our backup, got it?"

"Yup, no problem," Yufei says in that high-pitched voice of his while he gives Xi a salute with his left hand. Half the time, Xi can't tell if Yufei is making fun of him or if he's just that stupid. He better hope it's the latter, otherwise they'll be hell to pay, cousin of Shin or not.

Xi follows Haitao out of the car, and they both stand in front of their vehicle with their hands clasped one over the other in front of them. Xi's Glock hangs tight in the harness just under his jacket. He can have it out and aimed in less than a second if necessary. Haitao's not as fast, but he's capable. He may be something of an asshole, but Xi would rather he be out here than Yufei or any of the other idiots back at the shop. As the car ahead of them rolls to a stop, Xi can't stop thinking about what the bigger man said.

Too good to be true.

The car sits idle a moment; its quiet engine barely audible. It's a newer model BMW, one of those that's either hybrid or completely electric, Xi doesn't know which. But he does know they're expensive, which bodes well. This is going to be an expensive transaction. It's reassuring to see the other party isn't going to have a problem with funds. But the fact they're not getting out of the vehicle is beginning to raise the hairs on the back of his neck. All of a sudden, he's very aware of the light reflecting off the top of the car, the subtle smell of wet garbage coming from the dumpster on the other side of the alley. The light breeze blowing across his skin, though he's no longer cold. And the low rumble of the interstate, only about a block away. Despite the late hour, traffic is still going strong.

He fights the urge to look over at Haitao for reassurance. He's the one in charge of this situation, and he needs to be the one to *take charge*. He clears his throat and steps forward in an attempt to encourage the other party to exit their vehicle.

For a second, he thinks he might have to start banging on the hood before both front doors and one of the back doors all open at once, and three black shapes step out.

Three on three, he thinks. But they don't know Yufei is still in the back of the van. He's seen this before. It's probably an intimidation tactic, but a price has already been agreed upon. He won't renegotiate now, mostly because he knows any loss in revenue will be coming out of his cut and eliminate his place at the table.

The two dark shapes in front are both men, about the size of Haitao. Both are wearing designer suits with dark coats, and they look like they could be twins. Or at the very least, brothers. They stand as expressionless as stone statues. Xi would have to be an idiot to assume they're not packing, though he can't see the caliber of their weapons under their coats. They won't be small guns, no matter what. Could even be semi-autos.

But at the same time, he can respect these men. They're doing the same thing he and Haitao are doing: protecting their assets. Xi would have been surprised if they *hadn't* come without any kind of protection. He might have even been tempted to swindle them a bit, but he's not about to screw up

Shin's plan or his own future. Still, he can't get that creeping feeling out of the pit of his stomach, and he finds himself wanting this transaction to be over and done with already. He's done this dozens of times, but something about this feels…off. Usually, these kinds of meetings are a little less formal; everyone is on edge, but they're not *this* tense. They're not exactly relaxed, but it shouldn't feel as if one wrong move could result in bodies decorating the pavement. It's bothering him he can't read the faces of the twins behind their black sunglasses. They could be cyborgs for as much as they're moving. And they certainly aren't speaking.

The third figure steps out from behind one of the twins. She's about a half a foot shorter and dressed in all black herself with a long coat that reaches the middle of her thighs. It's cinched tight at the waist, and all Xi can see are the big buttons above and below as the woman approaches, her heels clicking on the pavement as she walks.

"You Huang?" she asks, looking at Haitao.

"Here," Xi says, gaining her attention. "I assume you're—"

"Let's not waste time." She says before he can finish. "I want to see the goods." She's stern and impatient, neither of which Xi likes about the woman. Her black hair is tied back, giving her already angular face an even sharper appearance. She wears no lipstick that he can see, but from what he can imagine, he can't help but think about what a tight little body she's got under that coat. Too bad she's a bitch, though.

Xi eyes the woman a moment. "Cash?"

She narrows her eyes, then returns to the vehicle and takes a suitcase from out of the back of the car. But she doesn't open the case, only holds it while staring expectantly at Xi.

"Get the crates," he says to Haitao, not taking his eyes off the woman and her posse.

Haitao hesitates a moment and heads to the back of the van. Xi just hopes Yufei isn't dumb enough to come out with him. Haitao can handle the crates himself, but Xi can just see Yufei coming along, trying to "help." The fact he's also armed doesn't make Xi feel much better.

Xi listens as Haitao opens the back of the van and lowers the ramp, though he keeps his eyes on the three people in front of them. None of them are expressing a single emotion; instead, they just stare forward, not even looking at *him*. The hairs on the back of his neck rise even further.

C'mon, c'mon, get the damned crate already.

A moment later Haitao returns, wheeling the crate in front of him. It's almost large enough to store a body in, but as Xi knows, it's much heavier. In fact, he wonders how the buyers are going to fit it in their vehicle. But after they make the exchange, that won't be his problem anymore. They can hire a U-Haul for all he cares.

"Open it, please," the woman says, though it comes across more like an order. Like Xi is working for her.

"First let me see the payment," he says, eyeing the case. He's also going to need to count it, but a good faith showing is the first step. They can inspect the contents of the crate while he and Haitao count. They should be large bills, so it shouldn't take long.

"Very well," the woman says. She unlocks the case, turning it in their direction and opens it. However, inside is only one measly stack with a one-dollar bill on top. There's no way that can be more than fifty bucks.

Xi leans in closer, thinking he's seeing things. "Is this some kind of joke?" he demands, his hand going for his weapon under his coat.

"No," the woman responds in that same monotone voice. But as Xi's hand wraps around the handle of the Glock under his coat, he feels three sharp punches, all to his chest. Except, they weren't punches. He looks down and can already see the bloom of crimson on his undershirt before the realization of exactly what's happened hits him. He feels his strength drain from his body as pain takes over, and he crumples to the ground. Beside him, Haitao is already on the ground, splayed out. He never even had a chance to go for his weapon. There's another sound like a cherry bomb, and Xi looks over to see Haitao with a brand-new hole in the middle of his forehead, his eyes glassy and distant. He looks up to see the woman standing over him, pointing a weapon right at his head.

He always knew this was a possibility, but he never actually believed it. He always thought there was a way out. Even now, he hopes that Yufei will step out of the back of the van and save him. *Someone* will come and save him. They have to.

But as his mind is running every scenario, terror fills his very being at the realization; his life ends here.

The woman…she smiles, then pulls the trigger.

Chapter One

So, this is what a murderer feels like.

I'm sitting on one side of a long table in a room with no windows and only one metal door. To my left is a long "mirror," but no one is fooling anyone here. Behind that mirror is a glut of recording equipment along with someone monitoring what few vital signs they can get from me without having me hooked up to anything. There's probably at least an infrared sensor back there, reading my heat signature. It might even be sensitive enough to pick up which parts of my body are hotter than normal. And right now, that would be my head because I have a raging headache that's been going for a solid hour— ever since I was brought into this room.

I take a deep breath and lean back in the chair, crossing my arms and legs while I stare up at the stucco ceiling with its two florescent lights. I know this game. I've played it on many occasions. It's just that normally, I'm the one on the other side of that door, trying to sweat out my subject by making them wait.

But I haven't been charged yet. Which means I've been able to keep all of my personal items on me, including my phone. And according to the time on the screen that I just checked a second ago, I've been in here exactly sixty-seven minutes. Just waiting. Who knows, it could be another sixty-seven until something happens. But it won't be longer than forty-eight hours, and if I have my way, it'll be a lot shorter than that. Because the entire reason I'm sitting here is ridiculous.

Ironically, I've been here before—right after I saved Avery Huxley's life and we discovered that the FBI had a mole within its ranks. I had disobeyed direct orders after all. So, I wasn't surprised when Janice hauled me in to interrogate me. I thought that night I would lose my job, and if she'd fired me, I might not have even argued with her.

But this? This is *stupid*. I shouldn't even be here.

And yet, here I sit. Counting the bumps on the ceiling.

I'm up to two-hundred-sixty-one when the door finally opens.

The man before me is tall, wearing a white button-down with suspenders holding up pressed, brown slacks. His tie is tight around his neck, indicating he's still fresh. Of course he is, he's probably been sipping coffee in the room beside this one, watching for me to make any move—any reaction that might lend credence to his agenda, whatever that might be.

"Special Agent Slate, sorry to keep you waiting," he says, closing the door behind him in a cool and calm manner. Detective Michaels strikes me as the kind of man who doesn't do anything without a purpose, and right now, he's showing me how collected he is. How *relaxed*. As if his state of being is supposed to make me angrier or at least more impatient that I've been stuck in here for over an hour at his leisure.

In one hand, he carries a brown folder file, and in the other a small Styrofoam cup. He doesn't look at me as he enters, instead heads straight for the chair opposite me and places both the folder and the cup on the table. I keep my arms crossed and stare at him, though the scent of warm coffee hits my nose, and I can't help my mouth watering just a bit.

"I'm sorry, the coffee machine in our break room is having some issues. If I hadn't already had a few sips from this one, I'd offer it to you." He indicates the cup without actually looking at me. Michaels is probably in his fifties, or maybe even early sixties. He's thin, and his skin is rough with age, small scars peppered across his clean-shaven face. A pair of glasses are folded in the pocket of his button-down, which he pulls out at the same time as he takes a seat.

"Hopefully we won't take up too much more of your time."

"Wednesdays often busy for you guys?" I ask. Though, given the size of Millridge and the surrounding counties, I doubt they have someone in this room even once a week. Millridge is a small Ohio community with a police department that can't be more than fifty hands strong.

If Michaels picks up on my sarcasm, he doesn't show it. Instead, he opens the folder, takes a quick sip from his coffee, and makes a big show of reading what's before him. As an investigator myself, I already know he's memorized everything in the file, and all of this is nothing more than a performance for my benefit. An attempt to cause some impatience on my part.

I have to give it to him; he's doing a good job because all I want to do is storm out of this place right now and call my lawyer. While FBI special agents are not above the law, we shouldn't have to sit through this little song and dance. Michaels wanted me here, I agreed. I had hoped he'd have enough respect for me to get straight to the point, but it seems I'm going to have to find out the hard way.

Detective Michaels was the man assigned to investigate the fire that destroyed my family's home. A family I didn't know I even had. Before the fire, I had received a series of letters, each more cryptic than the last. Because I was on an assignment in Louisiana when the most recent letter appeared, I asked Liam to go up and investigate it for me. Unfortunately, Liam was almost killed as someone set fire to the house while he was still inside, destroying what little evidence of my mother's family that had existed until that point.

As far as I know, the arsonist is still at large. That was what I *thought* the detective wanted to talk to me about when he called me in DC last week, asking me to return to Millridge.

Had I known I was going to end up in an interrogation room, I probably would have declined the invitation.

"As you know, we've been looking into the fire that destroyed the house at Forty-Six Crooked Brook Road. I just have a couple of questions I'd like to ask you about the house, if that's okay."

I shrug. "Not much I'm going to be able to tell you. I didn't know it existed until a month ago."

He looks up for the first time, his face unreadable, before returning his gaze to the folder. "Had you ever spent any time at the house, prior to the day it was destroyed?"

"No," I reply, pretty sure I just answered the same question twice. "Like I said, I didn't even know about it until recently."

"How did you first become aware of the house?" he asks.

"Via a letter," I tell him, "sent to my home in DC."

"A letter?" he asks. "From whom?"

"That's what I've spent the better part of three months trying to figure out," I reply. "The sender identifies themselves as my mother, however that is impossible as my mother died eighteen years ago."

"May I see this letter?" he asks.

"I don't have any of them with me," I tell him. "But I can show you a picture."

"There is more than one?"

I nod. "So far I've received five." I pull out my phone and scroll back through the pictures until I find the one I snapped of the first letter before I sent it off to the handwriting analysis unit at Quantico. "So far I haven't been able to determine who sent them." I pass the phone across the table. Michaels takes it for a moment, examining the image before passing the phone back to me.

"There's no address on this letter."

I nod. "They've been relatively cryptic."

"What is your relationship to Special Agent Liam Coll?" he asks, detouring in a new direction.

"We've been seeing each other for a few months," I tell him.

"How many months?"

"Four, give or take."

He glances down at his folder again. The edge pointing at me is raised just high enough so I can't see whatever Michaels sees. The folder could be blank for all I know. "And when did you receive the first letter?"

"About four or five months ago," I reply. "But you're not suggesting—"

"I'm not suggesting anything," he says, cutting me off. "I'm just gathering facts."

"You've been gathering facts for three weeks now," I say. "I would have hoped you'd have made some progress."

"I like to take my time with my cases. To make sure I don't miss anything." He glances up and gives me a peculiar look before returning his attention back to the folder.

He's messing with me, trying to get me to make a mistake. It takes all I have not to tell him what he can do with his case. Instead, I let out a long breath like this is the most boring conversation I've ever had. Though, that wouldn't be much of a stretch.

"How well do you know Mr. Coll?" Michaels asks.

"Well enough," I reply. In fact, I just spent a week in Virginia with his family as he was recovering from the injuries he sustained from the house fire.

"Any history of arson in his past?" Michaels asks.

"You know there isn't," I reply, deadpan. "Otherwise, he wouldn't be in the FBI."

"What about in his family?"

I grit my teeth, knowing the man is fishing. In all fairness, I'm not sure I'd put it past Liam's mother not to light something on fire if she were motivated enough. But this line of questioning just ridiculous. "Of course not. His father is a police veteran of thirty years."

"There is a statistically significant number of arsonists that come from some form of public service, whether it be working with a fire department or even part of a local police force. I'm surprised you don't know that."

"I'm sure that would have come up in the background check," I say, doing my best to maintain my calm.

He nods like it's the most obvious thing in the world, but continues to "read" the file. "I just find it curious you two began a relationship around the same time you began receiving these mysterious letters. Hadn't you considered that too much of a coincidence?"

"No," I reiterate. "Liam is not the one sending these letters. I'm one hundred percent certain."

He glares at me over the rims of his glasses just long enough to piss me off. "I'm sure you're right. But I have to follow the evidence."

"What evidence points to Liam having anything to do with this?" I ask.

"I would think that's obvious, considering he was the only person found at the scene of the crime. It also seems he knew *exactly* where to find this mysterious house, the precise address of which you claim not to have known," Michaels says. I begin to protest, but he pulls a few newspaper clippings from his file folder. There are four in total, two of which have been singed by the fire. And each of them is about *me*.

"What—"

"These were recovered at the scene," Michaels says. "I don't suppose you've seen them before."

"Of course I have," I say, staring at them. Each one accounts a previous case of mine, though they're all from different newspapers and span the past year. "I mean…I saw the AP articles when they were published. Some of these I haven't seen specifically."

"It appears that someone has an unhealthy obsession with you," Michaels replies.

"I don't know if I'd call it an *unhealthy* obsession," I begin, then realize I'm justifying the behavior of someone I don't know. I've fallen right into his trap, because now he's got me subconsciously wondering *if* Liam could have anything to do with this and needing to come to his defense before he's even made a formal accusation. "Whoever cut these out is probably the same person sending me letters. The person I've been looking for since December."

"It's funny," Michaels says. "Sometimes the thing we're looking for the most is right in front of us."

I glare at him. "It isn't Liam."

"What was Agent Coll doing near that property when it caught fire?" he asks.

"You already know that. You interviewed Liam in the hospital after the event."

"Humor me."

"He was there at my request. I was working a case in Louisiana and couldn't make the trip, so—"

He holds up a finger. "Make the trip?"

I sigh. "One of the letters told me to return to the town where my mother grew up. That I would find the answers I was looking for there."

"Uh-huh," he says, though the words are dripping with sarcasm. "But you didn't want to go."

"I told you," I say, balling my hands into fists. "I was working a case. I couldn't just pick up and leave. Liam had some free time and offered to go instead of me. If he had sent the letters, why volunteer to take my place?"

"Hard to say," Michaels replies. "Maybe he decided to change his plans, maybe something about your relationship changed, and he needed to pivot. Has anything significant happened in your relationship lately? Anything that might prompt such a change?"

The moment Liam asked me to move in with him and I rejected him pops in my head. That happened right before the last letter arrived—the one instructing me to travel to Millridge. At the time I felt blindsided by his offer—I'd been focusing on a case and wasn't even considering the possibility. But we've worked that out now, in fact, we're already planning on moving by the end of the month.

"Agent Slate?" Michaels asks.

"No, nothing," I reply.

He watches me for a moment, and for the first time in what feels like forever, I know I've been caught in a lie. He has no way to prove it, of course, but Michaels is no idiot. He knows something is going on. But if I tell him about us moving in together, he'll just string it along on his little circumstantial line of "evidence" as proof that Liam is plotting against me. When I *know* nothing could be further from the truth.

"Listen, are we done here? I have a job to get back to. If I'd known I was coming all the way back to Ohio for the third degree, I would have politely declined."

"I'm sure you're a very busy woman, Agent Slate," Michaels says. "Your accolades are of legend." He motions to the newspaper clippings in front of me. "If you don't mind, I'd like you to stay in town another day or so. I may have some follow up questions for you." I move to protest, but he speaks again before I can. "From what you've told me, sounds like you could use some time here in town yourself to investigate this...*mystery*. Mind if I clear it with your SAC?"

I want to tell him to stick it where the sun doesn't shine, but he's right. I have been itching to start my own investigation. I guess another day or two here wouldn't kill me, but it does give Michaels more time to build a strawman case against Liam. "No, go right ahead," I tell him. "I'm happy to offer whatever help I can."

"Thank you for your time today. I'll be in touch tomorrow." He makes a dismissive motion with one hand towards the door.

A few choice words get stuck in my throat as I get up and leave the confining room. I wait until I'm out in the hallway before I shake myself off, wanting to rid myself of the frustration and anger imparted by Michaels. I take a deep breath, remembering that they don't have anything—he was only fishing—and head to the lobby of the Millridge Police Station.

As soon as I pass the security door, a familiar face comes into view, smiling at me as I approach.

"So," Liam says. "How did yours go?"

Chapter Two

SITTING IN LIAM'S CAR, we stare at the small Millridge Police Station where both of us just sat for the better part of three hours. Obviously, Michaels wanted to speak with Liam first before taking a crack at me, and like any good investigator, he kept us separated until he was done so we couldn't "get our stories straight."

"This all feels like part of a practical joke," Liam says, glaring at the building.

"I wish that were the case," I reply, biting on the end of one of my nails. Immediately, I pull my hand away. I *never* bite my nails and realize the only reason I'm doing it now is because I'm stressed about what Michaels might try to dig up. I know there is nothing, obviously, but when has that stopped a nefarious investigator in the past? If he's determined to find something, who's to say he won't try to plant evidence somewhere along the way. And I doubt I can count on my boss back at HQ to back me up. Wallace and I haven't been on the best of terms lately; in fact, he was more than happy to comply with Michaels's request.

"He's just fishing," I repeat like a mantra, shoving my hand under my thigh so I can't chip away at the nail further.

"I don't think you and I had the same experience," Liam says. His voice still crackles slightly, his lungs still recovering from the smoke inhalation over a month ago. "He grilled me for a good hour before he finally let up."

"Grilled you?" I ask. "Like got up in your face?"

Liam nods. "The man is *intense*. I've worked with some hard investigators in the past, but I've never seen one that ruthless. Especially when he doesn't have a leg to stand on. He was acting like I had already been arrested and charged."

"Wow, no that wasn't my experience," I say, shifting in my seat so I don't pull my hand out again. "With me, he was more subdued. Still accusatory, but...simmering under the surface."

"Let me guess, he thinks I set the fire," Liam says.

I give him a sheepish look.

"Ugh. How many times do I have to try to explain it to him? It's like he's dead set on this theory and isn't willing to consider anything else. I tried telling him about the other woman I saw, but he just wouldn't even consider it."

"He's old school," I say, staring at the police station. I wouldn't be surprised if Michaels was watching us right now, glaring at the car between the thin blinds in one of the corner offices, his hands clasped behind his back, long shadows falling over the room. Just standing there, watching. Waiting.

"Whatever he is, he's not doing a very good job. Why on earth would I even set that fire?"

I don't mention Michaels's theory that Liam is the one sending the letters. Besides knowing that's not the case, I don't want Liam thinking I suspect anything. He'll wonder if Michaels is starting to break me, and I'm not about to let that happen. "It's not a very good theory," I say. "And it won't hold up. Not unless he invents something." I pause a moment. "Did he show you the clippings?"

"Clippings?" he asks.

I nod. "Apparently his team pulled some clippings from

the rubble that hadn't been burned. They were all stories about me."

"Those are the ones I found in the basement!" he turns, his eyes wide. "I'm actually surprised they survived. You would think newspaper would be one of the first things to burn in a fire."

He makes a good point. Still, Michaels had them, and I think it's the only thing he has to go on. "I told him about the letters. He seemed to think whoever is sending them is obsessed with me."

"It doesn't take a crack detective to figure that out," Liam quips, gritting his teeth. "And yet he won't accept there was someone else at that house? The *real* person who set the fire? It doesn't make any sense. It's like he's being intentionally obtuse."

"I agree, and I'd like to know why. But for the time being, I don't think there's a lot we can do about it. He hasn't charged you…or me for that matter. All he's done is conduct some preliminary interviews."

"But he has to know we're talking right now," Liam says. "He must have expected us to compare experiences."

"I'm sure he did," I say, though I don't know how that fits into his plan. Either Michaels is playing four-dimensional chess, or he's just throwing everything against the wall to see what sticks. Based on what I know about the man and this place, my guess would be the latter. "Maybe he's as frustrated as we are because none of this makes much sense. Why would a veteran detective and a current FBI agent set fire to a broken-down house in the middle of nowhere, Ohio? I'm sure finding those articles of me has only confused him further." I take a breath and sit back, pulling my hand out from under my thigh. "Part of me just wants to cooperate and get this over with."

Liam turns to me, his eyes wider than normal. "That doesn't sound like you."

"Aren't you sick of this?" I ask. "I've been getting these stupid letters for what, four months now? Whoever is doing this, I want them found and arrested. Obviously, they're not just going to show up and say 'Hi' like Camille did, so the more people out looking for them the better." I reach into my jacket pocket and pull out the photo Liam recovered from the house showing a black and white photo of my grandparents standing behind my six-year-old mother—my grandmother with a very obvious baby bump.

"You still think whoever is doing this is related to you?" Liam asks.

"My aunt or uncle is out there somewhere, and my bet is they are connected to all this in some way. Who else would try to pretend to be my mother? I don't know why, but it's more likely they would try to contact me than anyone else. I just need to find out who they are and what they want."

"Let's hope it's not money," Liam laughs.

"Yeah, they're going to be really disappointed if that's the case." I chuckle. "Of course, sending a bunch of cryptic letters is a bad way of asking for anything." I stare at the picture a few moments longer, studying the faces of the three occupants. I can't tell for sure, but my grandmother isn't quite smiling. I mean, there's a grin on her face, but it doesn't reach her eyes. It's like a forced happiness, like she's just pretending for the camera. My mother, however, couldn't be happier. And my grandfather looks like he's practically beaming with excitement, his hand on my grandmother's baby bump.

But grandma...now that I really look at her, it seems like she might even be worried. It could be nothing more than dreading the process, childbirth obviously isn't easy. I've never had to go through it myself, nor will I if I can help it, but I've seen it more than a few times, especially with victims who were pregnant and close to term. *Those* are particularly hard.

I'm speculating. It's just a picture, and I could be reading too much into it, but this is what I *do*. I read people for a living. And she looks like she might even be scared in some way.

"Em?" Liam asks. I look up to find him staring at me.

"Huh?"

"You okay? You look very...focused."

I screw up my features. "I'm just trying to figure out what was going through her head," I say, tapping the picture of my grandmother. "Is this new baby a happy occasion? Or an accident? And why the hell didn't I know about it?"

"You said your grandparents are dead, right?" he asks.

"Yeah, why?"

He hesitates. "Well, because when I was going through the town records before, I couldn't find death certificates for them. I searched for hours in the local courthouse, but I didn't see anything other than the property purchased in their names in the late nineteen fifties."

"What are you saying, that they're still alive?" I ask.

"Well, your mom didn't tell you about her brother or sister, right? So, what if what she said about her parents wasn't true either?"

"I..." The urge to argue that my mother would *never* lie to me is so strong that I almost let it slip through my lips. But he's right. Not telling me about her sibling was a lie of omission... what if what she said about my grandparents wasn't true either? What if they're still alive in this town somewhere? "I don't know."

"Maybe we can still find more information. They had to have known *someone* in town, right?"

"You'd think so," I say, though I'm still stuck on the fact that now I might not be able to trust anything my mother ever told me. I only had her for twelve years, but she had been my rock. As much as I loved my father, I never connected with him in the same way I did with my mom. Maybe that's typical for girls, we just relate to our maternal parent better. Or maybe it was just me, I don't know. But she was the most caring, the most loving person I've ever known. In the past, I've been accused of being too soft...of giving people too much leeway, often by burly agents looking to establish some sort of authority over the "girl" in the group. But I know my empathy is a strength, and it comes directly from my mother. She never had a harsh word for anyone, especially someone who was struggling. Instead, she would put herself in their shoes and see their challenges as her own.

People generally are always trying their best, Emily. But sometimes we all mess up. Try not to judge someone by their worst day. Instead, look for ways to help.

"We can do some digging," Liam says. "Even if they're not alive, there are still some people around who might have known them."

"Maybe. There has to be a record of them somewhere." I pause. "It's funny. Michaels encouraged me to begin my own investigation while we were here. I think he's planning on keeping us around for a few days."

"You mean he wants you to do his work for him." Liam rolls his eyes.

I give him a knowing look. "I think he just wants me to keep busy and out of his way. And if I happen to find something useful, I'm sure he wouldn't balk at it."

Liam turns the car's engine over. "So, what are we waiting for? The less time I'm around this station, the better. Where do we start?"

I furrow my brow. "You said you've already looked into the property records."

He nods. "And met probably the only nice person in this town. Amos, the town record-keeper. About ninety years old but still had a bit of spryness to him. He and I spent a lot of time together."

I nod. "We'll head back there if we need to. But I want to start with the local hospital. The same one that took care of you for your lungs. I want to find out who it is I'm looking for here," I say, tapping the photo of the baby bump again. "The hospital should have birth records, and based on how old my mother looks here, I don't think we should have too much trouble finding the baby's name."

His face darkens before he puts the car into gear. "Other than Amos, people in this town don't take kindly to strangers. I just wouldn't expect people to give you very many straight answers."

"How so?" I ask.

"Michaels isn't an outlier. When I was here trying to find the house in the first place...let's just say I had my work cut out for me."

"That's okay." I shoot him a wink. "I can be persuasive when I want to."

He grins. "Nice to see Zara is rubbing off on you." Taking his foot off the brake, we pull out of the parking lot.

I chuckle. "Just don't let her know. I don't want it going to her head."

Chapter Three

As we head to Hickory County Hospital, I can't help but feel a strange sense of déjà vu. The last time I made this trip, I was in a mad rush from the airport, trying to get to the hospital as quick as possible to check on Liam. This time, he's sitting right beside me almost a hundred percent healed. I remember doing everything I could during that drive not to let my thoughts manifest into that dark place that can sometimes take over when I'm not careful.

Given my history and how many people I've lost in my life, I have a hard time remembering that not everything is doom and gloom all the time when it comes to the people I love. Which means I also have to remember not every minute is consumed by a life and death situation. Sometimes life can be normal, where it's just me and him and neither of us are in mortal danger.

I look over at him as he drives, grateful that he wasn't hurt worse. I reach out, and he takes my hand in his, smiling. It's the small moments like these that I need to cherish.

When we reach the hospital, I find I'm not as anxious as I was at the police station. Some of that is probably proximity, and some of it is on purpose. I *really* don't want to go back for another round with Michaels. Not to mention I think it would be a colossal waste of time. I'd much prefer to focus on finding out whatever I can about my unknown relative. Strange that the answer could have been under my nose this entire time.

"Ugh, my mouth feels like cotton," Liam says, shutting off the engine.

"Bad memories?" I ask, smirking.

"Yeah, the kind you don't get rid of easily. They had me numbed for half the time I was in there so they could keep that tube in my throat. That's not a sensation I'm going to forget anytime soon."

"I dunno," I say. "I could always find Doctor Riley and ask him for a follow-up."

"And in that case, you'd be finding your own ride back to DC," he replies, getting out of the car at the same time I do.

"Don't worry, I won't make you stay in there any longer than necessary." I lead the way to the front doors, which slide open as we approach. Inside the main lobby is the same desk where I accosted the poor nurse last time, looking for Liam. Fortunately, a different nurse is on duty today.

"Good afternoon. We're looking for your records department," I tell her, showing her my badge. "I'm Special Agent Emily Slate and this is Special Agent Coll, with the FBI."

She looks up, but barely acknowledges us. Instead, she points with the rubber end of the pencil she's holding past me, down the hall. "Records will be the fourth door on the right. Buzz the door and someone will be with you."

"Thank you," I say. We head down the hall, which is in the opposite direction of the critical care unit where Liam was being held before. "See? Completely different part of the building. You'll be fine."

He just scoffs under his breath but follows along until we reach the fourth door on the right. The sign on the door says Authorized Personnel Only, though there is a small buzzer on the right side beside the handle.

For the first time, I feel a little nervous as I press the buzzer. Whatever is inside could hold the key to what's been happening to me the past few months. It might even tell me how to find what little family I may have left.

After waiting a minute and nothing happening, I ring the bell again. Then again, looking over at Liam, who just shrugs. "Maybe they're at lunch."

I grimace, then give the door one of my trademark "police knocks" as Zara calls them. The door rattles in its frame. I wait twenty seconds and am about to do it again when the latch clicks and the door swings open, revealing a middle-aged man with dark wild hair, thick black glasses, and a white lab coat on. He looks like a young version of a mad scientist and even has a collection of pens in his jacket pocket. A badge hanging from the other pocket identifies him as Dr. Shawn Walls. "*What?*" he yells, glaring at both of us.

Wow, Liam wasn't kidding when he said people in this town weren't very friendly. I show Doctor Walls my badge and calmly smile at him. "Good afternoon. I'm Agent Slate with the FBI here to take a look at the hospital records. Are you in charge here?"

"Of course not, do I look like a clerk?" he asks, his voice sharp.

"I'm sorry," a young woman says, trotting up to us. "I'm Melanie Kingsley, head of the records department." She turns to Walls. "I think I found the file you were looking for, Doctor. Back at the station where we were working?"

Walls gives us what I can only describe as a look of disgust as he turns and heads back inside the expansive room. "I'm sorry for him," Kingsley says. "He's been researching all morning and isn't making a lot of progress. I've been doing my best to help him. Doctor Walls is one of our best ortho-pedic surgeons."

"Hopefully we won't be as much trouble," I say. "We're looking for a birth record. It would have been around nineteen-sixty-seven to nineteen sixty-nine." My mother was born in nineteen sixty-two, and she looked about six in the picture, but a two-year margin of error won't hurt.

"I'm afraid you're going to have to be more specific than that," she says, giving us a hesitant smile. "There were a lot of babies born over that time period."

"The last name would have been Brooks," Liam says. "The mother was Janet and the father was Bill—William." I give him a look and he shrugs. "I spent a lot of time researching."

"Oh, good," she says, her face visibly relaxing. "Sometimes people come in here with the most obscure requests and they can be...difficult." She makes a small motion with her head in Doctor Walls's direction.

I know better than to ask what he's looking for, which would be a HIPAA violation, but I give her a knowing smile anyway.

"Here, come in," she says, closing the door behind us, the magnetic lock clicking on this side. "We can go through one of the computers." She leads us to a terminal in a line of four identical terminals, all on a desk in the middle of the room. There are more terminals along the back of the room, which has two more older, wooden doors. "We digitized most of our records back in the early two thousands," she says, logging in to the first computer on the table. "Though, there are some which were too damaged or too difficult to read. We keep those stored back in the rooms behind us in the event they might be useful."

"Glad to hear you've taken that step," I say. "A lot of places are still trying to play catchup."

"Thankfully the doctors run a tight ship here," she says. "We have some of the newest and best equipment for a hospital of our size in the entire state." She lowers her voice. "Even though they can be a pain in the ass, doctors like Doctor Walls really do care about this place." She motions to the doctor who has his face glued to the screen on the other side of the room. He's taken a seat and seems to have calmed down. I hope he's found what he's looking for.

"Okay," Kingsley says. "Brooks, between sixty-seven and sixty-nine. Let me see. Do you know the sex of the child assigned at birth?"

"No idea unfortunately," I say. I also have to consider the possibility the child was never carried to term. Maybe that's what had been in that expression on my grandmother's face. Maybe she knew there was something wrong with the pregnancy and was trying to put on a brave face. And if that's the case, my mother never lied to me at all.

I'm just starting to think I might have gotten this whole thing wrong when Kingsley pipes up again. "Here we go, I think I got it right here. Mother Janet Melissa Brooks, father William Donald Brooks, the baby was born on July fifteenth, nineteen sixty-nine."

I look over at Liam, who must see something he doesn't like on my face because his mouth turns into a frown and he mouths *what's wrong?*

I give him a subtle shake of my head and turn back to Kingsley, who is staring at the information on the screen. "What can you tell us?"

"Baby girl, approximately seven pounds, two ounces," she says. "Born at four-fifteen in the morning and by all accounts healthy on arrival."

A girl. Which means I have an aunt out there somewhere. An aunt who has been desperately trying to get my attention. But for what reason? Do you have a name?" I ask.

"Sure," she replies with a smile. "Emily Katherine Brooks."

∽

"Em, it's not that big of a deal. It's a common enough name," Liam says, following me back out the car. After gathering the information from Kingsley and retrieving a full printout of the birth record, I had to get out of there. For a minute, I felt like I couldn't breathe, like everything was collapsing in on me. But outside it isn't much better.

"It's *weird*," I yell back at him. "My mother has a sister named Emily, and she decided to use the same name for me? From a family she disowned and never talked to? A family I thought was dead? I mean, it's just…" I stop in the middle of the parking lot, trying to wrap my head around it. What could she have been thinking? Why name me after her *sister*? And did Dad know? Or was he an unwitting pawn? Did Mom just suggest the name out of thin air one day, and they happened to go with it?

Not only that, but now I have to contend with the fact that there's a very good chance the person who has been sending me these letters for the past few months is not only my aunt, is not only the sister my mother never told me about, but is also my *namesake*? How fucked up is that?

"Hey, at least she has a different middle name, right?" Liam offers.

I glare at him with enough force to bend steel, and he shrinks back, his hands up. "Just trying to help."

I rub my temples, closing my eyes. "No, I know you are. I just…ugh." I open my eyes again, holding out my hand. "Lemme see the printout again."

He hands over the printout of the birth record. There it is in black and white. *Emily K. Brooks*. Her hand and footprints are on the paper as well, though one of the handprints is slightly smeared. My guess is little Emily wasn't too happy about sticking her hands in ink and having them pressed on paper.

Everything else is just as Kingsley said. Weight, size, stats, time of birth…everything. Along with the current address of the Brookses, which just happens to be the same house that just burned down.

"What the hell is going on here?" I ask.

"I wish I knew," Liam replies. "But I'm willing to help you find out."

This is how I know he's not the one sending the letters. If there's one thing about Liam, it's that he is always helpful, sometimes to a fault. If he hesitated for even a second maybe, *maybe* I would have had cause to consider what Michaels said, but I wouldn't have wanted to give him the satisfaction. I can't wait until we find Emily or whoever is sending these letters so I can shove the facts right back in his face with a nice, big "told you so."

As I'm staring at the paper, a thought occurs to me. "Could Emily have been who you saw that day at the house?" I ask.

He shrugs again. "I mean, I guess. Though I still think she looked an awful lot like your mother."

"Well, they were sisters, right? Maybe they looked alike." Even though Emily was six years younger than my mother, I'm sure they had some family resemblance.

"Yeah, I mean, I guess that's possible," he says. "I was kinda out of it and trying not to die at the time."

I smile. "Good job at that, by the way."

"Thanks," he says, grinning back. "I worked really hard on that one."

I hand the paper back to him. "So then, do we think this is who had that little lair in the basement of the house? Where you saw the TV and desk and everything?"

"Makes sense, doesn't it? If she grew up in the home, she might have never left."

I dig my fingers into my palms. I just wish this woman would come out of the shadows so I could confront her. But if she really is the one sending the letters, she seems intent on making me come to her. Not to mention she picked the worst possible way to try and get in touch with someone. It's clear to me now that if this really is my aunt, then there is something terribly wrong with her. Maybe she suffered some kind of accident, or maybe it's genetic, I don't know. But whatever it is, it might be the reason my mother decided to cut off all contact with her family and start over with a new life. I have seen some of the darkest parts of humanity, so I know how malicious people can get. And I can imagine a couple of different scenarios that might have required such a drastic move. To think my mother had to endure something like that before leaving for good breaks my heart.

But then why name *me* after *her*?

"What are you thinking?" Liam asks.

"That this other Emily...she's dangerous," I say. "And it might not be smart to let our guard down." I have a sudden urge to call the dogsitter and check on Timber. I had to book her last minute, and I wasn't able to tell her how long we'd be gone. Normally I would have just had Zara keep an eye on him, but she's been pulling double shifts at the office the past few days, and I've barely had a chance to see, much less talk to her.

"Hey," Liam says, cautiously approaching and placing a supportive hand on my back. "This isn't Camille. Whoever this woman is, she's not an international assassin. You're a trained FBI agent; you can handle her, no matter who she is."

I appreciate the vote of confidence, but when you spend a good six months being hunted by someone determined to kill you, you tend to look at things in a different light. If this Emily wanted to contact me, to *really* get in contact with me, it would have been as easy as calling me on the phone. She obviously knows where I live. But instead, she's playing a game of some kind. And I don't know why or where it's leading me.

"How do you want to proceed?" Liam asks.

"Like we would with any other case. By gathering as much information as possible."

Chapter Four

Now that we finally have a name, I feel like it's enough to start a proper search. When Liam was here last time, he was grasping at straws. In fact, he told me himself it was dumb luck that he happened to find out about the house, that the man down at the public records office just happened to pull the right file they needed and saved him hours—possibly days —of looking.

Anxious to meet this clerk, Liam and I head back to the public records office. We know who we're looking for, so now we should be able to build a timeline of her life. There should be education records, DMV records, a social security number, and who knows what else. The more I know about her, the more likely I can predict where she's going to show up next. This time, I'm going to be ready.

Furthermore, I need to find out if my grandparents are still alive. While locating Emily is priority number one, tracking them down is a close second. If they are still living, they'll have to be in their eighties or nineties by now.

The public records building in Millridge isn't anything special, just a one-story brick building close to the town court-house in the commercial district. Millridge is one of those towns whose heyday has long since passed. All the stores downtown have been boarded up or otherwise abandoned, and the only businesses that look open are either gas stations, pawn shops, or quick-loan offices. I can imagine once it had been a bustling place full of activity, but sometime in the past few years, the town was left behind like so many other small towns in America. Big businesses come in and establish megastores close to the interstate which spells doom for a town that's built by mom-and-pop shops. Not to mention Ohio is one of the areas of the country hit hardest by the opioid epidemic. An increase in crime, lack of jobs, and an economic recession are all the ingredients you need to create a perfect storm that will annihilate a place like this.

Thankfully, the public records building isn't a victim of these kinds of forces. Somehow, the town government continues to march on. And generally, in a place like this, people don't ask too many questions. I kept waiting for Kingsley to ask us for a warrant or at least inquire about what kind of case we'd be working on that would need the birth record of a child born in the sixties, but she never did. Either she didn't care or she was too distracted by Doctor Walls to think of it. And given what Liam has told me about Amos the record clerk, it should be more of the same.

"Allow me, m'lady," Liam says, stepping in front of me to get the door. It's a large piece of oak with a detailed fresco carved into it, representing what I assume is the seal of the city. He pulls it open, and I step inside to find myself looking at a one-person desk behind a small partition. However, there isn't anyone at the desk and no sign indicating when someone will be back.

"Ummm..."

"Don't worry, it was like this last time too," Liam says, breezing past me. There's a half door in the partition which he swings open, indicating I should follow. Liam weaves his way through the corridor until we reach a set of stairs that heads down into a well-lit basement.

When I get a good look at the room, part of me feels a sense of familiarity. The room is full of rows and rows of floor-to-ceiling shelves containing nothing but files and banker's boxes. I've been in some variation of this very same room in almost every town I have a case in. Unlike the hospital, I'm guessing the town of Millridge *has not* digitized all their files yet. In fact, I don't see a computer anywhere. Which means this is going to take a while.

"Amos?" Liam calls out. "You down here?"

"Yup!" a voice yells back from somewhere in the stacks, but I can't see where. "Who izzit?"

"Liam Coll, we met a few weeks ago." He turns to me, lowering his voice. "Oh yeah, don't let him know you're with the FBI."

"Why not?" I ask, matching my voice to his.

"He doesn't like cops," Liam says.

I screw up my face. "Doesn't like—" but before I can finish the sentence, a frail-looking old man comes around one of the stacks holding a packet of papers in one arm while he supports himself with the other. He looks like he's about two steps in the grave already, given the gauntness of his face, but he wears a bright red sweater and a clean pair of slacks. I'm also surprised to see he doesn't have any glasses on, given his age.

"Mr. Coll, how are'ya?" he asks, beaming at us with a big smile. "Didn't think I'd see you again. You find that house you're looking for?" For comes out as *fur*.

"Yessir, sure did," Liam says, adopting a similar but not identical accent. I can't help but cock my head at him and give him a *what are you doing* look. He gives me a tight smile and a subtle shake of his head. "Amos, this is my girlfriend, Emily," Liam says.

Amos stops for a second, looking at me as if I was invisible to him until Liam said something. "Yeah? Izzat so? How're ya doin', Emily?" He extends a shaky hand and I take it, though I barely give it a squeeze for fear of breaking the frail digits.

"I'm…well. Liam told me a lot about you."

"Did'ee now?" Amos turns back to Liam. "Yeah, guess him and me got on pretty well last time. Lemme guess, you're here for somethin' else. Not comin' for a social call."

"Nah, wish I could say we was though," Liam says.

I wish I had a mirror so I could see my expression while Liam attempts to pull off an even *deeper* accent. In fact, I have to turn away to keep from laughing aloud and instead focus my attention to some very interesting looking boxes covered in what has to be twenty years of dust.

"Out with it, then," Amos says. "I ain't gettin' any younger. In fact, there's a good chance I might keel over any minute, so make it quick."

It takes everything I have to keep myself in check, given Amos's self-deprecating nature. At least he's not senile, that much is clear.

"We're lookin' for anyone else who might have lived in that house I was lookin' for. Particularly a young woman. Might have been the daughter of the people living there."

"Yeah, so whatcha need? Deed transfers?"

"If they exist," I say. As I'm looking at the stacks and stacks of files, a thought crosses my mind. "We could use anything the city has. Do you have old yearbooks here?"

"Sure do," he replies. "Aisle S, sections fourteen through eighteen. From the high, middle, and elementary school."

"Thanks," I say, heading off in that direction. At least the aisles are clearly marked.

"Em, don't you want—" Liam begins.

"Yeah, anything else you can find," I call back, anxious to get a look at this girl. It only takes me a minute to find the sections Amos mentioned, and I run my hands down the stacks and stacks of yearbooks, looking for the appropriate years. If she was born in nineteen-sixty-nine that means she should have been in elementary school by nineteen-seventy-five.

I pull the yearbook for seventy-five and have to wipe some dust off the top before I crack it open. The yearbook begins with the cursory images of the teachers, black and white photos of school activities, and teams before getting into the students themselves. It takes me a minute because the kids are all grouped by teacher homeroom, instead of fully alphabetical. But I find her. In Mrs. Clemons's kindergarten class of seventy-five. Emily Brooks, beaming in her picture.

I stare at the girl a moment, looking for any trace of my mother in her face. I pull out the picture Liam snagged from the house and place it right beside the picture of Emily. There's maybe *some* resemblance between my mother and my aunt at the same age, but not much. Not enough for me to even be sure they're related.

Furrowing my brow, I pull the next three books and look her up in subsequent years, seeing her grow before my eyes. Her hair looks to be a dirty blonde, though my mother's was auburn. And as young Emily comes into her face a little more, my mother's cheeks give her face some familiarity, but that's about it. By the time I get to her high school pictures, I can see the woman she will become, but her features are sharper and more angular than my mother, whom Dad always said resembled a cherub. I think he meant it as a compliment, though I'm not sure Mom ever took it that way.

But looking at the picture of Emily Brooks as a freshman in high school, I find it unlikely that anyone could confuse her and my mother. They just don't look very much alike.

When I pull the next yearbook, looking for her sophomore picture and hopefully some indication of where her plans might take her post high school, I can't find any mention of her at all. I go back to the freshman yearbook and find Emily was a member of the school's volleyball team and is present in the team pictures, but in the sophomore yearbook, she's nowhere to be found.

Gritting my teeth, I move on to the junior yearbook, but there's no mention of her in it either. Even though I suspect the same, I check the senior yearbook, and again, there is nothing. I set the book aside, deflated. What happened to her?

At some point while I've been searching through all these books, I've ended up sitting on the ground and hadn't realized it. Yearbooks are scattered around me, and I doubt very much that Amos would appreciate me leaving everything like this. I flip back through and snap a picture of Emily at each age before getting everything back in order.

Something must have happened between her freshman and sophomore years, between nineteen-eighty-three and eighty-four. Maybe she transferred schools or moved to a different town. My mother had been out of high school a couple of years by then and could have already moved to Washington. Or possibly Emily wasn't enamored with school and ran away. But then came back to live in her childhood home? I guess that's possible, though it's going to make finding anything else about the woman a lot more difficult.

"Any luck?" I ask, coming up on Liam and Amos as they're going through what look like DMV records.

"Nothing yet," Liam says. "You said she was born in sixty-nine, right? So, there should be some record of a driver's license here from eighty-four or eighty-five."

"I don't think you're going to find it," I say, explaining what I found in the yearbooks.

Amos puts his hands on his hips, thinking it over. "If she was a runaway, ain't gonna be no records here."

Liam must see the look of dejection on my face because he immediately brightens. "Let's keep looking. Maybe she just…I dunno. Obviously she came back at some point, right?"

"I guess," I say. Where before I was confident we could create an entire backstory for this woman, now I'm not feeling very sure. "Let's start with all the newspapers from that time. Maybe there's something about her going missing or leaving town. I don't know what happened to her, but that would be the most logical place to start." I turn to Amos, staring at him expectantly.

He pinches his weathered features before speaking. "That'll be a job I'm 'fraid. All the papers are on microfiche in that cabinet over there." He points to a large wall-to-wall cabinet along the back. "Every issue from eighteen-ninety-six until two-thousand-eight when the paper went under."

He's right. We don't have a tight timeframe. She could have left anytime between when the freshman pictures were taken for the yearbook and when the following year's book was published. That's going to cover at least twelve to maybe even sixteen months of daily newspapers.

"Please tell me you have one more than one microfiche viewer," Liam says.

"Nope, jus' the one," Amos says, pointing to some old library desks on the side of the room. "I'll get it and dust it off for you."

Liam and I exchange a groan.

Chapter Five

GOD, it's like the damn autobahn around here, Zara Foley thinks as she picks up the pace, walking just fast enough not to be considered running. She's been a part of the FBI's Violent Crime Unit for almost a full year now, and she's *never* been this busy, not even when she was prepping to go undercover to face Simon Magus. There was a time when she thought she might never work in this department again, that she was better suited to Intelligence, but Emily convinced her otherwise. As much as she hates to admit it, her friend was right. Zara loves this kind of work, but despises trying to squeeze so much in all at once. The past few weeks have been busier than ever, thanks to all the additional work they've been saddled with. She'd much rather take her time and do a proper investigation.

But since late February, something big has been brewing in DC, and her entire unit has been working their asses off trying to figure out what. It seems like major players of the drug underworld are moving the pieces around, but no one can figure out why or for what ultimate purpose.

And now she's going to be late for a meeting with the head

of the Violent Gang Forces. Not a great way to make a first impression.

As the glass conference room comes into view, Zara can see that almost everyone else from her department is already there, along with her boss and a bunch of other people she doesn't know yet. She gets to the doors as quick as she can, tapping on them lightly before Nadia Kane, one of her coworkers, notices and comes to open the secured door for her.

"Thanks," Zara whispers as they both return to seats that have been set up auditorium-style in the room, everyone's attention directed at her boss, Fletcher Wallace, standing with another woman, presumably the head of the VGF.

"—be working hand-in-hand with Agent Cervantes's division," Wallace is saying, though Zara missed the first part of it. "I'll let her go through the specifics with you, but just be aware the deputy director has given this operation the highest priority. We know we've already been putting in the extra hours on this one, but now I'm going to ask you to put your other cases aside for the moment and work exclusively with Cervantes's team. This is priority one."

Damn, priority one, Zara thinks. It must be something serious. She just hopes they don't need anyone to go undercover.

Wallace steps aside, allowing the other woman—presumably Cervantes—to take center stage. She's tall, maybe six-foot-two based on Zara's estimation, with her dark hair pulled back and clipped at the base of her neck. She gives off the aura of a woman on a mission—one who doesn't invite comment or criticism based on how tightly she's holding herself.

"Good afternoon, and thank you for being here," she says. For a moment, Zara thinks Cervantes might take the opportunity to glare at Zara for being late, but Cervantes doesn't even seem to notice her. "First of all, I'd like to personally thank

SAC Wallace and your entire department for the help you've given us so far. I hate to ask for more, but that's exactly what I'm here for. As you all probably know, there are five major criminal organizations in the greater Washington DC area, all with their own specialties and territories. It's our job at the VGF to monitor these gangs for criminal activity and threats to the general public. Unfortunately, as some of you already know, over the past few weeks there have been some monumental shifts in the power structures of these groups. I don't know about you, but when criminals start making major moves, I get nervous." She steps aside and clicks the remote in her hand, which brings up a map of DC divided into five colored screens.

"La Luna Roja, the White Hand, the Jefferson Kings, the Steel Dragons, and finally, but less consequentially, the Toscani family." She points to each color as she says a name. Zara's stomach does a little flutter when she mentions the Toscanis. She's had a few run-ins with them in the past while working cases with Emily. They used to be a powerful mob but lost a lot of that power when the head of their family, Marco Toscani, was caught and imprisoned for racketeering. The family has been headed by his nephew, Santino, ever since, but never regained the power or influence it had when Marco had been in charge.

"Each of these organizations is involved in a criminal enterprise of some kind, and it's our job to keep them in check. To take them down if we can. Many of you know it was my team responsible for putting Marco Toscani behind bars, thus greatly reducing the influence of the family on the city." She takes a deep breath and sighs. "But unfortunately, as you can see by the map here, shrinking the size of one criminal organization only encourages the others to grow in its place. As a consequence, both the Jefferson Kings and the White Hand have both increased their presence in areas that used to exclusively belong to the Toscanis."

She clicks her remote again and the image changes to a different map with two big red stars on it. "Over the past month, members of your team have been working with us to track the movements of associates of each of these organizations. We've been working under the assumption for a long time that when the Toscani operation was disrupted, it could potentially cause fallout as the others jockeyed for power in the city. And while the response wasn't immediate, we've been seeing a lot more movement lately. Thanks to your team, our people in the field have managed to keep tabs on and arrest some very high-profile members of these groups."

She pauses, looking around the room again. "So why am I here today? Because six days ago, two members of the White Hand were found gunned down in the warehouse district. Usually, this wouldn't be anything out of the ordinary, gang members are killed all the time. *However*, not more than forty-eight hours ago, two members of the Steel Dragons were also found dead in the exact same manner. Gunned down in an alleyway in the garment district." She clicks the remote one more time. Four faces appear behind her, pictures of the four gang members with pale faces and eyes closed in a bright, white room. Each of them has a bullet hole in the middle of their heads.

Nadia leans over. "Coroner pictures are always so clinical, don't you think?"

"Aren't they supposed to be?" Zara whispers.

"I know, that's what I like about them," she replies. "Clearly a close range, small caliber weapon."

Zara can't help but smile. Ever since Nadia Kane and her partner Elliott Sandel came into their department, Zara has felt like less of an outsider. She's always been a little quirky, but that had never been a trait encouraged by her parents, so when she came into the FBI, she'd sequestered herself away in Intelligence where she could just do her work and not have to talk to anybody.

But then Emily convinced her to apply for field work. While it was great when she was working with Emily, it was a lot harder when she was on her own. The addition of Kane and Sandel to the team have really helped Zara become more comfortable with herself because both of them have their own eccentricities, just like her.

"We believe that one of these organizations is attempting a power grab. The problem is, we don't know which one as none of our agents on the ground have been able to uncover a master plan. This is where you come in."

Zara's heart rate picks up. She can't be seriously about to ask them to go undercover, can she?

"We need your team's assistance in investigating the person making these moves and determining their ultimate goal. I don't have to tell you the death of four low-level gangsters doesn't bother me one bit. I have no trouble sleeping at night knowing that four more criminals are off the streets. What *does* keep me awake is the person pulling the strings behind the scenes. This was orchestrated, and we need to find the culprit before they strike again. Word in this town travels fast, and as soon as the other gangs figure out what's going on, it could be an all-out war out there." She turns to Wallace with a grim expression. "Thankfully, your boss was gracious enough to allow me to borrow you until we can get this buttoned up. I know this will impact your normal duties but trust me when I say that if we don't get a lid on this thing quick, a lot of people are going to be caught in the crossfire." She raises a hand. "Anyone remember the LA riots in the early nineties? Imagine that, but in our nation's capital."

Zara grimaces. She was born a few years after the riots happened. She might not have witnessed them personally, but she knows enough about their legacy that she doesn't want something like that ever happening again. Especially not in this day and age when so many people are on a hair-trigger. A spark like that could end up burning the city down.

Someone across from her and Nadia raises their hand but doesn't wait to be called on. "Why not just call in the National Guard now? It's not like people aren't used a military presence here."

"The idea is to not have Humvees patrolling the streets and causing a general panic," Cervantes says. "We need to figure out who is behind this and shut them down *before* it becomes an uncontrollable problem."

Nadia leans over to Zara again. "Looks like they're bringing everyone on board for this."

Yeah, Zara thinks. *Except Emily isn't here.* And given her history with Santino Toscani in the past, wouldn't it make sense for her to be working this case too?

"Alright, that's all for now," Cervantes says. "Thank you in advance for your help. SAC Wallace will coordinate your assignments with my team. Let's find these killers and find them fast." She clicks the off the screen behind her and heads over to gather a few binders on a side table. Wallace motions for his team to head back to their offices upstairs.

"Hey," Nadia says as everyone stands a low murmur fills the room. "Didn't you and Emily work on a case with the Toscanis once?"

Zara nods. "A few times, actually. I was just thinking she should probably be here for this."

"Well, maybe Wallace plans to bring her in on it later," Nadia suggests.

Zara gives her a terse look. "Wallace sent her off to Ohio with Liam because some detective out there wanted to interview them about the house fire Liam survived. She just texted me this morning. I don't think they have any plans of coming back soon."

Nadia frowns then looks over Zara's shoulder, motioning for someone to join them. Zara turns to see Agent Elliott Sandel approaching, his face dispassionate as ever. "Hey, El, do you think it's weird Emily and Liam aren't here for this briefing?"

Elliott considers it a moment, locking his hands behind him as he often does when he's thinking. "No. Obviously Wallace can't put *everyone* on this case. Perhaps he's reserved Agents Slate and Coll for something else."

"But Emily has worked Toscani cases before," Zara says. "We both have. Wouldn't it make sense for her to be a part of this?"

"What are you implying?" he asks.

Zara takes a deep breath, eyeing Wallace across the room, who is deep in conversation with Cervantes. "I don't know. Just that ever since Simon Magus and his group, Wallace has been doing everything he can to keep Emily out of this office."

"You believe he has some ulterior motive?" Sandel asks.

"Maybe we can find out right now," Zara says, stepping around Elliott and heading for Wallace. Her boss spots her out of the corner of his eye but doesn't stop talking to Cervantes. There was a time when Zara would have been too timid to come right up to her boss like this, but those days are long in the past. After her experiences undercover, she's found she can handle a lot more these days. "Excuse me, sir?"

Wallace hesitates a moment, then turns to her. "Agent Foley. May I introduce Gemma Cervantes. Agent Cervantes, this is Agent Zara Foley, one of my best field agents."

Zara takes a second to shake Agent Cervantes's hand. "Looking forward to figuring this one out," she says.

Cervantes nods. "I've seen your name on a few reports. You do good work."

"Thank you," Zara says, not willing to be deterred. She turns back to Wallace. "Sir, are you planning on bringing Emily in on this operation? She has a lot of experience with Santino."

Wallace flinches but gathers himself quickly before smiling at Cervantes. "Agent Slate is on another assignment at the moment. I'm afraid she's unavailable."

Zara is ready to protest, but Cervantes beats her to it. "You have an agent who has dealt with Santino Toscani personally?"

Wallace nods at Zara. "Agent Foley has as well. I'm sure she can handle—"

"Agent Wallace, I don't want to tell you how to run your team, but I can assure you I'd prefer access to *everyone* who has even had a run in with one of these organizations. Anyone who can make this process go smoother, I'd welcome them on board. Is her current assignment something that can be postponed?" Cervantes is practically foaming at the mouth. This isn't the response Zara was looking for, but she'll take whatever ally she can get.

Zara notices Wallace bite his lip, his face flushing. So, he hadn't planned on bringing Emily on this case after all. Interesting. She's sure Em will be *delighted* to hear that. "I'm sure we can arrange something," he finally says. "Though, it requires me moving—"

"Excellent." Cervantes turns to Zara. "I'd like to speak with both you and Agent Slate as soon as she's available. Is there anyone else who has had personal dealings with Toscani?"

"Not that I'm aware of," Zara says.

"Very well. You two might be just what I'm looking for," she says. "Wallace, keep me in the loop." She gathers her things and heads out of the conference room before Wallace can say another word. Zara turns to head back to Nadia and Elliott when she feels a hand wrapped around her bicep.

"Agent, you try pulling something like that again and I'll snap you back so hard you'll think you never graduated Quantico. Understand?"

Zara glares at the man until he releases her arm. "Try what? All I did was ask a simple question. And I got my answer." She leaves him standing there with a frustrated look on his face.

She can't *wait* to tell Em about this.

Chapter Six

WE'RE on hour four of scanning through newspaper microfiche one by one when my phone buzzes in my pocket. I don't even bother to look at the screen. My eyes are so tired I take the chance to close them when I answer.

"Slate."

"It's Wallace. Have you spoken to Agent Foley?"

I sit up, alarmed at the tone of his voice. "No, why? What's wrong?"

He hesitates a moment, and suddenly I'm wide awake again. "No reason. Nothing's wrong. Listen, I need you to come back to DC. We've had a situation here."

"What kind of situation?" I ask.

"Look, Slate, I'm not about to give you case details over the phone. Just get back to DC as quick as you can." He's frustrated...upset even. What the hell could be going on?

"What about Liam?" I ask.

"Agent Coll stays there. I've already spoken with Detective Michaels. He has no problem with you leaving town but wants to keep Coll around a few more days for questioning."

"Sir," I protest. "He doesn't have anything. He's trying to pin this arson on Liam and is just fishing for information."

"Well, apparently he has enough to want to keep Coll around for a few more days. I'm not going to sit on the phone and argue with the man. Now if he wants to press charges, that's a different story. But for now, Coll stays there, you get back here."

"But, sir—"

"I'm not going to tell you again, Slate. That's an order." He hangs up before I can get another word in. I look up to see Liam staring at me.

"Not good news I'm guessing," he says before his own phone buzzes. "Ah, shit." He pulls it out of his pocket, placing the receiver to his ear. "Agent Liam Coll." He pauses. "Uh-huh. Yes…yes, sir. I understand. No, sir. I will." He ends the call and slips the phone back in his pocket. "I guess that settles that."

"This is ridiculous," I say, standing. "He's just doing this to punish me because he knows we're together."

"Why would he want to punish you?" Liam asks.

"Hell if I know. I can't figure Wallace out. It's like sometimes he wants me on the job, and sometimes he doesn't want me anywhere near it. Who knows what's going on in that brain of his?"

"Did he say why he needs you back in DC?"

I pull out my phone again, preparing to text Zara. "Of course not. Why would he want to be transparent? But he did say to get back as soon as possible, which means I'm booking a flight."

Liam chuckles again, shaking his head. "You just love to poke the bear, don't you?"

"Hey, he deserves it," I reply. "After what he pulled back in Stillwater, I'm done playing Ms. Nice Guy with my boss."

"I wish I could be there to help," he says. "But it looks like I'll be stuck here until Michaels either decides to charge me or finally realizes he's looking at the wrong person."

I pause in the middle of my text. "What if you come with me anyway? What can Michaels do, really? I mean, if he had the evidence, he would have charged you by now."

He cocks his head at me. "Do you think that's smart? Especially after Wallace just told me to stay here as long as Michaels needs me?"

I sigh. "Probably not. I don't want to get you on Wallace's shit list too. He obviously has it out for me, we don't need you to be in his sights as well."

"You really think he has some personal vendetta?" Liam asks.

"Like I said, I have no idea what's going on in Fletcher Wallace's brain half the time." I finish typing out my text to Zara only for the three little dots to appear from her side before I can send it.

"It's okay," he says. "I can stay here and keep looking through the newspapers. Maybe I can find something on your grandparents too. It will probably take me another day or two anyway."

"Longer than that!" Amos says, walking by briskly, holding a stack of files. He's gone again before either of us can say anything. For a ninety-year-old, he's spry.

"I don't want you to have to do that," I say. "You've already risked enough coming up here for me once. I don't want you stuck in town, doing what I should have been doing in the first place."

"I guess I could just go back to the hotel and sit on my ass," he quips, shooting me a crooked smile. "Would that be better?"

I give him a placating look. "Okay, smartass. I just mean look what happened last time. Obviously Emily, or whoever, wants *me*. And if you get in the way again, you might not be so lucky a second time."

He holds up one hand and places the other over his heart.

"I promise not to leave the stacks or the hotel. I won't even go out to eat." I give him my best *I'm not convinced* look. "Promise. And once I find out what happened to her, I'll wait for you before taking any steps, deal?"

"I guess," I say, then look down as Zara's text comes through.

Get back home. Had to force Wallace to get you on board.

"What is it?" Liam asks. I look up only to realize I'm probably making a face.

"Just…more fuel for the fire." I turn the phone around and show him the text.

"You really *are* on his shit list," he says.

I nod. "Yeah, and I've just about had enough."

Four hours after leaving Liam in Ohio, my plane touches down at Reagan National. Thankfully, I was able to book a quick trip back, but it's already dark outside by the time I get my bags. I text Tessa to let her know I'm on the way and that she can leave Timber.

I try texting Wallace in the Uber, asking if he wants me to come in tonight—after all, I don't know how serious this might be—but I don't get any response. I'm not about to wait all night for him, but I'm a little peeved he was so insistent I come back and then shuts down for the night. Whatever it was, it clearly wasn't urgent enough to need me back immediately.

It's just another one of those little things that make me think I've done something to piss him off. It's not like our relationship started off in the best of places anyway, but I've done my best to be civil with him and at times have even trusted him like I once trusted Janice.

But with Janice, there was a mutual respect I've never felt

with Wallace. He's a very analytical kind of person, which makes it hard for me to relate to him. Usually, I can figure people out if I'm around them long enough, but Wallace has always been something of an enigma, even issuing contradictory orders on occasion. How he ever took Janice's place I'll never know, but this is starting to get ridiculous.

Dismayed to have come back early for nothing—I could have just hopped the first flight in the morning and continued to help Liam look in Millridge—I head back home, and I'm in the door by eight.

Timber almost knocks me over with his happy little wags, and I give him a good rub before checking the note on the counter from Tessa. "You've already been fed, so no begging," I tell him as he looks up at me with those adorable eyes of his. Still, he does it anyway, and of course, I cave like I always do and toss him a biscuit.

At least it's nice to be back home. But…this won't be home for much longer. Liam and I will be moving in together next week as if the stacks of half-packed boxes weren't reminder enough. While this has been a good apartment, it's also had its challenges. Like the fact I was held at gunpoint in here. It will be a nice reset to start over somewhere completely new. And given I have to be out by the end of the month, I should probably take this extra time to keep packing.

But honestly, all I want to do is take a hot bath and slip into bed. Between being stuck in Millridge with Michaels breathing down my neck, finding tidbits of clues about the "other" Emily, and then being called back to work, I'm exhausted.

It takes all the strength I have left to stay awake long enough to run the bath, and by the time the water begins to grow cold, I'm half asleep already. I take Timber out one more time before both of us are snuggled up next to each other in the bed. I guess Liam and I are going to have to get a king-size bed next week. Because there's no way all three of us will fit in a queen. Still, I haven't had a lot to look forward to lately, and this is a nice change of pace.

I drift off to sleep thinking about it, a smile on my face for once.

Chapter Seven

"HEY," Zara says, pulling me aside as soon as I come through the double doors to our department.

"Hey," I say. "What's going on?" She's leading me, looking over her shoulder like she doesn't want anyone else to hear us.

"We've got a meeting with Wallace and Cervantes this morning," Zara says.

"Cervantes from the Violent Gang Force?" I ask.

She nods. "We had a briefing yesterday. Our department is supporting theirs in some sort of manhunt. I'm sure she'll go over it."

"Okay, so why are you being so cagy?" I ask. "What's the deal?"

"Wallace originally didn't want you here," she says, her voice even lower. "If I hadn't told Cervantes about your experience with the Toscanis, you'd probably still be in Ohio."

"Wait, so it was Cervantes who wanted me here, not Wallace?"

She nods. "Yeah. And he's not happy about it either. I thought I should give you a heads up."

"Man, what is this guy's problem?" I ask. "I'm just trying to do my job here. But you know, he didn't want me on the

Magus case either. But that was you, he would have had to fire me to keep me out of that room."

"I dunno," she says. "Do you think we should take it to Janice?"

I wish I could say that was the best idea. "What are we going to say? Wallace doesn't like me, so he's keeping me off key cases? That's his prerogative."

"Not if it's detrimental to the department or the FBI. The whole time I was in that briefing yesterday, I couldn't quit thinking that you should have been there. Cervantes was looking for people with direct experience with these gangs."

"Wait, is this the case you were working on when Liam and I were in Stillwater?" I ask.

She nods. "We've been helping out for a few weeks, but it looks like something big is coming. I think—"

"*Slate!*"

I turn to see Wallace standing across the bullpen, his hands on his hips. He motions for me to follow him to one of our smaller conference rooms on the far side of our department, away from where most of the agent desks are located.

"Here we go," I say under my breath as Zara and I walk side by side in that direction.

"Just wanted to give you as much heads up as possible," she says before we're in earshot of Wallace.

It's a good thing she did too, because I was already coming in a little hot from last night. Knowing that I wouldn't even be here if it weren't for Cervantes gives me a little more leverage. And I'm sick and tired of holding back.

Wallace heads into conference room two, and we follow. I note that he doesn't wait to hold the door for us. Inside, he's already taken a seat at the large conference table. There's another agent there as well, and even though she's sitting, I can tell she has a long frame. I catch sight of her name badge as she looks up.

"Agent Cervantes?" I ask, holding out my hand.

"Agent Slate, good to meet you," she says, standing as she takes my hand. Wow, she is tall. "Agent Foley, good to see you again."

Zara nods. "Happy to be back." I don't miss the look she gives Wallace, but he does, given he's turned away from us in his chair.

"Please, take a seat, both of you," Cervantes says, resuming her position. "I'm sorry to pull you off another case, Agent Slate, but we're dealing with a time-sensitive matter here, and given your and Agent Foley's experience with Santino Toscani, I thought it best to be prudent."

Zara and I take a seat across from Wallace while Cervantes remains at the head of the table. "Not a problem," I say. "It wasn't anything urgent." I turn to Wallace. "Liam says hi, by the way." Wallace's features only darken.

"Let me give you the basics," Cervantes says, oblivious to the tension in the room. She briefs me on what I assume she talked with Zara and everyone else about yesterday. It's not long, but I understand her concern.

"So, you have four dead gang members, and you're worried about a turf war with a bunch of civilians stuck in the middle," I say once she's gone over everything.

"That's about it. The crazy thing is, despite having people embedded in most of these organizations, we can't figure out who is calling the shots."

"How certain are you that it *is* one of the five factions?" I ask.

"Seventy percent, give or take. I'll be honest with you both, I can't even rule out the possibility of a *sixth* faction that's decided to make inroads into DC. But, a new faction would have made some waves along the line. And that's what I need your help with. Specifically on Santino Toscani. He's kept his nose relatively clean since his uncle was sent to prison, but this could be the beginning of a power move. You and Agent Foley have some experience, what's your assessment?"

I shoot Zara a quick look. "Honestly? Santino Toscani is a small fish in a big pond. He tries to play a big game, but from what we've seen, he's not that much of a threat."

"Except the last time we ran into him," Zara says.

I nod, conceding the point. "That's true. We were investigating the disappearance of a little girl, and one of his drivers showed up on our suspect list. He was somewhat cooperative, but he gave the distinct impression it would be the last time. We may not be your best choice; our experience definitely didn't endear us to him."

Cervantes gives us a subtle shake of her head. "No, you're exactly who I'm looking for. I want someone he knows to put pressure on him."

"Given what I know about the local power structure, the Toscanis have a rivalry with the White Hand, but don't even cross paths with the Steel Dragons. Why would he go after them?"

Cervantes sits back a moment, regarding me. "I'm impressed, Agent Slate. You know this world better than you let on. I don't suppose you'd be interested in coming over to the VGF?"

Usually, I'd say no immediately, but if I could have this woman as my boss and not Wallace, the offer would be tempting. But I don't want to leave Zara and Liam. "I appreciate the offer."

Cervantes nods. "Have you ever had any dealings with the other gangs?"

"I helped break up that kidnapping ring early last year. I think that was being financed by the Dragons, wasn't it?"

She nods. "We believe so, but haven't been able to build a solid case yet." She opens a folder in front of her. "That's right, I forgot that was you."

"I didn't handle them directly, but I've done surveillance on both the Jefferson Kings and the White Hand," Zara says, "back when I was working Intelligence."

"That's good enough for me," she replies, turning to Wallace. "Any objections?"

He hesitates a moment then seems to give up, shaking his head. "None."

"Objections to what?" I ask.

Cervantes taps the file folder in front of her a few times. "I've been going over both your records. Between the two of you, you have a higher close rate than anyone else in this office. When I say I need people on the ground, *you're* who I'm talking about."

I exchange a quick glance with Zara. "To what end? I mean, this isn't a normal investigation."

"No, it isn't," she says matter-of-factly. "It's much more important. Whoever is doing this is looking to ignite a powder keg in this city, and it's my responsibility to keep that from happening. Which is why I'm willing to give the two of you carte blanche authority here. Do a deep dive into these deaths. Perform your investigation as you see fit, and find out who is trying to start a turf war. Then, me and my people will take them down."

I shoot a terse look over at Wallace. "Are we cleared for that?"

He hesitates again, but after a stern look from Cervantes, he nods.

Full authority? As special agents, we're already allowed a certain amount of autonomy, though it seems like mine has been curtailed lately. But this would mean we would have the same authority as a supervisor in our position, and it means Zara and I can make calls in the field we normally couldn't make.

Honestly, I'm surprised Wallace has agreed to this. It's just more of his back and forth that I don't understand. "You realize that we can't guarantee success," I say, leaning forward. "We have plenty of cold cases on our desks too."

"Speak for yourself," Zara says, shooting me a sly smile. "Some of our stacks are actually small."

I'm about to remind her that's only because she hasn't been a field agent as long when Cervantes speaks up again. "Frankly, I don't care what you do, but we need to get a lid on this. Trust me when I say tensions are already riding hot in this town with the new administration taking over. The last thing we need is more chaos."

I turn to Wallace. "What about the rest of the team?"

"They'll continue to coordinate with Cervantes's people. We're ramping up everything we've been working on the past month. But this isn't without risk. By publicly investigating these deaths, you'll be putting targets on your backs, likely from whichever gang is looking to gain the most power here."

I'm not about to let a few low-level criminals scare me out of doing my job. "I think we can handle that."

"Very good," Cervantes says. "You'll be reporting to me on this one for the sake of time and clarity." Maybe I imagined it, but I feel like that comment was directed at Wallace. Cervantes may not have liked that he tried to "hide" me from her investigation.

"Anything else?" Wallace asks. Normally he's not so impatient, but I feel like he's itching to get out of here and get on with his day.

"No, I think we're done, thank you," Cervantes says. She turns to us. "You should have access to all the case files we've compiled so far. Let me know if you have any questions." She passes a business card to each of us, her cell phone number scrawled on the back.

Cervantes seems apprehensive, more than I would expect for an operation like this. Then again, maybe that's just her demeanor. But I understand the urgency. These aren't minor street gangs—they are well-organized, well-funded criminal enterprises whose reach extends beyond just DC. Igniting a firestorm here could have dire consequences.

"Thanks," I reply. "We'll get right on it."

Cervantes nods and begins to gather her things while Zara, Wallace and I stand to leave. This certainly wasn't what I was expecting when Wallace called me back from Ohio, but I'm more than happy to track down the culprit behind these murders.

It will also provide a welcome distraction from Detective Michaels and his maddening theories.

"Agent Slate," Wallace says once we're out in the hall. Both Zara and I stop, turning in the man's direction. "I need to speak with her alone," he adds, glaring at Zara.

"I'll meet you back at our desks," she tells me, then narrows her eyes at Wallace before walking away. I half expect her to throw up a pair of middle fingers in his direction, but that probably wouldn't look too good on her record.

"I want to make something very clear," Wallace says once Zara has turned the corner. "I am not in favor of this proposal. Your history of recklessness and disregard for the rules of this office make you the *last* person I would want to put in charge of this. But Agent Cervantes is running this show, so I have to give her all the resources I can manage."

There are some people who just have punchable faces, and Fletcher Wallace's face is looking like a bullseye right now. Then I remember what Doctor Frost said about unchecked anger. I think it might be time to schedule another session with him. "I'm not reckless," I say.

"You are. While you may think you have all the authority to run this investigation as you like, I'm going to be keeping a close eye on things. And if I don't like what I see—"

"I'm sorry," I say. "Are you threatening me?"

He blows me off. "Do the investigation, but keep it clean. I don't want to hear about any slip-ups, understand?"

"Oh, you mean like when the bomber you're looking for has been part of the ATF team you've partnered with from the beginning?" I ask.

I know it was a low blow, but I have been dealing with whiplash from Fletcher Wallace for the better part of three months now, and I'm sick of it. I'm sick of *him*.

"I'm warning you, agent——" he begins, his face going completely red.

"Listen to me, I'm not about to kowtow to you or anyone else. Nor am I about to break the law. I don't know what it is you have against me, but I am *done* being tossed around like I don't matter. As soon as this case is over, you can bet I'm taking this conversation up the ladder. You can only bully yourself so far in this job. Eventually, you have to face the consequences."

"Is that so?" he growls. I've never seen him so…angry before. But if he's ready to throw a punch, I'm ready to take him down.

"We done here?" I finally ask when he doesn't move. He's wound as tight as a rubber band.

"We're done."

"Good, because I have a case that needs my attention." I turn and leave the man in the hallway, half expecting a knife in my back.

Chapter Eight

WE SPEND the better part of the rest of the day going through the case files, familiarizing ourselves with all the information collected so far—some of it by Zara herself. Cervantes has given us full access, but between yesterday and today, my eyes feel like they're about to fall out of their sockets by the time six o'clock rolls around. Zara and I agree to take a pause and head back to my apartment, seeing as I need to keep packing anyway.

For the second time in two days, I'm almost knocked over by Timber as I get in the door. He's just so happy to see me I can't help but stop a minute and give him some love. Zara comes in right behind me, and the butt wagging goes off the scale.

"It's my boyfriend!" Zara yells as soon as she's in the doorway, and Timber half wiggles-half runs over to her as she holds her arms wide open, bracing for the impact. Before I can even get up from where I was petting him, he has slammed into her and is covering her with licks all while threatening to shake himself apart with happiness.

"Okay, okay," I say after they love on each other for a few minutes. "Let's get you outside before you pee all over the floor. The last thing I need is another cleaning bill before I move out." I get his leash and take him outside while Zara heads for the kitchen. By the time I bring him back in, she's got a pair of glasses out of one of the boxes I already packed and is pouring me a bourbon before hunting in the fridge for an open bottle of wine.

"Your fridge is ridiculous, Em," she says, opening the door all the way so I can see how empty it is inside.

"Yeah, well I won't be here much longer."

"Okay, fine. But where did you pack the wine?"

"I have no idea," I say, looking around. "Give one of these a shot," I say, tapping on my glass as I round the island to get Timber's dinner together.

"Ugh, no way," she says. "That's like drinking gasoline. Don't worry, I'll find 'em." She heads into the living room, looking through some of the boxes I've already packed. I'm about halfway done, but I'm going to need some serious help if I'm going to finish before move-out day.

"Hey, do you think you could help me this weekend? Assuming we're not bogged down with this case?"

"Sure," she says, her head in one of the boxes. "Here we go, found one." She pulls out a bottle of Pinot from a box I packed last week and had neglected to label. She brings the bottle over and sticks it in the freezer before grabbing a stray sharpie from the counter. Heading back over to the box she writes ALCOHOL in letters as large as the side of the box before capping the sharpie and placing it back where she found it with a big grin. "Now you won't forget."

I chuckle. "Thanks. How long for your wine to cool down?"

"About fifteen minutes," she says. "At least, that's as long as I'm willing to wait. Mama needs some relief, and I'm impatient."

"Tell me about it," I say pulling down a can of Timber's food. I measure it into his bowl and head over to his food station. I can barely get it on the ground before he's going at it like a wolf. "What do you think about this whole case?"

"The more important question is, what do you think Wallace is going to do?" I've already told her about the "advice" he gave me in the hallway earlier, but we agreed it was best not to talk about it at work. I wouldn't put it past Wallace to put a listening device somewhere on my desk without me knowing, especially after today's little tantrum.

"I don't know," I say honestly. "And right now, I can't focus on that. Whatever game he's playing, I don't want it to distract me. I've got too much else going on right now."

Zara holds up her phone with a delivery app on it. "Pizza?"

"Works for me," I say, taking a sip of my drink.

"How is Liam faring in Ohio?" she asks.

"I haven't heard much from him yet today," I say. "But I would hope he'd let me know if Michaels had called him back in for another interview."

"I can't believe he was willing to stay there," Zara says, hopping up on the edge of the island and perching herself there. "From the way you described it, it didn't sound like the most fun place."

"He's determined to find this woman he saw at the house," I reply. "Almost more than I am. "Not only because it will clear his name, but he wants to prove to Michaels he's not delusional. And it's not going to be an easy job. We had a good five hundred newspapers to go through, and when I left him yesterday, we'd only made it through about fifty of them."

She lets out a low whistle. "He really is too good."

I nod, taking another sip of my drink. "I can't believe Michaels had the gall to suggest he was the one sending the letters."

"Wait, what?" I look over to see her perched on the edge of the island like she might fall off.

"Right? Michaels suggested it was Liam himself who had

sent the letters and had been using that basement. All because he found clippings of news articles about me in the rubble."

"But that doesn't even make sense!" she yells.

"I know!"

"Ugh, fine, gimmie that," she says, indicating the bourbon bottle. I pass it to her, and she takes a swig before almost gagging and dropping it back on the counter. "That's the most ridiculous thing——" she starts before coughing a few times and clearing her throat. "——I've ever heard."

"I thought so too," I reply. "And when I pressed him on it, his argument kind of collapsed. The man has nothing of substance, and instead of looking for the real arsonist, he's fishing for fake evidence. It's all a waste of time." I stare off into the distance for a moment, thinking. "When Liam is done with the newspapers, I'm going to tell him to come home. Michaels can't keep him there indefinitely while he manufactures evidence against him."

"What about Wallace? Didn't he order Liam to stay in Ohio?" Zara asks.

"Screw Wallace. I think maybe your first instinct was right —we should have gone to Janice earlier. His behavior is getting out of control, and he needs to be stopped."

"*Finally*," she says. "I know you don't like to go to other people for your problems, but I think this is a different case. It needs to go to HR as well."

"You're probably right," I reply. "I'm just too hardheaded to see it sometimes."

"I'll drink to that," she says, hopping down from the island. "Speaking of which…"

"But it hasn't been fifteen minutes yet."

"Eh, it's enough. I need a palate cleanser after your death in a glass." She pulls the wine out of the freezer. There is a thin layer of condensation on the surface. "In the meantime, we need to figure out how we're going to navigate this…snake pit."

I nod. Going through all the files this afternoon, I didn't learn anything I didn't already know except the names and conditions of the victims. "I say we treat it like any other investigation. Start at the bottom, head to the crime scenes. The one from the Dragon killing is sure to still be relatively fresh."

"And the bodies. Did you see the wound pattern?"

I nod. "I found that interesting too. I'm assuming that's why Cervantes thinks these were all done by the same killer, but I want to take a closer look to be sure. I know Cervantes wants us to start with Toscani, but I want to make sure we're not heading in the wrong direction first." I pause before taking another sip. "Did you order the pizza yet?"

"Are you kidding? I'm *starving*."

I have to agree. It feels like I haven't eaten anything all day. Timber is already done with his food, as he usually finishes it in under a minute, and is already staring up at Zara with his big eyes. "Oh, do you want dessert, boyfriend?" she asks.

"You!" I point to her as she goes for the biscuit tin, and she freezes in place, her eyes wide. "You're the one who got him to start doing that. He never wanted dessert before you started babysitting him."

She gives me a wicked grin as she takes a single biscuit out of the container. "Was your mean ol' mama starving you? She was, wasn't she?" she coos to Timber who just laps it up. He waits until she gives him the command before taking the biscuit. "That's a good boy. That's right, Auntie Zara will spoil you forever. Yes, she will!"

"Do you know how long that's going to take to train out of him?" I demand, though I can't help but grin at how obedient he was to her.

She gives me a noncommittal shrug. "Eh. Life's short. Eat the biscuit."

I roll my eyes and drain my drink, figuring she's probably right. "Speaking of boyfriends…how's that coming along?"

"Can't talk about it," she replies.

"What? Why can't you talk about it?" I say a little too loudly. I'm starting to feel the alcohol.

She pulls her fingers across her lips. "Can't. Top secret."

"Ugh, well you have to tell me at some point, right? And not on the wedding day."

"Whoa," she says, hopping back up on the counter. "Who said anything about a wedding?"

"Aha!" I say, pointing at her. "So it's not serious yet?"

She narrows her eyes at me. "Oooo, that was sneaky. You better watch out; I'll get you back for that one." She sighs. "It's…okay. We just really haven't had a lot of time to connect since…well, since the whole bomb thing. But he keeps in touch."

"Let me guess, he's overseas working on something classified." I take the bottle and pour another drink.

"Usually, yeah," she replies. "I'm still not a hundred percent sure what he does."

I wiggle my glass at her. "You need to find someone boring. Someone who collects insects and sits around the house all day thinking up new math equations or something. At least they'd be around."

She gives me a smile, but I'm not convinced. "You mean someone like me."

"What?" I reply. "You're like the least boring person I know."

"No, I'm not. I basically sit in my apartment in my free time and play video games. And when that gets old, I work on cases all day long. I'm not exactly a catch."

"Pssh," I say, wrapping my arm around her. "You are definitely a catch. You just haven't found the right person yet. Sometimes, even when you think you've found the right person, you're still wrong." My thoughts want to go there, but

I pull them back. "Maybe Andrew will turn out to be the one after all."

She smiles again. "Who needs anyone else when I've got you?" Her eyes go wide. "That reminds me, how are you feeling about moving? We've barely had a chance to talk about it since you popped the question."

I nod, feeling like I'm trying to convince myself more than her. "Good. I think. It's just…it'll be weird living with someone again. I mean we practically live together already, but getting a place together, living under the same roof…it's different, you know?"

"Yeah, it means you have more time for *action*, right? You can set up permanent fixtures. Hang a sex swing on the back of the door. You know, make it homey."

I just about spit out my drink. "We do *not* have a sex swing."

"Maybe you should get one. I hear good things." She winks at me.

"Wait, do *you* have one?"

"Of course not, what am I gonna do, swing by myself?"

"Well, I don't know how they work! You're the one talking about hanging it on your door. How does…I mean how do you…" I bust out laughing before I can even finish the thought. My mind is flooded with mental images of naked people scrambling to fight each other off of a playground swing. Zara chuckles along with me until we're both full out belly laughing, probably mostly from the alcohol.

At some point the pizza comes, and before I know it— between me, Zara, and Timber— we've polished off the entire thing.

I needed this. A break from everything. Just a night to relax before diving headfirst into another case. Not to mention all this stuff going on in Ohio.

"Hey," Zara says, holding up her wine glass, which is almost empty. I check my tumbler and see it barely has half an ounce of liquid in it, but I raise it anyway. She clinks hers against mine. "Here's to you and Liam. I know you two are going to be very happy living together."

"Thanks," I say giving her a second clink for good measure. We both drain our glasses and flop back on the couch. "I think you're right."

Chapter Nine

ZARA ENDED up taking an Uber back to her place sometime last night. I tried to convince her it was fine if she stayed, but she's the kind of person who likes to sleep in her own bed, and I can't blame her. My days of staying over and sleeping on people's couches are over. But we did have a fun night, and for that I'm grateful. I've had too few of those in my life lately, and as I'm getting ready the following morning, I resolve to have them more often.

I end up arriving at work early, wanting to get a jump on the case. After talking with Liam this morning, I was disappointed to learn he hadn't made any progress on the "other" Emily or my grandparents. He's made his way through more than half of the newspapers for the year, and there's been no mention of a runaway or indication that anyone even knew she left.

I can't imagine a girl of that age could just pick up and leave without anyone noticing, but the eighties were a different time. Parents weren't as watchful of their children, kids had a lot more autonomy to go out and do what they wanted, and of course, no cell phones. If a kid ran away, there was virtually no way for the parents to find them. They could just be...gone. But wouldn't my grandparents have at least put out an ad in the paper looking for her? In a town that small, wouldn't there have been a story about a missing high-school student?

Then again, maybe I'm going about this all wrong. There's no evidence that says she ran away. She could have transferred to another school with my grandparents' permission, and no one would have ever made a stink about it. Or she could have graduated high school early and headed to college.

Whatever happened, something serious must have occurred between then and now, because the person sending me these cryptic letters does not seem like the same happy, carefree girl I saw in those yearbooks.

I just hope he can find *something* in Millridge. Because if he can't...we're back to square one.

Instead of heading to the office, I make a detour to the medical examiner's office first. The bodies are being held in the Bethesda wing under the supervision of Bjorn Jameson—a medical examiner I met on a previous case. That was the case I worked with Detective Rodriguez, though I try not to think about what happened to her. Every time I do, I send myself into a guilt spiral. Doctor Frost tells me I need to accept that what happened wasn't my fault, and no one could have predicted what would happen.

Still...

Jameson isn't in the office yet as it's still early, but I manage to get access from one of his colleagues who directs me to the morgue freezers. I'm going over the autopsy reports when Zara comes trudging in, dark circles under her eyes and a coffee in one hand.

"Morning," I say. "Sleep well?"

"How are you so chipper this early in the morning?" she asks. "Don't you have a headache or something?"

"Maybe a little one," I admit. I did have a couple more

drinks last night than I'd intended to. "Did you get your car yet?"

She lets out a noise I take to mean I'm an idiot for even asking before she slumps down in the chair beside me. "My head is pounding. I think I'd be a hazard if I tried to drive right now."

"Guess I get to be your chauffeur then," I say, returning to the autopsy reports on the computer. I will admit, it's a little hard for my eyes to focus this morning, but I push through. Cervantes is counting on us to get this right and I don't want to let her down.

Zara takes a sip of her coffee, rubbing her head. "Find anything yet?"

"Just got started," I say. "But this all looks standard. I'm not seeing anything here that's out of the ordinary."

"What are you looking for?"

"I don't know," I admit. "I just wanted to make sure everything was on the up-and-up. You know how sometimes these things can go sideways."

"Yeah," she says, taking another sip. "Shall we defrost the subjects?"

I nod. Even though there are pictures in the file, I want to see the bullet patterns for myself. Not because I think the medical examiner missed anything, but I've found when I can see the victims in person, I have a better understanding of what might have happened, as silly as that sounds. Sometimes images on a screen don't amount to the real thing.

Zara leaves her coffee behind and we head to the wall of freezers marked with names and IDs. Our first two bodies are in the bottom row, and we pull them out one by one.

Each victim is naked, pale, and their eyes have been closed. A large y-shaped incision runs down the middle of their sternum, indicating where the autopsy was performed.

"Tight grouping of shots," Zara points out on both victims, right in the middle of the chest.

"And one to the head, each," I say, noting the clean bullet hole dead center on each of them. "These were executions. The shots to the chest would have killed them in short order, but the shooter wasn't taking any chances."

"Richardson and Weiss," Zara says. "Local members of the White Hand."

I furrow my brow and go to the next two. When I pull them out, they're virtually identical to the first two. "Huang and Tao. Members of the Steel Dragons." Both men have been executed in the same way—tight group of shots to the chest, one to the center of the skull. "I'd say Cervantes was right. There is no way these weren't all killed by the same person."

"But is it one of the other rivals?" Zara asks.

I stare at the men for a moment. "Maybe. The reports state tire tracks were found in both areas where the men were killed, but no vehicles were left behind. So how did these guys get there in the first place?"

"Someone took off with their vehicles," Zara says.

"Which are probably scrap metal by now, but it might be worth looking at the junkyards as well, assuming we can get a description of the missing vehicles," I say. "But what were they doing when this happened? Neither was at a known hangout spot for either gang."

Zara heads back and retrieves her coffee. "Probably meeting up for a deal that went wrong," she says. "Someone got greedy."

"Or someone set them up," I say. "The White Hand deals in mostly hard drugs, right? Opioids and similar stuff. But the Steel Dragons deal in weapons. Given that we know it was the same shooter, we have to assume the killer set up both meetings."

"Okay," Zara says, taking a seat as I close the freezers. "So was the purpose of the meetings to kill the gang members or get the goods?"

"At this point, I'm not sure we can say. The goods could have just been a bonus. Cervantes seems to think this is a power play by one of the other groups...but what if it's simpler than that? What if it's a buyer who couldn't or just didn't want to pay for the deals they made?"

"It's a big risk," Zara says. "Obviously the gangs would have known who they were making a deal with, right? Wouldn't the killer be risking a lot of retribution?"

I nod. She's right. "Unless they didn't know who they were really dealing with. I know Cervantes wanted us because of our experience with the Toscanis, but I'm not sure the Toscanis had anything to do with this. While they have a rivalry with the White Hand, they don't have any relationship with the Dragons. But the Jefferson Kings *do*. They have rivalries with both organizations going back a decade or better." I join Zara back at the computers.

"I didn't see anything in the files about the Jefferson Kings," Zara says. "At least nothing other than a couple of reports from agents embedded in their organizations noting that nothing seemed off lately."

"These gangs aren't stupid...they know most of their recruits can't be trusted, not really, until they've proved themselves. I'm betting Cervantes's people haven't made it far enough up the chain to really know what's going on. We're going to have to go directly to the source."

She scoffs. "Wait, you mean just walk up to the leaders of the Jefferson Kings and *ask* them if they just ripped off two rivals? Do you *want* to get shot?"

"Well, no, maybe nothing so simple. But I don't think we're going to get a straight answer if we try anything else."

"C'mon, Em. Even if we do end up talking to someone in charge, it's not like they're just going to come out and admit they killed four people and stole all their stuff."

"That's not the point. I want them to know we're here, looking into it. That's what Cervantes brought us on board for.

To put on a very public investigation. I want to make them nervous enough that if they *did* have something to do with it, they make a mistake and show their hand."

"How so?" she asks.

"Maybe by moving some ill-gotten gains around with less care than normal. Maybe enough so that Cervantes's embedded agents catch wind of it." I sigh. "If this was any normal robbery, we could just go to the affected parties and ask for an inventory of everything that was stolen. But somehow, I doubt either gang is about to give us a detailed list of the illegal contraband they lost."

"That *would* make it easier," Zara says, draining the rest of her cup. "So, what do we need to do? Figure out where the Jefferson Kings call home?"

I nod. "Let me check with Cervantes, I'm sure her department has data on that. In the meantime, we'll head back to the office and gear up. Like you said, going in there is going to be treacherous. I want to make sure we both have as much protection as necessary."

"Aw, man," Zara whines. "I hate those body armor panels. They're so bulky—they make me look like I have a really small head."

"Better than getting killed," I say.

"Easy for you to say, they actually fit you," she replies.

"C'mon," I say, getting up. "Let's get going. The sooner the better."

She pauses. "Em, what happens if the Jefferson Kings aren't behind this? What if they didn't have anything to do with it at all?"

I consider the question for a moment. "Then I guess at the very least we can warn them. Because anyone could be next."

Chapter Ten

AFTER REACHING out to Cervantes for any additional information, she gave us access to the Jefferson Kings' full file in the FBI. It's long, and despite being under a clock, Zara and I take the time to go through the highlights. I don't know a lot about their organization as I've never really worked on the side of town the Kings operate, but the more I read, the more fascinating it all becomes.

"Hey, did you see the Kings were originally formed as a response to police brutality in the eighties?" Zara asks, looking over her computer at me.

"I guess that makes sense," I say, though I've decided not to rely fully on the FBI file. I've also taken to doing my own research on the Kings online. If we're headed into the middle of a den of vipers, I want to know exactly what I'm getting myself into. "From what I can tell, they originally began as a type of community protection guild. Not only that, but they provided outreach for at-risk youth, helped raise money for the community and provided protection whenever it was needed. Centered around the Fort Jefferson neighborhoods."

"Where are you reading that?" she asks. "I don't see that anywhere in here."

"Wikipedia," I say, grinning over the top of my screen. "Look who's schooling the computer whiz."

"I wouldn't call looking something up on Wikipedia *schooling* anyone," she replies, sarcasm tinting her voice.

"Still did it first," I call back. She really must be tired, I rarely get a leg up on Zara about anything, but I hear her furiously typing away, no doubt in an attempt to catch up.

"Well this is just great," she says. "It says here they believe all the police are corrupt and that they can only count on themselves to protect their neighborhoods. I'm going to go out on a limb and assume that means the FBI as well."

"Probably," I reply. "And honestly, I'm not surprised. Given how this country has historically treated African Americans."

"And with the White Hand being primarily Aryan and the Dragons obviously Chinese, those rivalries aren't out of the ordinary," she replies. "Maybe this is the start of a race war."

"In which case, we need to be careful. It means they have a lot more drugs and guns in their possession right now."

"Em," Zara says, and I look around the computer again. Her face is pulled back and terse. "We can't just walk into that neighborhood hoping to speak to—" she cuts off and turns back to her screen. "Intelligence says their current leader is a man named Damian Drummond, and there's no way we're going to get in and out of there alive. Not as FBI officers anyway."

I nod. "You're right, I've been looking into that. Drummond operates a club in downtown DC. And it is Friday, after all."

"Wait a second," she says, and I hear that trademark smile in her voice. "You said you'd never step foot into a club again." Before I know it, she's up and around both our desks, perched on the edge of mine. "Does this mean I get to put you in a dress again? I've got this new one that would be perfect for you, comes up to right about here." She moves her hands to the middle of her thigh. If she thinks I'm getting back in a dress that short, I might have to commit her.

"No way in hell," I say, "Don't even think about it. As much as I *love* the club experience, after what happened in Stillwater with Liam, I'm not about to step foot into a loud, noisy, overcrowded room full of drunk people again."

"Then how do you plan on using Drummond's club to—"

"Oh, trust me, I have a plan. One where you might not even have to wear a bullet-proof vest. Though you'll still want to leave the dress at home."

Her eyes light up. "This I can't wait to hear."

AT ALMOST TEN P.M., WE'RE SITTING IN MY CAR ABOUT A block from Drummond's club, aptly named *The Circuit*. Zara and I have been keeping watch, and from what I can tell, this is a happening place. There's been a constant line since about eight-thirty, stylish cars roll up every twenty minutes or so and they even have someone outside directing traffic when necessary. People have been flowing in and out all night. I imagine it has to be a madhouse in there.

"I can't believe you don't like places like this." Zara is practically fogging up my windows with anticipation.

"I can't believe you do," I tell her. "You can't even hear yourself think in there."

"I know, that's the best part," she says. "It drowns out all the extra noise and then it's just you, and the dance floor."

"And all the grabby hands, and the leering looks and the guys trying to drop stuff in your drinks…" I look up, checking the corners of the buildings. I don't know what I'm looking for, but it's partially out of habit. If we're going to pull this off, there can't be any surprises. And that means I don't want someone tipping Drummond off. Supposedly, he's in there every Friday and Saturday night, but there's no telling when he'll show up or if he's already here. And we can only wait so long.

"Okay then, Ms. Buzzkill," Zara says, crossing her arms. "I'm gonna start my own club. No guys allowed. Just loud music and dancing. None of the other stuff. Then you'll *have* to come."

I chuckle. "Women are just as capable of doing those things as guys are."

"You really know how to kill a mood," she says.

"That's my specialty," I say absently as I finish checking on all the corners. I grab the radio in the center console. "Hare Leader to Hare Two, come in."

"Hare Two here, copy."

"Double-check the second-floor windows on the building directly across the street. I can't tell for sure, but there might be a lookout up there."

"On it, Hare Leader."

Zara peers out the windshield. "I don't see anything up there."

"I thought I caught movement," I say. "Just want to be sure before we head in. Like you said, it's not like we'll be welcomed."

"Yeah, better safe than sorry," she says. We wait a moment in silence before the radio crackles again.

"Clear Hare Leader. All the rooms are empty."

"Thanks. All eyes up. Five minutes until we're live."

"What if Drummond isn't here yet?" Zara asks. "Some of these guys keep late schedules."

"And what if he isn't the kind of guy who stays out late? If he leaves, we lose our window. And I really don't want to do this again tomorrow, do you?"

"No, not really," she says.

I wait until the clock on my dash says 10:10 before grabbing the radio again. "We're going in. Clocks start now."

"Ten-four, Hare Leader," the voice on the other side says.

I look over to Zara, who gives me a reassuring nod, and we both get out of the car and head in the direction of the club.

The line stretches all the way down the block and has to be at least sixty people long, but we bypass it, heading for the front doors. There are two men taking names as we approach. Before they can say anything, I show him my badge. He hesitates a second, but apparently decides letting us in is easier than trying to argue. But now we're *really* on the clock as I have no doubt he will inform his boss who just walked into his club.

Inside, the place is jumping. Literally. Everyone is jumping to some song at the same time while the lights go crazy. The bass is so loud I can feel my teeth vibrating. I lean down to Zara. "We need to find Damian as quick as possible. As soon as you get eyes on him—"

"I know!" Zara yells. "Good luck!"

"You too," I call back, and we both head off in different directions into the club. I find myself pushing my way past people and squeezing through small openings in the crowd. I'm hoping to get to the VIP lounge where I'm more likely to find Drummond sitting at a table. He could also be in this crowd somewhere, but I haven't spotted him yet.

The worst part is I swore I'd never step into a place like this again, but here I am, two weeks later, right back in one of these Godforsaken hell holes. Maybe if this all goes south and Wallace decides to fire me, I might never have to visit one of these again.

Finally, I get through the main throng of people who are continuing to jump and yell and spill their drinks as they sweat off the stress of the week. I've just never been able to relate to people like that. Probably because I'm never really "off," so I have to take a more…tempered approach to stress relief. I would much prefer a night like last night with Zara to whatever this is.

As I'm beginning to think I've pulled the trigger too early

and Drummond isn't here, I spot him in the very back of the club. He's in a section that's been cordoned off by velvet red ropes and two more large men standing guard. Drummond—or at least what I can see of him—is seated in the very back of the circular booth with a woman on each side of him. On the table in front are some very distinct white lines of powder. While it's probably not an opioid in the traditional sense and more than likely is just cocaine, it's enough to give me probable cause, though it's not enough to prove my theory.

I pull the radio out of my pocket just as one of the bouncers spots me and his eyes go wide. "This is Hare Leader. NOW!"

The bouncer turns to say something to Drummond, just as the fire alarm in the building goes off. All the emergency doors fly open at once and the place is flooded with a combination of police and fire personnel, all yelling at the patrons to get out. I make a beeline for Drummond as I hear a second alarm go off—which wasn't part of the plan—and all of a sudden, every sprinkler in the room erupts, showering the entire place in an indoor rain.

It's uncontrolled pandemonium as people are yelling, screaming, trying to keep from getting soaked, and I see Drummond attempting to jump over the back of the booth and head for what I assume is some sort of exit. I run at the bouncers who are blocking my way. Even though no one can hear a thing over the alarms, I try yelling out, "FBI," and going for my badge, but I catch one of the bouncers look at my hand going into my coat. His eyes go wide and immediately I know he thinks I'm going for a weapon. Crossing the distance between us in a few short steps, he attempts to grab on to me, which I manage to deflect and instead deliver a roundhouse kick to his midsection, taking him down. The other bouncer already has his weapon out, but I manage to grab his hand despite the water-slick floor, sliding my finger between the trigger of the weapon and the handle. I feel him squeeze just as I manage to disarm him, but fortunately, the gun doesn't go off. I deliver a solid punch to his neck, and he collapses immediately.

With the two bouncers out of the way, I finally have a clear path to Drummond, who, instead of running, is back in the circular seat while the two women who were with him are nowhere to be seen. At first I'm confused, but when I see Zara appear from my right with her weapon trained on Drummond, I understand why he's not going anywhere.

People are still yelling and screaming behind us as the fire marshal and police escort everyone out, but someone finally shuts off the alarm. A minute later, the sprinklers cut off. I'm absolutely drenched, as is Zara, Drummond and everyone else. And officers are already putting Drummond's bouncers in handcuffs as the man himself just stares at me, his eyes burning.

"Get that one some medical attention for his neck," I tell the officer attempting to cuff the second bouncer who is still struggling to get air. "He took a hard hit."

The officer nods and helps to escort the bouncer away as the fire marshal comes up beside me. "Agent Slate."

"Chief." I nod. "Perfect timing."

"Someone pulled the sprinkler on us, but we got everyone out quickly enough." He turns to Drummond, holding out a piece of paper. "I believe you're the proprietor of this establishment. You are hereby in violation of the fire code."

Drummond screws up his face and turns to the man. "Fire code," he spits.

The Chief nods. "You had at least four hundred people in a building that's only rated for one-seventy-five. Overcrowding is a five-hundred-dollar fee. We'll also be charging whoever pulled the sprinkler alarm." He turns to me. "Assuming we can find them."

"Thanks, Chief," I say, not taking my eyes off Drummond. The Chief nods and excuses himself without another word.

"You destroyed my club for a fucking five-hundred-dollar fine?" Drummond asks.

"Oh, no," I say, stepping over the soaked velvet rope that had been knocked over in the chaos. "It's much more than that."

Chapter Eleven

DAMIAN DRUMMOND IS a big man in the sense that he probably could have been a linebacker in college. He's got to be at least two hundred and thirty pounds, and from what I could tell when he was trying to get out of the booth, is probably six-one or six-two. And it looks to me like practically all of that is muscle. He might be carrying a little extra around the gut, but I definitely wouldn't want to take a punch from the man. His hands look to be as big as my face.

Still, I'm not about to be intimidated by him. Now that he knows he can't get away, he's adopted a more relaxed posture in the booth, even going as far to extend both arms out and leaning back into the cushions, even though they have to be absolutely drenched.

Personally, I don't mind getting wet, but the sprinklers probably dropped three inches of water in under a minute. The water is already starting to send chills up my body. Still, I remain steadfast and don't let Drummond see a second of weakness in my eyes. Zara is positioned to my right where she'd emerged, cutting off Drummond's method of escape.

"So?" he asks, holding his hands up without moving his arms. "We gonna do this or what?" The citation from the fire marshal sits on the table in front of him, all the cocaine I saw earlier now washed away. But if Drummond thinks this is a drug bust, he's in for a big surprise.

"Mr. Drummond, I'm Special Agent Slate with the FBI. This is Agent Foley."

"Yeah, so does that mean the FBI is going to pay for fucking up my club?"

I shoot him a look. "You heard the fire marshal. This place was overcrowded. That's a clear violation, besides, we didn't set off the sprinklers. Any repairs will be your own responsibility."

"That's bullshit and you know it. Every club is over-crowded. It ain't just us," he says.

"Guess you just got unlucky," I say.

"Yeah, big surprise," he replies. "Seems like my people *get unlucky* a lot. Just how it goes."

I didn't mean to get into a political argument here; I need to pivot quick if I'm going to get anything out of Drummond. "Mr. Drummond, we don't care about your club. We're here because of the recent hits on the White Hand and the Steel Dragons."

He grins, showing me a set of jewels embedded in his teeth. "Heard about that. It's a shame, ain't it?"

"Did your organization have anything to do with it?"

"No," he says, still grinning. I didn't expect anything less, but I don't like how confident he is when he says that. Even though I know he's not upset about what happened to two of his rivals, I was hoping I'd get a better read on him. "We done here?"

"As much as I'm sure you'd like that, we have a few more questions. If you weren't responsible for those killings, who was?"

"How should I know?" he asks, holding up his hands again, though his smile fades somewhat. "Ain't my business."

"And yet, the Jefferson Kings are bitter rivals with both

organizations," I say, crossing my arms. "If it wasn't you, someone did you a big favor."

He shrugs. "Guess they did. But I didn't tell 'em to."

"Aren't you worried about retribution?" Zara asks. "If we could put two and two together, I'm sure the other gangs will too."

Drummond smiles again. "What have I got to worry about? We protect our own down here. Don't nobody get in unless I say so."

I look around. "Except us, it seems." His smile immediately disappears. "I'd think you'd be taking this a little more seriously. Because if you weren't behind these deaths, then it means you're potentially in the crosshairs of whoever is."

"Like I said," Drummond growls. "We can take care of ourselves. We don't need no fancy cops coming around *offering* help." He motions to the club around us. "You've already done enough."

"Except we *will* get involved," I tell him, "when the turf war begins. Do you think all this is just going to go away? What would you do if you knew either one of those groups was responsible for the death of your men?"

He finally sits forward, his face stern. "Look, I know you think you're big and bad, coming down here and beating up my guys. And you," he says, motioning to Zara. "You kept me in my place. But that's only because I'm not about to kill two cops—"

"Agents," I remind him.

"—*cops* out here with so many witnesses. You try this shit down in Fort Jefferson, see what happens."

"That's exactly why we're here, and not there. But threatening the lives of two FBI agents isn't the best play, don't you think? Not when you're looking like a good mark for both sets of murders."

"*Goddamn pigs*," he says under his breath. "Listen sweetheart, I've already had to deal with a load of shit from both of those assholes. You think I like meeting with people who don't even think I qualify as a person? No, but I don't want a war either. So guess what, I've been out there doing your job for you, keeping the peace, and you repay me by coming in here and costing me thousands of dollars in damages. Now how am I supposed to respond when you accost me?"

"You've already met with the Dragons and the Hand?" I ask.

"Didn't have a choice," he replies. "Unless I wanted to wake up to find my house firebombed. Look, we all may hate each other, but at least we have enough mutual respect to stay out of each other's way. What business do I have getting into Aryan bullshit? Or Dragon? They deal in drugs and guns, neither of which we care about."

I give him a skeptical look. "You're telling me if you fell into a trunk full of weapons, you'd just throw them away?"

"'Course not, I ain't stupid. But I'm not about to risk starting a war over them either. We got plenty of money for weapons, and no shortage of them anyway. And we don't sell. They're for community protection only."

"Uh-huh," I say. "Like your friend there who tried to shoot me a few moments ago."

"He didn't know who you were," Drummond says, leaning back again. "Simple mistake. I'm sure you've shot people you haven't 'meant' to. I see it all the time."

"I'm not sure that's how a judge will see it."

He gives me a condescending look. "Somehow, I think you're probably right. Seems like they never do see it that way, do they?"

I have to give it to him; Drummond has a big chip on his shoulder, and I'm sure it's deserved. But I'm not sure how much I can trust what he's saying. "Even after all this, you don't believe either organization will retaliate?"

"Why would they, we didn't do anything," he replies. "I know you don't believe it, but it's the truth." He opens his arms wide, looking up as he speaks. "This whole operation is one big ecosystem. If one of us tries to overstep, it doesn't just fuck me, it fucks *everybody*."

"You really expect us to believe you all just live in some kind of harmonic balance?" Zara asks, incredulous.

"What can I say? We're progressive. This is the twenty-first century. It doesn't do me any good to be the last man standing if there's nobody else left. We've had a beef with Hand and Dragons in the past, but they don't come into our neighborhoods anymore, and we don't go into theirs. That's all I want. I ain't out there lookin' to be the next kingpin or Scarface." He grins again. "Live and let live, I say."

"Someone obviously doesn't feel that way," I tell him. "And more than likely if it's not you, then you could be next."

He waves me off. "My people aren't little bitches like those other guys. Anyone comes up on us is in for a world of hurt."

I pause a few moments, pretending to examine the destruction all around us. I'm cold, wet, and I'm not getting very far with Mr. Drummond. And while I knew we probably wouldn't, it's still frustrating to get more male posturing than answers. Drummond is an asshole, that much is for sure, and I don't trust him for a minute. I'm reasonably confident this "meeting" he's talking about either didn't happen, or it was much more...intense than he's describing. He can't be stupid enough to think just one meeting with his two biggest enemies is all it will take to prevent them from raining hellfire down on him. But if that's about to happen, we would least have some warning from our agents on the ground.

"Okay, Mr. Drummond, just a few more questions and we'll be done," I say. "I'm going to need the whereabouts of both you and all your...enforcers on the nights March twenty-third and March tenth. As soon as you can provide that, we'll be out of your hair."

"Yeah, I ain't giving you shit without a warrant," he replies. "Not to mention I should sue your asses for all this."

"If that's how you want to play it…" I begin, though I know I don't have much of a leg to stand on. I've done what we've come to do, getting any additional information now would be a bonus, but isn't necessary. I just hope we've applied enough pressure for Drummond to start moving some things around, including any recently ill-gotten gains. Then again there's always the possibility the Kings really didn't have anything to do with the murders, in which case all I've done is waste everyone's time.

"Yeah, I think that is how I'll play it," he says. "Now get the fuck out of my club."

Zara and I exchange a look before heading out, our shoes making sick squelching sounds as we leave.

Chapter Twelve

"I'D SAY there's only about a twenty percent chance he won't sue the FBI," Zara says, leaning back in her chair back in our office. After the events of last night, we decided to call it since we were both soaked and there was little good in taking any more shots at Drummond or the Kings. I think we made our point. Now we just have to wait and see if anything comes of it.

"If nothing else, it was a pretty bold move," Nadia says. She and Elliott have joined us this morning back in the office. I thought it might be a good idea to get a couple more opinions, and since both Nadia and Elliott have been helping to track the gangs over the past few weeks, they were the perfect candidates. Not to mention they are some of the only people in the office I actually trust. When they first transferred in a few months ago, I wasn't so sure, but after everything we've been through, I'd be hard pressed not to trust them at this point.

"I guess," I say, leaning back in my own seat and staring at the ceiling. I have an urge to find an old number two pencil and throw it up to see if it will stick, just like I used to do back in middle school.

"You effectively destroyed his club," Elliott says, his tone completely emotionless per usual. "As moves go, it's hard to think of something more...intense."

"It was pretty cool," Zara says. "Emily coordinated with the Bethesda police and fire departments to bust in all at once. We just hadn't counted on someone pulling the sprinkler alarm too. We actually planned on keeping the damage to a minimum."

"I certainly didn't need *another* reason to antagonize him," I say. "The man was hostile enough already."

"From what I know about Drummond, he sees himself as more of a community leader than the head of a criminal enterprise," Nadia says. "He'll want to downplay what happened at the club in favor of all the churches his organization helps support. I don't think you have anything to worry about."

"How do you know all that?" I ask.

"They assigned me to Drummond back when we first started working this case. I've been following his moves, watching where he goes and where he doesn't. He spends a lot of time in church. Trust me, those people love him. He won't want to make a big deal out of the club."

I fold my hands behind my head, still staring up. "I guess gangs just aren't what they used to be. At least they're not like they were when I was growing up."

"That's what happens when you get old," Zara says.

"Yeah? I wouldn't be talking. Guess who has a birthday coming up?"

Nadia turns to Zara. "When is it?"

Zara rolls her eyes. "Not until November. Emily is just grumpy that I have almost an entire year her."

"I have a question," Elliott says, seeming to come out of nowhere. When he first transferred here, he started out more bullheaded and strong-willed. I don't know if he was trying to prove something, but after Simon Magus attacked three cities on the East Coast back in January when he was in charge, Elliott seems to have become more reserved. At least, the two of us haven't butted heads nearly as much, and I've warmed up to him. But sometimes, he does seem to change the conversation just out of the blue. "Why not just go to Toscani directly? Isn't that what Cervantes brought you on board for?"

I pitch my chair back forward. "Part of the reason we went after Drummond was because he has rivalries with both gangs that were hit. Toscani doesn't."

"The bigger problem is," Zara says. "No one seems to know where he is. Emily and I looked into it yesterday before the raid just in case things didn't pan out. Neither one of us could find anything on his current whereabouts. He's been out of town for weeks and hasn't been seen since."

"That doesn't mean he's not out there, directing other people to do his dirty work for him, but until he pops up, we have to proceed without him," I add.

Elliott nods thoughtfully. "So you've decided to start with the most likely suspects. That makes sense."

"Yep. Like I said, there's probably a fifty-fifty chance anything will come of it. But if they aren't responsible, at least they have a little warning in case whoever came after the others comes for them."

"I'm sure Damian Drummond wasn't very appreciative of the heads up."

"*That's* putting it mildly," Zara says, doing revolutions in her chair. She's got her legs up so that she can spin around quicker.

"So, what's your next move?" Nadia asks. "If it's not the Kings—"

"That leaves Toscani, La Luna Roja, or some unknown player in the game," I say. "La Luna has a mild rivalry with the Dragons, but nothing as deep as the Kings. And the Toscanis are rivals with the Aryans and La Luna, so if they're responsible, why go after the Dragons?" I rub my eyes, tilting back again. "It's like trying to solve a puzzle from the inside out."

"Why not ask the victims themselves?" Elliott offers.

"First of all, I don't consider anyone who tattoos a swastika on themselves a victim," I say. "I'm not about to go to the White Hand and ask them who they think did it because they'll just point the finger at whoever they hate most right now. I don't need them thinking we're a tool to take out their competition."

"And the Dragons?" he asks.

"Probably a better chance of getting a real answer…but still, odds are about as good as with the Kings."

"The Dragons might know of anyone else looking to muscle in on the territory," Elliott replies. "The reason I bring it up is because I have a contact."

Nadia turns to him. "You do?"

"A man who was an informant for me a few years back. He helped us take down a small smuggling ring before his children were killed in retribution. He joined the Dragons shortly after, and I haven't spoken to him since."

I stare at him incredulously. "And this is the person you think you can trust to give us solid information?"

"He's an honorable man, I believe that," Elliott says. "He might provide a foot in the door. A chance for you to speak with them on even terms."

Zara's stopped spinning long enough for me to shoot her a look. "Cervantes has people embedded, I'm sure we could—"

"But that could risk their covers," Nadia says. "And if it doesn't work, you're no worse off."

It would be helpful to have a way in to the Dragons so we don't have to pull something as drastic as we did with Drummond. But I still don't know how reliable the information will be. These are professional criminals after all. Their entire lives are built on lies and subterfuge. "How will we know if whatever information they give us will be accurate?"

"That's the problem with informants, sometimes they lie," Elliott says. "I don't know if my contact is willing to provide anything useful, but I would have been remiss in not mentioning it."

"It's worth a shot, I suppose." I toss a balled-up sticky note at Zara. "You ready to get your hands dirty again?"

"Just so long as I stay dry this time," she replies.

"I HATE DÉJÀ VU," I SAY, STARING UP AT THE TWO-STORY building in front of us. It's an unassuming commercial building down in the garment district, not far from where the two Dragons were murdered.

"Whaddya mean?" Zara asks. She places a stick of gum in her mouth as she asks.

"I mean, this is going to be exactly like last night. We're going into a loud club with lots of music, lights, drinking, and assholes to get a pile of nothing in return." I say. "These guys are all alike. They love to show off their fancy clothes, cars, watches. Why can't we ever meet anyone in a library?"

She stares up at the building, arching an eyebrow while she chews. "Doesn't look much like Drummond's place to me. There's not even a line outside."

She's right, but I still don't want to go inside. "I'm not even sure this is going to work."

"Stop being such a grump. It's where Elliott's contact wanted to meet us," she replies.

I check my watch. It's a quarter 'till nine. Almost twenty-four hours after we raided Drummond's place. I guess the good news is we haven't felt any blowback on that yet. Maybe Nadia was right and Drummond won't want to make a big deal about it.

"Fine, I guess we might as well get it over with."

"That's the spirit," she says, popping her gum one more

time before taking it out and tossing it in the nearest sewer grate. "C'mon, let's go try not to get killed."

"Can't wait." I follow her to the main doors, which are locked. Undeterred, Zara heads around the side where there's another smaller service door. She tries this one, finding it unlocked, and heads inside. I follow and find myself in something of an antechamber with her, with another steel door in front of us. It sports one of those sliding metal portals at the top. I'm preparing to ask her if we should knock when the panel on the other side slides open and a pair of eyes stare out at us.

"What?"

"We're here to see Zhao," she says.

The metal door slides closed, and I hear a latch thrown on the other side. Zara smiles at me as the metal door swings inward.

The first thing I see is a tall man dressed all in black sporting a semi-automatic Uzi that's strapped over his shoulder. Another man, presumably the one who opened the door, stands off to the side. "Any weapons stay here," he says.

"No deal," I reply.

"Then you don't get in," the man with the Uzi says.

I pull out my badge and show it to him.

"We know you're FBI," he says. "Weapons stay here or leave."

I exchange a glance with Zara. My weapon never leaves my side, but she seems to think there's something we can use here. Maybe she's right, and I should just trust her. She has faith in Elliott. I should as well.

Begrudgingly, I remove my pistol from the holster under my arm and place it in the glass box as indicated by the man with the Uzi. Zara does the same. The other man closes and seals the door behind us.

"This way," the man with the Uzi says and we follow him down a short hallway to a metal detector. We both remove our badges and anything else with metal out of our pockets before passing through. Thankfully the machine doesn't ping, and he hands us our items back before leading us up a flight of stairs, which takes a sharp right. Just past the turn at the top are a pair of metal doors which require a keycard to open. He pulls one out from his belt which is on a retractable wire and swipes it, turning the pad green.

"Enjoy," he says, opening the door for us.

I'm prepared to be blasted back by more heavy bass, but I'm pleasantly surprised to find only a soft classical number drifting through the air. The room itself is clad in dark woods with gold highlights and red accents all over the place. There are about a dozen tables set up, five people around each, all playing different versions of games. Some are playing with cards, others with mahjong tiles and some with dice and what looks like a piece of paper with different animals stamped on it. The air has the hint of smoke and something else, and I catch a few people smoking cigarettes or…other things.

"Oh, shit," Zara says. "Em."

"Yep." Illegal gambling operation.

My first instinct is to call Wallace. Then I remember. We have full authority here. I don't have to report it to anyone. But that just doesn't sit right with me. We *have* to report it; there's no way we can sweep something this big under the rug. Even though we'll be signing our own death warrants when we do.

A few heads turn to look at us, but most people, the dealers included, pay no attention. Guards stand at each of the entrances and exits, all with the same issue Uzi as the man who brought us in here. Two FBI agents, alone and unarmed, in a room full of criminals and killers. No way out without a firefight. I *really* hope Elliott knows what he's doing.

"Why would Zhao want to meet here?" Zara asks. "He's just exposed this entire place."

"Maybe he doesn't expect us to leave here alive," I tell her.

"What do we do?"

I'm frozen, trying to figure out how to handle this. The fact no one seems to even care we're here bothers me. It bothers me a lot. When two FBI agents walk through the front doors, people should scatter in a place like this. But they're all just going about their business, quietly playing their games.

Finally, I see one of the men with an Uzi approach. I brace myself; this could have all been nothing but a setup—a way to take out two nosy agents. We should have brought Kane and Sandel for backup.

"Mr. Zhao is at the bar," the man says in a heavy accent, then indicates the large wooden bar along the end of the room. "He invites you to join him."

"What the fuuu—" Zara says as we follow him to the bar. We're already here, right?

In for a penny, as they say.

Chapter Thirteen

THE MAN NAMED ZHAO—or at least who I presume is Zhao as he's the only one at the bar—is dressed in a tailored suit that probably cost what I make in half a year. His dark hair is perfectly styled, and he can't be older than thirty. Maybe even younger. He wears dark sunglasses that he removes as we get closer, and I'm struck by how green his eyes are. They complement his skin tone, and I notice his tie has specks of green in it, adding a nice touch.

"Agents Slate and Foley," he says with a perfect English accent, standing and shaking both our hands. "I am Jun Zhao. Join me, won't you?" He offers two seats along the bar. I let Zara take the closer one to him; I'm her backup on this one.

"You're Elliott's contact?" Zara asks.

Jun chuckles. "Not what you were expecting?"

"The man Elliott described to us was…less poised," I say.

"Too true," he replies. "Back when I worked with Elliott, before all this," he motions to the room behind us, "I was in a bad way. But whoever said money doesn't buy happiness was clearly broke." He motions to the bartender for three orders. Of what, I have no idea. "Thank you for meeting me here. It's my favorite bar in the city, and they do a tequila sunrise like nowhere else."

"Mr. Zhao—"

"Please, call me Jun," he says.

"Jun—I hope you understand we can't just…" I look out at the room of gamblers, going about their business. "I mean, this is a major operation. By bringing us here—"

"I've potentially exposed a massive illegal gambling operation, is that it?" he asks.

I give Zara a worried look. The man doesn't seem fazed at all. "Yes, that's correct."

"Allow me to direct your attention over there," he says, pointing to a framed plaque on the wall.

I furrow my brow and get up, going over to read the document. Zara appears beside me, and we scan it together. I turn to Jun when I'm halfway through. "This building has been annexed by the Chinese Consulate? Is that even legal?"

He smiles.

As I scan the words, I can barely believe what I'm seeing. This took an act of *Congress*. They approved this building as an official extension of the local Chinese Embassy in Van Ness. And apparently, it's been that way since two-thousand-sixteen. "How did we not know about this?" I ask Zara.

"I'm not sure anyone knows about this," she replies.

"As you can see, we are under Chinese jurisdiction now, so we are not breaking any local laws," he says, motioning to the room again.

"But I thought gambling was illegal in China," I reply.

"Ah, one of the benefits of our…fluid nature here. I hope once we finish our business, you might stay for a game or two. I'd be happy to stake you. No risk."

"Maybe another time, we're on the clock," Zara says, shooting me a glance. I don't think either of us can exactly believe what we're seeing. This is just a broken-down old building in the middle of the city. No one pays any attention to it. And, as I think about it, I guess that's the idea. Hide in plain sight, as they say.

The bartender delivers three tequila sunrises, placing one in front of each of us as we take our seats again. "I hope your jobs aren't so strict you can't share a drink with me," Jun says, taking his by the stem.

We probably shouldn't, but I get the distinct feeling that Jun isn't about to tell us anything unless we play this little game with him. He wants to be the host, to make sure we have a good time. Zara shoots me a strained look, and I shoot her one right back. This is why it's fortunate we're on this together. Thankfully, we've learned to read each other over the past year, and it's developed into something of a shorthand. She's thinking the same thing I am.

"One drink," she says, taking her glass as well.

"Excellent," Jun replies. "Take a sip and tell me that's not the best sunrise you've had in your life."

I finally give in and take a sip from mine as well, and I'm pleasantly surprised to find he's right. It's delicious. I tend to stay away from tequila, but the sharpness isn't there, just the subtle warmth. A drink like this is *dangerous*.

"Jun," Zara says after blinking a few times too many. I hope it isn't too strong for her. This is a lot stronger than her usual wines or the occasional cosmo. "We're here because of what happened to members of your…"

"Gang?" He smiles, taking another drink and relishing it for a moment. "It's alright, you can say it. We're under no pretense here. And remember, you're on Chinese soil. American laws don't apply."

My ass they don't, I think but manage not to say aloud.

"Yes, it's a terrible tragedy," he continues. "Have you made any progress in finding the killer?"

"That's what we wanted to ask you about," she says. "Who would want to kill your people?"

Jun examines his drink again, thinking. Or, at least,

pretending to think. "There are the usual suspects, of course. The Kings. And the Lunas. I'm sure you've spoken with them."

"It's on our list," I say.

"Not really their style though. Damian isn't much of a cold-blooded killer and Felix...well, Felix is ruthless as you know. But he doesn't generally go for unprovoked attacks. He'll retaliate with the fire of a thousand burning suns, but he's no instigator. No, I believe it is the work of someone else."

Unfortunately, I don't know much about Felix, who I assume heads La Luna Roja. From what I know about them, they can be cold-blooded and merciless, and I'd hoped to stay off their radar until absolutely necessary. But he's right, the Lunas don't typically initiate. And it wouldn't make sense for them to go after the Hand either unless there's a new rivalry we don't know about.

"Who do you think is behind it?" Zara asks.

"I don't know, but I haven't seen work like that before. At least, not in a while. A couple of months ago, my people ran into a contract killer. A very interesting woman with blonde hair who had a unique accent. I was thinking—"

"She's dead," I say without hesitation before taking another sip of my drink. It really is delicious, and I need the distraction from thinking too much about Camille.

"Ah, very well. She was my first guess, given how clean the kills were."

He's right. But Camille didn't waste bullets. She wouldn't put three in the chest then one in the head unless necessary. She'd just go for the head every time.

"Since you've already lost it, and no longer have posses-sion, I'm curious what was taken," Zara says.

Jun smiles at her, and I think he knows he's on shaky ground. Even though we're not technically in America, that protection will only go so far. Finally, he drains the rest of his drink. "Unfortunately, we lost a two-thousand-nineteen

Mercedes Sprinter Van. Dark blue in color. I can also provide a license plate if that will help."

"And what exactly was in this van?" I ask.

He holds up both hands, his face innocent as can be. "Nothing, as far as I know. I believe it to be a carjacking that went very, very wrong." He's over-enunciating every word, clear in what he's implying. They lost a shit-ton of weapons they illegally imported into the country, and now they have no idea where they are. Not only that, but they didn't even get paid for them.

"I don't suppose you have any witnesses to the crime," I say.

"Well, there was one other man in the van when they left to…go out for the night."

I furrow my brow. "Another man?"

He nods. "Named Yufei. He was…how do I put this delicately? Well, he was an idiot."

"Was?"

"He is dead," Jun says. "We found his body about a mile and a half from where the van was taken."

"And you removed it?" Zara asks.

Jun grimaces. "Yufei was related to Shin, who runs our organization as you know. Shin didn't want his cousin's remains…taken by the authorities. It's a personal matter."

"Can you elaborate on that?" Zara asks.

"No. As I said, it's a bit sensitive because of his relationship to—"

"Or the fact there was something in Yufei's bloodstream you didn't want anyone to find," I say, knowing the accusation will probably only make things worse. "Removing a dead body from the scene of a crime is not a small offense."

"Agents, I am attempting to be completely transparent with you here. I could have kept quiet and you would never have known about Yufei at all."

"So why say something in the first place?" Zara asks.

"To let you know that I am trying to be helpful," he says. "We want to catch these killers as much as you do. Yufei was just an unfortunate consequence of a bad situation."

"You don't seem too upset about it," Zara says.

He purses his lips. "Maybe I should be, and maybe that's cruel. But I didn't like him very much. However, Xi and Haitao were my friends. They were good men who didn't deserve to die."

I hold my tongue again. It's always hard to judge the morality of criminals. No, they probably didn't *deserve* to die, but how much suffering did they cause by being part of this criminal organization? The Dragons aren't a bunch of puppy dogs, despite what Jun would like us to believe. Their trade is weapons. How many people have died because one of the weapons they illegally imported wound up in the wrong hands? And because they aren't registered, have no serial numbers. Anyone investigating those deaths would have a very difficult time tracking down the culprit.

"Since you're being open with us, I don't suppose you know who might be behind the killings?" I ask.

"There has been talk of a new faction moving into town, but unfortunately, I don't have any information on them. We know nothing because we've heard nothing."

Not exactly helpful. "Anything else?"

Jun gives us a noncommittal shrug. "I wish I could be of more assistance. Can I get either of you another drink?" My glass is still half full, and Zara has barely touched hers.

"No, but thank you for meeting with us," Zara says. "We'll do our best to recover your lost vehicle."

"I'd much appreciate that," he replies, grabbing a nearby napkin and producing a Montblanc pen from his inside jacket pocket. On the napkin, he writes down the license number of what I assume is the missing van before handing it to Zara. "I don't suppose you'll be staying for that game."

"We really need to get back to it," I tell him. "But thank you for the invitation."

He raises his drink to us. "It's open anytime. And tell Elliott I said hello. He and I should catch up as well."

From the way Elliott made it sound, he and Jun weren't on good terms. In fact, he was skeptical Jun would even take his call. But from the way Jun is acting, they're old besties. Then again, I'm not inclined to believe a word of what this man has said.

Zara and I stand, only to find another one of the guards close to us. "If you'll come with me." He leads us back to the same doors we came through and we go back downstairs and through the metal detectors, this time setting them off because we still have our badges and phones on us. Our weapons are returned to us at the entrance, and we're escorted back out into the alleyway. It's such a stark difference from inside of the building that I can hardly believe we only took a dozen steps instead of crossing a dozen miles.

"Well that was a bust," Zara says. "Sorry, I thought he might really have something."

"We had to check it out, and maybe he was telling the truth about this mysterious new faction as much as I'm not inclined to believe it." We head back over to the car, and even though I didn't have very much, I can feel the alcohol in my system. That was some strong tequila. I can't imagine what might have happened if we'd ended up drinking the entire thing.

"What now?" Zara asks as I pull away from the curb and head back toward the mall.

"Unless you want to go back to the office, I think we need to call it for the night," I say. "Your car is still at my place; I can just head there."

"Aw, c'mon. It's Saturday night. Can't I interest you in a nightcap somewhere? The Roxy? I know how much you love getting up on stage." She gives me a soft elbow.

"No, I really need to get back. I was supposed to finish packing today because we're supposed to have everything out next week. Now I'll have to do it all tomorrow."

"Want some help?" she asks.

"Sure, I'd—" I'm cut off by the immediate flash of bright lights and squealing tires. I barely have enough time to see the car coming up on my left, fast. It barrels down on us, and I swerve to avoid being sideswiped. The car blares its horn as it passes before correcting itself and going back into its lane.

"Six-John-Nine-Ocean-Four-Four…Zebra…I think," Zara says, squinting as the car speeds away.

My heart is hammering in my chest. "What the hell was that?"

"Drunk driver," she says. "Wanna go after them?"

"Call it in to the local police," I say, feeling more rattled than I should. Thank God for my reflexes. "It was an older car. A Pontiac maybe?"

"Yeah, I'm not sure," she replies. "I don't know cars that are two decades older than me." She picks up the in-car radio and calls it in to the local PD, giving them our location. They'll put a BOLO out on the vehicle and hopefully stop it for reckless endangerment. Part of me has an urge to stop it ourselves, but I really don't feel like getting into a high-speed chase in the middle of DC on a Saturday night. There are pedestrians everywhere, and you never know what could go wrong. But I also don't like the idea of letting a drunk driver roam the streets.

"Em, you're shaking," Zara says.

I look down at my hands and see she's right. Something like that shouldn't have spooked me this bad, but I feel like I've just escaped a near-death experience in the span of five seconds. "Yeah…I, I think I'm still wired from the casino."

She puts her hand on my shoulder. "Do you want me to drive? I can get us back home. No nightcap."

"No, it's okay," I say, taking a deep breath, trying to reset myself. I'm stronger than this, and I'm going to get us back home. "I got this."

But as we head back in the direction of my apartment, my heart just won't slow down.

Chapter Fourteen

"YOU'RE COMING BACK?" I ask, the phone up to one ear as I stuff coffee mugs into a brown box. It feels like I've been doing this for an hour. Why on Earth do I have so many fucking coffee mugs?

"Yep, Michaels finally said I could leave," Liam replies. "Well, I kind of had to drag it out of him, but I think he's admitting defeat. I should be back home this afternoon."

"Great, you can come help me pack," I tell him. "I'm still a day behind."

"As much as I'd love to, *I* have to pack," he replies. "Both of us are moving out of our places, remember?"

Right. Between his injury and the time we had to spend in Ohio, Liam hasn't been at home much. As soon as we came back from Stillwater, we managed to find a place that would suit both our needs. The only catch was we had to take it at the beginning of the month, which at the time, was only two weeks away. Now it's less than one. We've both had to scramble to get everything together in time, and being called to Ohio didn't help matters any.

"How much can you have? Really? I've seen your place, it's mostly bare."

"You didn't see the closets," he replies. "I'm a secret packrat."

"Whatever," I say, giving up on the coffee mugs and instead deciding to donate the ones I haven't packed up already. "If that's true we're going to have a problem. I need a clean house."

"I'd love to hear your definition of clean, considering *I've* seen your bedroom."

"The bedroom doesn't count," I reply, grinning.

"So, what you're saying is we each get one trash room."

I get that longing in my gut which tells me we've been away from each other too long. Damn, I didn't realize just how much I missed him until this very moment. "I can't wait to see you."

His voice softens. "I can't wait to see you either. I'll stop by on my way back in town. It's only about a five hour drive. And bonus, if you're done packing by then you get to come help *me*."

I look around at the apartment, with most everything I own still out where it's always been. "Yeah, no promises on that one." I pause a moment. "I'm guessing you didn't find anything in the records about Emily Brooks or my grandparents."

There's a pause on the other end of the line. "I'm really sorry, Em. I looked through everything I could. Amos and I got through all the newspapers and all the town's DMV records. Nothing on any of them. It's like they just...disappeared."

"Damn," I say, plopping down on one of the stools that's beside my kitchen island. Timber looks up from his bed, whining. "I thought for sure there'd be something there. Something more than a few yearbooks, anyway."

"We'll find her," he says. "I know we will. You haven't gotten any more letters, have you?"

"No...nothing yet," I say, staring at my door as if I could

see through it to the mail hanger outside. The letters had been arriving with some regularity, but no more after the fifth. Maybe after burning down the house, my aunt lost everything, including her ability to send the letters. It's not much of a theory, but it's something.

"Em, you still there?" he asks.

"Yeah, just…distracted," I tell him. "Be careful on your way back home. See you this afternoon?"

"Count on it," he replies. "Love you."

"I love you too," I say before hanging up. I let out a long breath and set the phone on the counter. At least that's one monkey off our backs. Detective Michaels must have finally concluded he didn't have anything on Liam. Either that or he couldn't reasonably keep him in Millridge anymore. Whatever the reason, I doubt either of us will be going back there anytime soon.

Timber lays his head back down but is still looking up at me. I smile and slide off the chair and sit down beside him. "I'm okay, bud. It's just a lot right now, you know?" I rub his head and behind his ears, and his little foot kicks out every time I hit the right spot. His coat is short and soft, though I can feel his tummy is a little larger than last time I checked. "Uh oh, looks like Auntie Zara is trying to get you into trouble. We're gonna have to cut back on the cookies, okay?"

At the word "cookie," he stops everything and looks at me intently, halfway getting up.

"Whoa, okay either that or you and I are going to need to start going on runs together again. How does that sound?" When it becomes apparent I'm not going to give him a cookie, he relaxes back down and enjoys the rubs and scratches. But a second later he jumps up, almost knocking me over and runs to the door, his nose inches from it.

Just as I'm getting up, the doorbell rings. Wow, the dog has uncanny senses. It still blows my mind that Camille ever got past him.

I open the door to find Zara and Nadia standing on the other side, Zara holding a cradle of coffee cups in one hand. "Good morning!" she says. "We're here, ready to pack."

"Thanks for coming," I say, opening the door for both of them. "I really appreciate the last-minute help. I thought about just hiring people to pack for me, but—"

"That's just a waste of money," Nadia says, coming all the way in and looking around. "Wow, I don't think I've seen your place before." She looks down at Timber who is in the middle of his regular round of love from Zara. "I forgot you had a dog; I *love* dogs."

"He's *very* lovable," Zara says, then takes Timber's face in her hands, squishing all his skin together. "Aren't you, boyfriend?"

Timber's butt is going at about a hundred miles per hour, his short little tail wagging as hard as it possibly can. Nadia bends down and starts rubbing his back, and I think he's probably going to explode from all the attention.

"I'm glad someone is here to provide the entertainment," I say. "This for me?" I indicate one of the cups that Zara set on the counter.

"The one marked Lilly," she says. "I told them Emily, but they never get it right."

I shoot her a look, then take the cup. It's still hot and just the way I like it. "You could have made a good career as a barista."

"Didn't make it, just picked it up," Zara says, heading into the kitchen. "So how's it going? You're already done, right? So we can all go out for mimosas and brunch?"

"I wish. I gave up on the coffee mugs."

She peers into the cabinet where I store them all. "You have *a lot* of mugs."

"I know, and I don't even know where they all came from. I think they sit in there and multiply." The coffee is doing wonders for my system. Liam's news deflated me, but this is doing a lot to help.

"This should be easy," Nadia says, her hands on her hips as she looks around the room. Other than my birthday party a few months ago, I think this is the first time she and I have done anything social outside the office. It's actually kind of strange to have more than one other person in my apartment at the same time.

"Did Elliott bail?" I ask, though I didn't even really expect Nadia to come. When I told Zara I needed help, I didn't realize she'd be out recruiting.

"He had a family matter come up," she says. "But really, I think he's more concerned about your meeting with Zhao last night."

"That *was* weird," Zara says, perching herself on one of my stools. "I couldn't figure out his game."

"Neither could I." I take another sip of the coffee and head over to one of the empty boxes beside the mantle. Now that Timber has had his moment, he's made it back over to his water dish where he's furiously lapping, getting water all over the kitchen floor.

"Elliott doesn't like it when people don't make sense," Nadia says. "It gets under his skin."

"I think that's something we all have in common," I say.

"Okay," Zara says, clapping her hands. "Let's get to it. The quicker we get this done, the quicker I can get some eggs benedict with a side of screwdriver."

"Ugh, at this time of morning?" I ask.

"It's Sunday, it doesn't count," she says before sticking her tongue out at me. "Where do you want me to start?"

"Umm…"

Nadia takes charge. "Zara, you start in the kitchen. Wrap every glass and plate with newspaper or foam pads. Stack them neatly. Emily, you head back to the bedroom and work there. I'm guessing you want to take care of that stuff yourself."

"Well, yeah I guess——"

"I'll start here in the living room with the largest items I can fit in boxes first, then working my way down to the smaller ones. I will do my best to keep everything grouped as it is now, so that when you're unpacking, you have some idea where everything is."

"Oh, wow, I mean you don't have to——"

She comes over and places one hand just below my left shoulder. "Trust me. I love organizing things. This is what I do. We'll have you packed up in no time. Is there anything that needs to be left out for you to use before you move?"

She's a little bit shorter than me so I'm looking slightly down at her, but Nadia can have a commanding presence when she wants to. "Just one set of dishes probably."

"Done."

"And probably better not pack up Timber's toys yet. He'll just want to pull them all out again anyway."

"A man after my own heart," Zara says.

"Don't worry, Emily. We've got this handled. I estimate it shouldn't take more than a few hours."

"Yeah, who needs those stinky ol' boys anyway," Zara laughs.

"Thanks Nadia," I say. "That really helps." I was low-key dreading this entire process, but having them here is making it a lot easier. "This is kind of a big deal for me."

She nods. "I get it. When I moved in with my partner, we had a hell of a time. It's a big step, bringing two lives together. Especially when you're doing it for the second time."

I find myself becoming more emotional than I'd expected, and tears begin to well in my eyes. "Aw, Em," Zara says, coming around the island and wrapping me in a hug. "It's gonna be okay. Don't worry."

"I know," I say, wiping my eyes with one arm as I have

another wrapped around her. "It's just…after everything, it's a lot."

She takes a step back from me. "It is. But you got this. You and Liam are going to *love* living together."

I give her a reassuring smile before we get to work. It really is hugely helpful to have them here. We each take our assignments, and because I'm not trying to do everything at once all by myself, the work goes faster than I expect. Just as Nadia predicted, we're practically done in under three hours. I guess by the time Liam stops by, I *will* be able to go help him pack. I'm debating bringing Nadia along with us, just because she's so damn organized.

When I look around at all the work, I notice each box has a code on it, written in sharpie. Nadia explains the first letter indicates the room, the second number indicates its packing order and the final letter indicates if it is part of a "set" or not. Normally I would have just marked each box with the name of the room it went in, but I can see the wisdom in a system like this. It will help keep everything organized when it's time to unpack again.

Despite it being early afternoon, Zara convinces us we can still find brunch somewhere, though just as we're getting ready to head out, my phone buzzes.

"Slate," I say, picking it up.

"It's Cervantes," the woman says on the other end. "Get down here right away. Someone you'll want to speak with just walked in."

Chapter Fifteen

AT SOME POINT in the recent past, I can remember promising myself I would stop doing this—coming into the office over the weekend—making work my first priority. Or at the very least, start giving myself one full day off per week. But this job doesn't necessarily work that way all the time. Sometimes things happen that require our immediate attention. And this seems to be one of them.

Because Nadia was already with us, I figured another pair of eyes couldn't hurt. She's been integral to our investigation so far and might as well get some face time. Especially if what Cervantes says is true and we might actually have a witness on our hands.

The entire way there, I can't help but think this is awfully convenient. Last night, Jun told us about a possible witness, but in the same breath, mentioned he's already dead. And then the very next day, a witness shows up at our doorstep? I'm not convinced Jun wasn't playing us. It might explain his strange behavior, at least according to Elliott. But to what end? What was the point of it all?

We head into the office, going through our normal security checks. As it's the weekend, jeans, a long-sleeve t-shirt, and my coat will have to do. Plus, most of my clothes are packed now anyway.

"Agents," Cervantes says as we head into her department. There are a few other agents milling about, still working on the case, I assume.

"Agent Cervantes, this is Special Agent Nadia Kane," I say, motioning to Nadia. "I don't know if you've had a chance to meet personally."

"I know the name. Pleasure," Cervantes says, taking Nadia's hand before releasing it quickly. "He arrived about an hour ago. Turned himself in."

"Who is he?" Zara asks.

"Some lowlife named Conrad Garza. I ran him through the system; he's got a rap sheet about half as long as my arm. Been in and out of prison for the past ten years for a variety of minor offenses."

"Dealing?" I ask.

She nods. "Distribution, robbery, theft, assault. The usual suspects."

"So why is he here?" Nadia asks.

"Claims he saw what happened the other night. He has some details that make me think he's telling the truth. But I want your take on it." She looks over her shoulder at another agent who nods and heads off in another direction.

"He doesn't happen to have an alias, does he?" I ask.

"Not that I found in the system, but you're free to ask him. Look, I've got an appointment. He's in interview room six. I don't have to tell you that if he did witness the murder, he could be our lynchpin. Get everything you can out of him. I don't care what it takes."

"Yes, ma'am," I reply, nodding.

"Good. Nice to meet you Agent Kane," Cervantes says before rushing off to follow the other agent.

"Busy woman," Nadia says.

"There's someone who definitely *doesn't* need more coffee," Zara adds.

"Okay, let's get this done," I say. "Nadia, I want you in the booth watching. Keep an eye out for anything we might miss. Whoever this Conrad Garza is, I find his appearance to be a little too convenient."

"I was just thinking that," Zara says, giving me a sly look. "*Awfully* good timing."

Nadia heads off to the viewing room beside interview six while Zara and I make our way straight there.

"Hey," Zara says as we're almost to the door, then motions to her hair.

I stop and feel my head, a lot of my hair has come loose in all the work we were doing earlier at my apartment. I gather all my hair back up, resetting the ponytail so nothing is out of place. "Good?"

She gives me two thumbs up and we head inside.

A man with a thick five o'clock shadow sits at the table inside, halfway slumped over. He's wearing a dirty gray jacket, and his hair is shaggy and oily. He has the look of someone who hasn't had a good night's sleep in a few weeks. An empty Styrofoam cup sits beside him. As soon as we enter, he looks up, and there are dark purple circles under his eyes.

"Conrad Garza?" I ask.

He nods. "Who are you?"

I don't waste any time. "I'm Agent Slate, this is Agent Foley. We understand you might have some information for us."

"Yeah," he says, scratching at his neck absently. From the marks on his neck, I realize now Conrad isn't sleep deprived, he's an addict. And it's been a while. Which means he's desperate. "Yeah, I just thought…maybe there'd be a reward or something."

"A reward. For what?" I ask. As usual, Zara has positioned

herself behind me and is watching Garza carefully while I sit down across from him and attempt to study the man.

"For, you know, info. I saw some people get killed."

I turn to look at Zara, my movements exaggerated. "Did you?"

"Yeah. And I knew they were Dragons. No one else dresses like those guys."

"Okay," I say, folding my hands together. "Tell me what you know."

"What about the reward?" he asks in sort of a pitiful voice. Generally, we don't give out rewards to informants or witnesses, but if we don't at least offer him something, he might not talk at all.

"We'll discuss that once we've heard your story," I say. "If it's credible, we can talk about a…reward."

He scratches again. "Yeah, okay. Where do I start?"

"At the beginning. When was this? What were you doing?"

More scratches. "Right, right. Yeah it was uh…Tuesday, I guess? Or it could have been Wednesday. No, no it was Tuesday 'cause Jerry had dropped me off because he works Tuesday nights."

"Jerry?" I ask.

"Yeah, he's…my roommate." He squeezes his eyes closed and rubs on them a minute before opening them again.

More than likely he's Garza's dealer, but I don't press the subject. "Keep going."

"So, I had to walk back to my place, which is over on Twenty-First. He was running late and dropped me off at the liquor store on Isherwood so I could get something for later. You know it?" I shake my head. "Well, I was heading back and I heard this loud noise, like a firecracker. At first, I thought that's all it was, so I didn't pay it no attention. But then it happened again and again, so I hauled my butt over there, wondering what was going on."

"Let me get this straight," Zara says. "You heard something that sounded like a firecracker, or maybe something else, and you ran *toward* it?"

"Yeah...I mean...I'm a concerned citizen. I thought maybe..." he trails off.

"Conrad, we're not going to get very far if you lie to us," I say. "And there definitely won't be a reward if you do."

He inhales sharply and lets it out. "Okay, okay. I didn't run toward it. At first, I hid. I figured it was somebody gettin' capped for some reason or another. What do I care? But you know sometimes how when people are in a hurry, they forget stuff?"

I narrow my gaze at him. "I suppose."

"When I didn't hear anything for a minute, I thought...I thought maybe the shooter had left. I thought maybe I could go over and see what happened."

"And why would you do that?" Zara asks.

"Cause...someone might have been hurt," he says. "Right?"

"Conrad..." I warn.

"Okay, okay," he says, putting his palms on the table. "I thought maybe if something had gone wrong, there might be something there for me."

"Something like..."

"I dunno, like they might have missed a wallet or some-thin'. Half the time people get killed in this city and the killers don't even take anything. Just shoot 'em and leave."

My stomach turns. "You were looking to scavenge."

"Well, I mean, what's a dead guy gonna do with a wallet?" he asks, giving us a weak smile. "Right?"

I have the urge to walk out of here and leave this little bastard behind, but we need this information, no matter how much gut-churning I feel sitting in this weasel's presence. "Is that what happened? Did you find someone's wallet?"

"No, that's just the thing," he says. "When I came around the corner, I saw there was a bunch of people still there. I couldn't get a good look at 'em, but I saw two bodies on the ground, and I knew those guys were dead."

"Keep going," I say.

"There was another car, but I didn't get a good look at it. And a van. A blue one, I think. Some guy was getting in the driver's side, and a second later he took off behind the other car."

"Did you get a good look at this guy?" I ask.

He holds up one hand, making a little motion with it. "Not really. It was dark and there weren't no streetlights in that alleyway."

"Was he tall, short, Caucasian, Black, heavyset, thin...you have to remember something."

"On the tall side, I guess. But not too much. I couldn't even really see his face. But he was wearing a hat."

"A hat?"

"Yeah, like one of those old wide-brimmed ones, like gangsters use to wear back in those old movies."

"A fedora?" Zara offers.

He snaps his fingers, pointing at her. "That's it. A fedora. He was wearing that."

It's odd, but not completely indistinguishable. And it's not a lot to go on. "What about the other car. Not the van. Anything? Was it a sedan? An SUV?"

"Uh, sedan, I guess? Looked kind of fancy from what I could tell. Black, maybe?"

This is frustrating. He was right there at the scene, but he can barely tell us anything about what happened. "Did you happen to see a third body anywhere? Other than the two on the ground?"

"No, why?" he asks.

I turn and shoot a look at Zara. The terse look on her face tells me she doesn't know if we can trust what Garza is telling us. I tend to agree. I turn back to our "witness," "Conrad, do you have any aliases you've used in the past?"

"No, why?"

I highly doubt this is the case, but I have to ask anyway. "Does the name Yufei mean anything to you?"

"I don't think so…" he replies. "Should it?"

He certainly doesn't look like someone named Yufei. "Routine question. Have you told this to anyone else?"

"Yeah, my roommate Jerry. We talk about everything, but I don't really talk to many people other than him." He starts up the scratching again.

"Why not go directly to the Dragons and tell them?" Zara asks. It's a good question.

I nod. "I'm sure they would have been willing to give you a reward as well."

"Nah, nah," he says, pushing back from the table. "I don't mess with the Dragons. Don't mess with none of those guys. Can't trust 'em. Plus, word on the street is the Hand got hit too. I figured the cops would rather know. But when I went to them, they sent me to you."

That's because Cervantes has arranged for anyone with information pertaining to this case to be brought directly to us. "I'm sorry, I just have a hard time believing you came in of your own free will. Reward or no."

"B-but," he stutters. "It's the truth. I-I seen it. You guys give out rewards when it leads to arrests right? And that money would really help, man."

"I can see that," I say. "Which is why I have a hard time trusting you. How do we know any of this is the truth and you're not just making it up because you heard about some high-profile murders?"

"Nah, man, nah. I was there. That alleyway between Merchant and Idlewild, right? It's got that laundromat on the corner that's open twenty-four-seven." His eyes are wide, and I can see he's beginning to panic because he's about to lose his golden goose. "Look you gotta believe me, okay? Listen, listen." He scoots closer, breathing more erratically. I'm on alert, but I keep still, waiting to see how this plays out. "Okay, the first guy. He was kind of big, right? Bald? And he had on this leather jacket over a—it was like I dunno, like a wife-beater. Black. And the other guy, the smaller one. He was wearin'…it was like a black and yellow track suit, but it had some writing on it." He smacks the middle of his forehead a few times. "It was something like…I dunno, Gonesy or something."

"Guanyu," I say.

He snaps his fingers. "Yes! That's it."

I sigh. That is an accurate, if crude, description of what the men were wearing. Garza would be hard pressed to know exactly what they were wearing unless he saw them in person. But, I'm still not sure I buy this whole story. Something about it feels off and I don't know why.

I tap the table a few times, noticing Garza's leg bouncing almost uncontrollably. "Wait here."

"Sure, sure," he says. "Hey can I get some more coffee?"

I stand and head for the door, Zara right beside me. "We'll see what we can do."

"Thanks, man. 'Preciate it."

Once we're back out in the hall, Nadia rejoins us from the monitoring room next door. "Thoughts?"

"He's obviously lying about something," Zara says.

"Heatmap backs that up," Nadia adds. "But it isn't exactly conclusive. He's all over the place—looks like the early stages of withdrawal."

I nod. "He probably came in here looking for a quick turnaround so he could go pay his dealer. Which makes his witness statement questionable at best."

"So, what do we do?" Zara asks.

"He hasn't really given us much." Before I can say anything else, Garza is banging on the door, looking through the window at us.

"Hey! I remembered something else."

I take a deep, calming breath and return to the door. This man is trying my patience. I open it to find him standing close, hugging himself. "What do you remember?"

"The guy, getting in the van to drive it away. I think I've seen him before. I think he works for the Toscani Family."

Chapter Sixteen

DAMIAN DRUMMOND SITS behind his desk, going over the repair quotes he's received so far for the club. And already they're not looking good. He's a good ten grand in already just on water mitigation, and that doesn't even include any tear out and repairs.

Fuckin' feds. He ought to sue their asses. But a court battle would put a spotlight on the Kings, and he doesn't need that kind of heat. The feds know that, which is why they think they can just come in and bust up his place without consequences. Well, the next time he sees those two little darlings, he ain't gonna be shy about letting 'em know who's boss. A badge can only give you so much protection. Sometimes bad things just happen to "nice" people.

"Hey D, about ready?" He looks up to see Lamar standing in the doorway. He's already got his jacket on.

Damian checks his solid gold watch, the one that cost him more than most people pay for a car. Yeah, it's big and flashy, and that's the way he wants it. Tells people he's not to be fucked with. That, if he can afford this kind of watch, he can afford pretty much anything. But now he sees they're going to be late if he doesn't get a move on. "Damn man, why didn't you come get me earlier?"

"I figured you were working," Lamar says. "You said you didn't want to be bothered after what happened the other night."

"You wouldn't want to be bothered either if you saw what some of these people want to charge me," he says, driving his finger into the papers on his desk. "I practically built this community, and this is how they repay me?"

Lamar rolls his shoulders back until they pop. "Want me to set up a collection? This community owes us."

Damian shakes his head as he joins Lamar. "No, not for the club. I don't want their money paying for that. This deal tonight should cover it."

"You really think it's smart going out tonight?" Lamar asks. "After what those FBI agents—"

He doesn't get to finish the sentence because Damian's back-hand cuts him off. Lamar rubs his jaw, checking for any blood from his lip. Given the size of the ring Damian wears on his right ring finger, he's surprised he didn't draw any. "I don't give a *fuck* what those agents said. They destroyed the club. You really think we can trust them? If there is someone out there targeting us, we're gonna be ready. Where're Nine and Cordell?"

"I sent them ahead," Lamar says, though Damian can hear the resentment in his voice. He better watch that tone unless he wants another blow. Damian isn't about to suffer any fools. So far, Lamar has been good, but he's young and ambitious and might need to be put in his place a few more times.

"Good. We're gonna make sure this thing goes off without a hitch," he says. "And then we'll use the money to help fix the club up. Once that's done, we can get back to business as usual." He heads down the hallway to the garage.

"You think those feds know what's going on? Do they know what we're moving?"

"Doesn't matter," Damian replies. "As long as they don't catch us with it." He goes over to the steel cabinet beside the van parked in the garage, opening it with a key and pulling out two Glock 20s. He hands one to Lamar before tucking the second one into his front belt. No one is going to get the drop on Damian Drummond. "Get in."

"Still don't know why you need me," Lamar says, getting in the passenger seat.

"Like I said, we're not taking any chances. And Calvin's as slow as his damn mother sometimes," Damian replies, starting the van and opening the garage. He pulls out of the building only a few blocks away from the club. The place has been boarded up for the time being; he'll get something more permanent in there later this week. And a new sign, letting people know about the new and *improved* club. If those feds had known how close they'd been to the real action, he'd be sitting in a federal prison right now. But he'd played it cool, and all they seemed to care about was finding out if he'd been responsible for what happened to those racist fucks and the Chinese.

Does he wish he could take credit? Sure, but he ain't about to say he did something when he wasn't the one who did it. He'd like to thank whoever did, though, 'cause it's really thrown a wrench in things for both of them. He doesn't know all the details about what happened, he just knows a couple deals went bad. Which usually only happens when you're in a desperate situation like the one he and Lamar are in right now.

But Damian isn't stupid. He's actually counting on this meet being a setup. Because if it is, and he can take down those responsible, and it will lead him to a treasure trove like nothing the Kings have ever seen before. He'll have weapons, illegal goods, and more drugs than he'll know what to do with. The Kings will be unstoppable. He looks behind him at their "product" and smiles. All it will take is a couple of boxes of fake watches.

He drives over to Easton and finds the meeting location: a large parking lot of an abandoned shopping center. They're out in the open where there won't be any surprises. Damian smiles as he brings the van to a stop, cutting the engine.

"I hope you're as good with that thing as you are with those damn games you play all day long," Damian growls, staring out the window, waiting for fate to come meet them.

"This?" Lamar asks, holding up the Glock. "I've been handling these since I was fifteen. You don't have to worry about me."

Damian hopes he's right. But even if Lamar is a lousy shot, he's got Nine and Cordell in place. At least, that's the plan. He pulls out his Bluetooth earpiece and calls Nine on his phone.

"Speak."

"You in position?" Damian asks.

"Can see the whole parking lot. Front to back."

"Good. Stay on the phone. If something goes wrong, you take them out."

"We got your back, Big D."

That makes him feel a little better, but even so, he's still nervous. It's a feeling he pushes down and uses to ignite his anger, thinking about how he can't wait to break down those little FBI girls. How dare they come into his place of business like that. When he's got things back up and running, they better start watching their backs.

"D."

Damian looks up and sees the headlights headed for them. Lamar moves to get out of the van. "Hold up," Damian says. "Let them get out first."

Lamar sits back and waits. The other car pulls up and Damian notices it's a BMW M8. That's a nice car. It takes a minute, but finally the doors of the car open and two men step out at exactly the same time. Damian notices they haven't turned off their engine. Maybe they're looking for a quick getaway.

"Nine, get ready," he says and motions for Lamar to get out. Damian follows, and the two of them leave their doors open in case they need to dive back into the car. Damian can already tell there's something wrong with these two men. Other than looking like carbon copies of each other, they're completely expressionless like robots or something. He doesn't like it.

"Hey, where's the lady I spoke with on the phone," Damian demands.

"She's otherwise engaged," one of the two twins says.

"You'll be dealing with us instead," the other one adds. It's like they're the same person, just split in two. Damian takes a step back toward his van.

"I don't think so. I don't change the deal after it's been made." But before he can go for his gun, he's knocked back by what feels like a punch to the middle of his chest. He finds he's lying on the ground, and when he pulls his hand away, he feels the sticky warmth of his own blood. "Nine!" he yells into his Bluetooth. "Take them out!" He's bleeding out, fast. How did they pull a gun on him so quickly? He didn't even see it. "Lamar!"

One of the twins appears over him, holding an ATI GSG pistol. He recognizes it because he's bought the same one from the Dragons before. Are *they* the ones behind this?

"Lamar is dead," the twin says. "And so are you."

Damian doesn't let the man see his fear. Instead, he just stares right up into the twin's dead eyes until he squeezes the trigger.

The world explodes in light and sound. And then...nothing.

Chapter Seventeen

"Shit," I say, looking at the dead body of Damian Drummond in the middle of an empty parking lot. His eyes are still open, gazing up at me. What I wouldn't give to see the last thing he saw.

"This throws that theory out the window," Zara says behind me. "Guess the Kings really weren't behind it after all."

It's early Monday morning, just after sunrise. We got the call not more than an hour ago, and after interrogating Conrad Garza for most of the afternoon yesterday then cutting him loose sans reward, I'm grateful to have some time outside.

Though, this isn't exactly what I was hoping for.

I bend down, examining the body as a couple of officers tape off the scene, and crime techs begin to search for evidence. The call came from a security guard who patrols the building next door. He just happened to see the bodies after he was done with his regular rounds.

Drummond's is practically swimming in his own blood. It's formed a pool beneath him, but he's also covered in it. It's as if his heart was pumping with the pressure of a steam train.

"Doesn't this look like a lot of blood for the caliber of weapons we saw before?"

Zara bends down to take a look. "I guess?"

"And I'm only seeing one tear in his shirt here." I motion for one of the crime scene techs to come over and get some pictures. "Capture all this real quick, I want to cut his shirt off him."

"Yes, ma'am," the tech says and snaps a few photos while I pull on a pair of nitrile gloves.

"Do you have a knife or scissors?" He heads back over to his case and returns with a sharp knife that should do the trick.

"What are you looking for?" Zara asks.

"I dunno," I say.

"He's still got the bullet to the forehead, just like his buddy over there," she says, pointing to the other body on the ground. We've already identified him as Lamar Douglas, another member of the Kings. His wallet was still in his pocket, so I guess Garza wasn't too off the mark when he said the killer just leaves everything behind.

I carefully cut the fabric of Drummond's shirt away, revealing the dark skin underneath. There is a *lot* of blood. But instead of three bullet wounds as I'd expected, all I see is one golf-ball sized wound. "He was only shot once," I say.

Zara wrinkles her nose. "That is a gaping wound all right."

I look around. There aren't any tire tracks on the parking lot, which means no one left in a big hurry. They killed these men, and then just like with all the rest, took their vehicle and whatever was contained inside.

But they couldn't have been standing that far apart when Drummond got out of his vehicle. Douglas's relative position to Drummond suggests they were standing on either side of the vehicle they arrived in. The distance indicates the vehicle was mid-size, but again, we have no idea what we're looking for. There is already a BOLO out for the Dragon van based on Jun's description, but presumably we have two other vehicles missing now.

Someone is gathering a collection.

"What are you thinking, Em?"

I look over at Zara, both of us still squatting over Drummond. "That whoever shot him couldn't have been close," I say. That's not the kind of bullet that comes from a pistol or even a shotgun. That's a rifle round, and given the size, I'd say it's a long-range rifle at that."

"Long range from where?"

I look over my shoulder again at the building the head of the parking lot. It used to be an old Circuit City years ago but closed when the company went out of business. I wonder how difficult it is to get up on the roof of that building. "Here, come with me."

We head off for the building, circling around the side until we reach the back where we find a fire escape going up to the roof. The lock has been broken and the ladder pulled down out of the cage. But I have no way of knowing if that was recent or not.

"Keep your gloves on," I tell Zara and I carefully make my way up the ladder, making sure to use the far sides of the rungs as much as possible. I don't want to smudge any possible fingerprints.

When we reach the top, I see a dark shape near the front side of the building. "Is that—?"

"I think so." Given what the body is wearing, it looks like another one of the Jefferson Kings.

"Three shots to the chest and one to the head," Zara points out. "*Here's* our MO."

"Yeah," I say, looking around. There's another dark shape in the adjacent corner. When we reach him, it's more of the same. Exact same pattern as the other man. "These two were providing cover."

"Looks like they didn't do a very good job," Zara says.

"Someone got the jump on them. Our killer. And then they used the high position and even the weapons these two brought to take out Drummond and Douglas. The impact from a long-range rifle would have knocked them back and is exactly what would have left a hole of that size in their chests."

Zara tsks. "So, Damian thought he could outsmart the killer, maybe even take them down before they got to him." She stares at me. "Do you believe it was the Toscanis?"

"What choice do I have? Garza fingered them. and they're only one of two gangs that haven't been hit yet. If anyone actually *knew* where Santino Toscani was at the moment, I would very much like to talk to him."

"Em, we need to find him. This is turning into a blood-bath. Cervantes is right, this city is going to erupt if we don't stop it. What do you think the Kings are going to do when they find out someone killed their *leader*?" I can tell from the way she's pinching her features that Zara is worried. I am too. The other hits have been low-level goons. But this is something else. The killer is ratcheting things up a notch. Did they just kill Drummond because he happened to be here? Or was he the target all along?

"Yeah, you're right." I turn and wave, getting the attention of some of the techs still down in the parking lot. "Get a team up here!" I yell out.

"So what's the plan?" she asks.

"Find Toscani. No matter how long it takes."

WE SPEND THE BETTER PART OF THE DAY DRIVING TO ALL OF Santino Toscani's old haunts. Despite intelligence telling us he hasn't been seen in weeks, I'm not convinced. If Garza is right, and he is behind all these killings, then he is close. And if he's not, then he's just another target, like Drummond.

His warehouse, which sits in the industrial area of town, is a bust. We pull up, and even though the warehouse is running business as usual, there's no sign of Santino. I'm actually surprised and a little suspicious, how easy it is for us to get in, considering the treatment we've received the other times we've tried coming here. And given Zara and I were never Santino's favorite people, I figured he would have put an embargo on us ever entering his warehouse again.

But his people let us in, escort us around, and even allow us to examine the place on our own. It's a huge warehouse, and there are any number of places Santino could hide, but he's not that kind of person. He wouldn't be holed up in some little storage room. No, he'd be in his office, projecting the kind of strength he thinks he needs to maintain control of this organization.

Somehow, I just know he's not going to be there. They wouldn't be that open and transparent if he were. I'm always suspicious of people who are *too* anxious to help us out. Kind of like Garza. Generally, people are altruistic, but not so with the kind of people we tend to deal with.

Next, we head downtown to places Santino is known to frequent to see if anyone has seen him lately. After a lot of interviews and greasing a few wheels, we find that Intelligence was right. There's been no sign of the man for weeks.

Finally, even though I know it's fruitless, we head to his home outside the city. It's a gated property but the service staff let us in. A quick conversation with them reveals they don't know when he'll be back, only that he's been gone since the end of February.

"I don't like any of this," I tell Zara as we head back to my car after doing a thorough check of the Toscani estate. "Why would he just up and leave his company and everything else behind? Taking over the business from his uncle would have been very lucrative—one way or another."

"Maybe he just decided to take a vacation," Zara suggests. "He's certainly rich enough."

"And then all of these murders happen while he's away?" I ask. "No, something is definitely wrong. We need to bring Garza back in. Show him more mugshots, see if he can identify the man he saw that night."

"He's never going to be a credible witness," she says, checking her phone. "He's a crack addict who may or may not be high when we interview him again. Maybe he did see something, but he could just make it all up to waste our time."

"He's all we've got," I say. "We could always…I dunno. Find his dealer?"

"Well, *that's* not happening," she says. From the tone of her voice I can tell she knows where my mind is headed: put pressure on Garza's dealer to get Garza what he needs to even himself out. Even if we tried it, it wouldn't get us anywhere. Not to mention is illegal.

I wince. "I know, I know. I'm just…frustrated and angry. I need answers, but there doesn't seem to be anyone around who can give me any."

"We can still check with the Lunas," she says. "There's always the possibility they're involved. They still haven't been hit…as far as we know anyway."

I start the engine and pull away, heading down the neighborhood road to the main street. "They're going to be a tough one to crack. I don't know anyone in Luna, do you?"

She gives me a small shrug. "Maybe Elliott does? He seems to have contacts everywhere."

"Yeah, contacts that both love and hate him at the same time? What was that about?"

"I have no idea. Maybe Jun was looking to establish a new FBI connection. You know, something to impress to his bosses."

"Like we're the assets and he's the handler?" I ask.

"Something like that. Andrew says foreign governments try to do it all the time. They embed their own people in the local cartels or triads or whatever and work rival governments from there."

"So, you're saying the Chinese Government is trying to get American state secrets by planting an agent in the Steel Dragons to act as a liaison?"

"I mean…it sounds crazy when you put it like that," she replies.

"That's because it is crazy. Andrew actually *told* you this?"

"Well…he more of…suggested it," she says with a sheepish smile.

"Z, I didn't want to say this, but I think you need to be careful with him. Especially given how you two met. We still don't know a whole lot about him. *He* could be the foreign asset attempting to work you over." I pause, letting the silence fill the car between us. "Have you even done a background check on him yet?"

She doesn't answer.

"Z?"

She blows out a breath, which puffs her hair off her forehead for a second. "No, I haven't done a background check on him yet."

"But you do checks on everyone you meet. You even did one on Liam, remember?"

"I just…I wanted this one to be different," she says. "I didn't want to know everything about him before he had a chance to tell me. Don't get me wrong, knowing a person's full digital history before you say one word to them is *great*, but I wanted to find out the old-fashioned way."

"I get that, I do. But this man was part of Simon Magus's group. He's said he's part of MI6, but we have no idea if that's true, and you really don't know anything about him."

"That's the best part," she almost yells. "I *like* not knowing anything about him. Do you know how much research I did on Raoul before we started dating? I knew where he went to school, who his parents were, who his friends were, what he studied in college, what extracurricular activities he undertook, his co-workers, how much he paid for his house. Everything. I could almost tell you what he was going to say before he said it. And you know what? It was *boring*. I didn't want that with Andrew. I want to be surprised, for unexpected things to happen."

We're quiet a few more minutes as I drive. I don't really know what to say. I get that she wants spontaneity. I would get so tired if Liam and I were the same all the time, if I could predict what he was going to do and say. I just don't know if the man she met undercover working for a terrorist is the one person she shouldn't investigate.

"I know it's a risk," she finally says. "I'm just afraid the minute I learn too much about him, he's just going to become another one of those guys, and I won't have any desire to continue the relationship. The not knowing is what's keeping us going." She pauses. "At least, it's what's keeping me going."

"That's understandable, it really is," I say. "I just want to make sure you're careful. I don't want to wake up one day and find you missing because suddenly something happened."

She smiles. "Thanks, Em. But I'll be okay. I'm not scared anymore. Not like I was before."

It's a relief to hear that. There was a time when I thought Zara might retreat all the way back into her intelligence shell and never come out again. She's such a free and fun spirit when she's her best self, and I would hate to have seen that lost. Thankfully, it seems like she's managed to clear that hurdle.

But still, I can't help but worry.

We pull up to a stop sign and I check both ways before going, only to realize another car has pulled up behind us.

"Z," I say, looking in my rearview.

Her eyes go wide, and she turns around. "That's the same car that almost hit us the other night!"

"Can you see the driver?" I ask.

"No, looks like the windows have been tinted. I can't see anything inside."

I'm debating how long it would take me to get out, dash to the other car and break open their driver-side door. The driver would either have to back up or rear-end my car to get away quick enough, but there's no guarantee I could do it. And what are the odds of running into them again?

Unless it's not an accident.

"What are you going to do?" Zara asks.

I weigh my options and decide to act like everything is normal. I pull through the stop sign and head to the next intersection. The car behind me does the same, following the traffic laws exactly, which is a far cry from the other night. "No plates on the front," I say.

Pulling up to the next stop sign, I press the brake to the floor, ready to throw the car into park and get out just as soon as the other car is close enough not to be able to get away quickly. "I think you're right. It's a Ford of some kind. An old one."

"I'm looking it up right now," she says, tapping away on her phone.

That pit in my stomach is back as I keep glancing back at the old vehicle. There's a familiarity to it I can't place, and yet at the same time, I've never seen that car before in my life. My FBI brain wants to tell me this could be Jun's work. After our meeting, I just thought it was a drunk driver. But now I've obviously got to revise that theory. We still don't know what his ultimate plan is, maybe he's having us followed to keep tabs on our progress.

Then again, I don't know if a Chinese gang would necessarily choose to drive a nineteen-seventies American-made

Ford. In fact, the longer I look, the more I'm convinced that isn't the case.

"Got it," Zara says. "It's a Ford Granada. Manufactured from nineteen seventy-five until nineteen eighty-two."

"Time to meet our mysterious driver." I throw the gear shift to park at the same time I open the door and get ready to run at the car behind us. But the driver is ready, and pulls the Ford to the right, rounding my car and speeding off.

"Oh, no you don't," I say, jumping back in my car. I peel away from the curb, hot on the car's trail.

"Em, the plates—" Zara points out.

As I'm rushing to keep up, I realize the plates don't match the car that almost sideswiped us the other day. "What the hell?" I ask.

"Could it be another car?"

I shove the accelerator to the floor in an attempt to catch up with the car. For an older model, it sure can move. It's weaving around other cars in traffic with no regard to public safety. "I don't know, but call it in. We're not letting this one get away. We can figure out what's going on once we've stopped them."

"Got it," Zara says, pulling out her cell phone as I try my best to keep up with the driver. You'd think the driver was a professional with how they are expertly moving through the slower traffic, avoiding all the obstacles. But why? And what would two identical cars with different license plates want with me?

"I've got the locals on it, and have given them our position," Zara says.

My knuckles are white as I grip the wheel, still working to keep up. "Good," I say, gritting my teeth as I almost clip a Prius that's blaring its horn at us. "You got the plate?"

"Got it," she replies.

"There can't be that many Ford Granada's driving around these days, right?" I ask as my tires squeal in a hard right turn, following the Ford down Connecticut Ave. All of a sudden, I see flashing lights in my rearview and a DC Police car passes us at high speed. Finally, I let off the accelerator, thankful to let the local cops handle it.

Another cruiser comes screaming past, and both of them are hot on the trail of the other vehicle. I slow enough to get us back into normal traffic as Zara's phone rings in her hand. She answers and confirms with the local cops the details of the chase.

Again, my heart is in my throat.

"They've got them on the run and will let us know when they have the driver in custody," Zara says. "Man, what the hell, right?"

Finally, I just pull over and put the car in park so I can take a breath.

"Em, you okay?" Zara asks.

"I think...I think it's her. I think she's finally decided to come after me."

"Who?" Zara asks.

"Emily."

Chapter Eighteen

"TELL me you've made some progress," Cervantes says, coming in and rounding her desk. We've come into her office first thing this morning after realizing we weren't making any headway on finding Toscani. I had hoped yesterday would have been more productive, but it turned out to be a complete bust. The man is off grid.

Worst of all, the local DC cops lost the car following us. And even though they have the make, model, and plates of *both* cars, neither has showed up again on any traffic cameras in the city. How that's possible, I have no idea. The more I think about it, the more I'm convinced it's Emily. She's finally tracked me down and is what...stalking me? That's the only explanation that makes sense. I just hope DC Police finds the car...or *cars* soon.

And as much as I'd like to pull additional resources and make looking for that car my focus, we have a more pressing problem: finding Toscani. I managed to convince Nadia and Elliott to help go through all the surveillance tools we have in an attempt to find the man. After the hit on the Kings, it's looking more and more like he might be the actual culprit behind all this.

"I wish we had better news," I say, sitting forward in one of the chairs across from Cervantes's desk. "But Toscani is AWOL. I think you might have been right from the beginning. The only problem is no one can find him. We spent the entire day yesterday going through all his operations, and there was nothing. Everything looked squeaky clean."

"The last time we spoke with him, he didn't seem interested in reentering the criminal world. He said he was going to right his uncle's mistakes," Zara adds.

Cervantes scoffs. "I don't believe that for a second, and neither should you. He's out there somewhere, we just need to press harder. Regardless, even if he's not here, the killer is. Any progress on that front?"

"It's someone highly trained," I say. "They know how to handle a variety of weapons, including long-range sighted rifles. Their kills are always quick and clean. And based on what we saw, I'm guessing it was quick. Drummond and his boys didn't have time to even fire off a shot. Their weapons were fully loaded. And we've spoken with CSI, and whoever it is, they aren't leaving behind any evidence."

"You contacted a representative of the Dragons?" she asks, seeming to pivot.

I nod, giving her the rundown from Jun Zhao. "He mentioned something about another, new faction but didn't have any details. And we also have a 'witness' who we plan on bringing back in for another round."

"Conrad Garza," she says, flipping her pen between her fingers. "I'm not so sure he's credible."

"Us either," Zara says. "But at the moment, he's all we have. He *did* provide an accurate description of the victims."

"And he pointed the finger at Toscani as well. We had him run through a couple of mugshots before he left, but nothing stood out. I want to take another crack at him."

Cervantes takes a deep breath then puts her pen down.

"So, you've eliminated the Kings as possible assailants, which only leaves two possibilities."

I nod. "Toscani, which, until he pops up or we catch his guys in the act is a non-starter. And—"

"La Luna Roja," Cervantes finishes for me. She swears, staring out her window. "I didn't want to have to get involved with them. But we can't ignore the possibility they could be behind this as well."

I exchange a glance with Zara. "Their reputation is hard to ignore."

"It's well-deserved, trust me," she replies. "I used to work the Lunas back when I was still a new agent. I've seen just how brutal they can be. You do not want to be on their bad side." She pauses a moment. "We could never prove it, but we found a shallow grave once. The bodies had been run through with chains."

"Run through?" I ask.

She nods. "Someone had threaded chains through the bodies like they were sewing them up. We only found everything after the fact, but from the way the chains had been positioned in the bodies, they'd been hanging by the chains for a while. Long enough for scavenger birds to pick apart the meatier bits." She points to her eyes and mouth. "Wasn't a pretty sight."

"The Lunas did that?" Zara asks.

"Again, no direct evidence, and we couldn't ever build a solid case, but my gut said yes. We believed the victims were nothing more than homeless people who had asked the Lunas for some food and shelter."

I shoot Zara a worried look. "Doesn't sound like they'd be too happy with us barging in and accusing them of murder then."

"Definitely not," she replies. She taps her fist on her desk a few more times, still looking out her window before turning back to us. "How confident are you Toscani is behind these killings?"

"Right now? I'd say maybe fifty percent," I say. "Zhao's possibility of a new faction moving in is something to look in to as well."

Cervantes nods. "Don't leave the stone unturned. We need to talk to the Lunas, if for no other reason than to see how they're reacting to the murders. But I'm not about to send you in there alone."

"We can handle it, we're——" she holds up a hand, cutting me off.

"No. This is different. You go in there without a contact, you may not come back out. FBI agents or no."

"They wouldn't just kill us," Zara says.

"Look, the Lunas are an arm of one of the biggest Mexican Cartels in the US. And there are certain…considerations." She picks up the phone, but only hits one number, then speaks into the phone. "Yeah. I need to speak with Armaz. Tell him it's urgent." She hangs up, checking her watch. "What's on your agenda today?"

"We were going to take another run at Conrad Garza, assuming we can find him again. He sort of disappeared after we let him go the other night," I say. "And continue to look for Toscani. A couple of our fellow agents are reviewing surveillance footage. We're trying to figure out when he left DC."

"Scratch that," she says, getting up. "If we're going to do this, we're going to be quick about it. I don't want to linger."

"Do what?" I ask.

"Speak with the head of the snake," she replies.

I'm sitting in the back of Cervantes's black Chevy Tahoe while Zara is in the passenger's seat. Cervantes has been driving us for about forty-five minutes outside of the city, giving us the rundown on the Lunas as she drives.

I like Cervantes, she seems like an action-oriented kind of agent. You'd never find Wallace getting his hands dirty by going out to meet a drug lord. And that's what we've learned about the Lunas and their leader, a man named Felix. He originally grew up in a city called Tlaxcala, Mexico. From there, he either joined or formed the Lunas, the intelligence is shady on which, before moving operations into the United States. He's been operating in the DC area for almost a decade now. But of course, he's never been stupid enough to get caught with his hand in the cookie jar.

"Whoa, this can't be it," Zara says as we pull up to the address. It's a house...I think, but it looks more like a small town. A large stucco wall encircles the property, cutting it off from the outside world. But over the wall, I can catch sight of the tops of three or four different buildings, all of them as big as a mansion, and each featuring modern Spanish architecture. It's a compound all right. What's surprising is the amount of flowers surrounding this side of the wall, given the time of year. I didn't think most flowers would bloom in the DC winter, but then again, we are on the cusp of spring. But it tells me the Lunas have money to burn. If they can spend this much on *gardening*, how many weapons are they going to have trained on us in there?

"This is it," Cervantes says, pulling up to a large iron gate. There's a keypad beside the gate, but before she can even roll the window down, a man appears on the other side of the gate, brandishing a fully automatic M-16. That thing could punch holes in this car and us under two seconds flat. In fact, it *should* be illegal because it's fully automatic. But because it's an older weapon, made before the mid-eighties, they can still be bought and purchased. Though, I know they're not cheap.

"Let me handle this," Cervantes says, getting out of the car and closing the door behind us. She walks up to the gate to speak to the man, who doesn't seem to be responding to whatever she's saying, only listening.

"Em, what the hell is going on here?" Zara asks.

"I have no idea. But I don't like any of it."

"Do you think Cervantes knows what she's doing?" Both of us watch as she continues to talk to the man outside. As she does, it begins to drizzle, the sky having turned a foggy gray as the morning marches on.

"I hope so," I say. "I just can't figure out why such a large and ruthless organization is allowed to continue to operate here," I say. "Some of the others I get…the Kings, the Hand…they're less organized, smaller time, more of a community. And the Dragons seem to have some kind of official-slash-unofficial governmental support. But this is a different level, it's like a fully operational military base." I nod to Cervantes who has started making motions with her hands to the guard. Finally, he nods, and she turns back and gets in the car again.

"Sorry that took a minute," she adds, opening the glove box and pulling out her service weapon. "I need you two to be on guard when we go in there. We're all going to watch each other's backs."

"Ma'am, I don't mean to be indelicate, but how much danger are we putting ourselves in by going in there?" I ask. As I do, the gate opens from the inside, the man with the M-16 still standing close and watching our vehicle.

"Just…be on guard," she says. "It would be very, very stupid of them to try something. But I wouldn't put it past them if we manage to piss them off. Just play it cool and follow my lead."

I find myself holding my breath as Cervantes inches the car forward until we're past the main gate. Even though the back windows of the Tahoe are tinted, I feel like the guard is watching me, eyes are glued to the vehicle as we pass. The man barely even blinks.

Usually, I'm not intimidated in these types of situations, but I know we are going to be far outnumbered here, and we're not in a place where our badges will necessarily protect us.

"No sudden movements; don't give them a reason to suspect you. We probably have about half a dozen weapons trained on us at all times. You won't see them, but they're there," Cervantes says. "Be aware, but try to pretend like everything is normal."

"Sure, piece of cake," Zara says turning to me and shoving a finger in my face. "Pretend like you're not five seconds away from death, and how about we make it look convincing this time?"

"Yes, ma'am," I say.

"Here we are," Cervantes says as the car slows to a roll. We've pulled up in front of what looks like the largest of the buildings, a mansion decorated in ornate detail and ironwork that must have cost a fortune. "Like I said, we're just here to see if we can get any useful information out of them. Don't accuse them of anything."

I think both Zara and I understand how serious this is. "We're not going to slip up."

"I know you won't," she replies. "Otherwise, I'd never have brought you with me." She cuts the engine as three more men with M-16s show up, surrounding the car. I take a deep breath and open my door.

Chapter Nineteen

ZARA and I are on one side of the Tahoe, while Cervantes is on the other side. "Good to see you again, Armaz," she calls out to one of the men. The drizzle has continued, and while it's cold, I feel like I'm sweating under my jacket.

"Wish I could say it was mutual," the man replies. He's dressed in all black and speaks with a slight Mexican accent. He's sporting a goatee, and his short black hair is slicked back. "Every time I see you, I always regret it."

"Just here to ask a few questions."

Armaz motions to us with the end of his weapon. "Who're they?"

"We work together at the Bureau."

He hesitates a minute like he's trying to decide whether to shoot us or not. I don't take my gaze off him. Instead, I offer a simple nod. He barely reacts, then turns to one of his compatriots, speaking something into his ear that none of us can hear. The man turns and heads off while we remain in a staring contest with Armaz. I don't know if this is going well or not, but I don't dare start looking around. I know they're up there, somewhere, with beads on the back of my head in case we make one wrong move.

I hate to think what would have happened if we'd tried to come here without Cervantes.

My phone goes off in my pocket, and Armaz's gaze locks on mine as he tightens his grip on his weapon.

"Just my phone," I say.

"Show me," he says.

I reach into my jacket slowly, and deliberately before pulling out the vibrating device. He relaxes his grip, before motioning to the phone with a tilt of his head. "You're okay. Answer it."

I really don't want to be on the phone right now, but I can see from the screen it's Liam. "Hey," I say. "Can I call you back?"

"Sure," he says. "Didn't mean to interrupt. It's nothing urgent."

"Thanks," I say and end the call, slipping the phone back into my outer coat pocket. I feel like I'm on a hair-trigger here. One wrong move and that's all she wrote, folks.

"He has the worst timing," Zara whispers to me as the man Armaz originally spoke to comes walking back up.

"It's my fault," I tell her. "I didn't tell him what's going on."

"He's not going to be happy about that," she says.

"I know. But this all happened kind of fast."

"Okay," Armaz says. "All three of you, come with me." He turns toward the house and Cervantes follows first, me behind her and Zara bringing up the rear. One of the other guards steps into line behind Zara while the third remains near the vehicle. The drizzle is only getting worse and it's like someone has laid a wet blanket on my hair.

Instead of going into the house, we wind around the side, following a concrete path where the lawn has been landscaped beautifully. As we reach the back of the home, it opens up into an expansive vista looking out into the distance, and the entire area has been decked out in what I can only describe as an homage to Greco-Roman architecture. Large marble statues frame a square pool, along with columns that seem to be nothing but decorative, as they're not holding up anything, they're just...standing beside the statues. There's not a blade of grass anywhere back here, the entire area hardscaped. The pool itself is still covered for the season, and lounge chairs surround the pool itself, but they are covered as well.

We're led past the pool toward a large structure off to the back right of the house, which looks like a massive greenhouse of sorts. Green iron girders frame out the glass throughout the entire structure and condensation turns everything inside to colored shadows dancing behind a mirror. Armaz leads us to the double glass doors, opening them to reveal *another* large pool, one completely enclosed in the greenhouse. Where the structure is attached to the house, a large indoor bar runs along the stucco and opens up into a covered sitting area with wall-mounted televisions, each showing a different soccer game. The place reads like a private country club, except there are no shortage of automatic weapons being brandished.

As we step inside, I'm struck by how warm it is. It's like going from the refrigerator to the sauna, and sweat beads on my forehead immediately.

Inside the greenhouse are at least a dozen people, half of which are women in skimpy bathing suits. They're mostly lounging around the pool, though one is swimming and another leans back beside the pool, looking bored as she taps the water with her foot. A barrel-chested man hovers over a table close to the pool, a cell phone at his ear. He's wearing a dark suit, though his jacket is off, and his blue shirt is unbuttoned halfway down, revealing a hairy chest. Another, younger man dressed all in white relaxes nearby while four other men crowd around another table close by, playing a game of cards.

It's not hard to guess the barrel-chested man is Felix. And

I'm willing to bet the men nearby are all bodyguards. What I don't know is who the younger man is. A relative, perhaps.

"Wait here," Armaz says, indicating we shouldn't move from our spot.

"They didn't check us for weapons," Zara whispers.

"I don't think they need to," I say, checking my peripherals without actually moving my head. Even though we're in a glass building, I bet we still have plenty of eyes on us.

Armaz stands close to who I assume is Felix until the man finishes his call. He places his cell phone on the table beside him, then motions for us to come join him. Armaz steps back and Cervantes leads the way. Zara and I keep an equal distance between all of us.

"Felix," Cervantes says.

The man stares at her a moment before standing. "Gemma. What an unexpected pleasure." He looks over her shoulder at us. "And who are your friends?"

"This is Emily Slate, and this is Zara Foley. They work with me."

Felix appraises us as I give him the same nod I gave Armaz. "Needed a little backup, huh? I guess after what happened last time, I can't blame you. Take a seat." He motions for the younger man to get up so Cervantes can have his seat, which he does without another word. However, he doesn't invite us to do the same, so Zara and I stay put.

Cervantes sits, and when she does, I can clearly see her sidearm in the folds of her coat. I don't doubt that Felix sees it too, but the man seems unperturbed. "To what do I owe the pleasure?" he asks.

"We need to talk about the murders," Cervantes says. I'm listening intently, only to realize the other man who was sitting with Felix has come up beside me.

"Business can be so boring, don't you think?" His voice is strong, but also sultry and I have to work to control my features. *Who is this guy?*

I shoot a quick glance at Zara, whose eyes are wide. "I...suppose."

"Come, join me for a drink. The least we can do is stay cool while we wait," he says, getting close enough that I can smell his cologne. It's something expensive. "You don't want to just stand here, do you?"

I get the distinct feeling this isn't so much a request as it is a requirement. Felix's men may not want more than one armed FBI agent standing so close to him, even though they definitely have us in their sights. I'm also not thrilled about leaving Cervantes to fend for herself. Though, she and Felix obviously have a history.

"Very well. Lead the way," I say.

He gives me a tiny smile then heads for the indoor bar, which the woman has vacated. Zara and I follow while Armaz stays close to Felix and the other man who had been bringing up the rear, hangs back, though he sticks with us. This feels less like a house and more like a prison.

"You look young to be in the FBI, both of you," the man says as he reaches the bar. "Though I can't imagine Gemma would bring new agents here."

"We get that a lot," I say, joining him at the bar without actually sitting down. Zara is close behind, though I can't see her right now.

"You're Emily, and you're Zara, right?" The man asks, taking a seat, and I'm struck by a bit of déjà vu. This is eerily similar to our experience with Jun. The only difference is the setting. "I'm Javier." He holds out his hand, and I give it a quick shake. Zara does the same, though neither of us have taken a seat. "You look hot, do you want to remove your coats? It's about eighty degrees in here."

"We'll be fine," I say. "Thank you. Are you and Felix related?"

"My father. Everyone says I resemble my mother, though," he says. "May I offer you a fresh lemonade?"

"Um…sure." I chance another glance at Zara. Is this how *all* these guys act towards women?

"You're here because of the killings, am I right?" Javier asks. "The gang murders?"

"That's right," Zara says.

He glances down, shaking his head. "It is a difficult business. Lots of risk." The bartender brings over three lemonades, setting them on the bar. I am fully sweating under my clothes now. I'll be lucky if I'm not soaked by the time we get out of here. I just hope it's not showing on my face too much.

Javier smiles, handing us each our drinks. "You sure you don't want to remove your coats? The weather outside may be bad, but it's always nice in here."

"I've never seen anything like this," I say, indicating the greenhouse, fully aware that if I remove my jacket, my weapon will be on full display.

"A necessity when we're here. With the weather not cooperating half the year, my father decided he needed a place he could relax, even in the winter months. But our place down in Puerta Vallarta is beautiful year-round." He emphasizes the last two words, making a quick kissing motion with his hand and mouth before taking a sip of the lemonade.

I figure it's probably fine to drink—drugging us would do them no good, so I take a sip and it immediately cools me down. Zara has already finished half of hers. "How often are you here?"

"As often as we need to be," he replies. "But that's not really what you want to talk about, is it?" He leans a little closer, lowering his voice and I catch that cologne again. "Who do you think is doing it?"

I glance back over at Cervantes and Felix who seem to be having a civilized conversation, but while both of them may seem relaxed on the outside, I'd be willing to bet they are on hair triggers, ready to go off at a moment's notice.

"We don't know," I say honestly. "We were hoping your father might have an idea."

"Ah," he says, leaning back and taking another sip of lemonade. "So, you came all the way out here, braved all of this, just to gather information."

I nod. "Pretty much."

He leans around me to look at Zara. "But that's not all you've come for, is it?"

"What do you mean?" she asks.

"You want to know if we had anything to do with it," he says and immediately my hackles rise. Javier holds up a hand. "Calm yourself, you're not in any danger here. Not yet, anyway. It's a reasonable assumption. You have victims from three different gangs, it only makes sense you question the rest of us."

"We're not here to question you," I say, trying to reassure him.

"That's because you're on our territory," he says, smiling. "With four different high-powered weapons sighted on that beautiful black hair of yours as we speak." He leans forward again. "But don't lie, if I were in one of your interrogation rooms, in the middle of the most secure building in the city, you'd be asking me the question."

I bite my lip and set my lemonade down, having lost any desire to finish it. I just want to get out of this alive. Maybe the best way to do that is to be honest. "Yes. We would."

He holds out his hand as if to say *See? It's fine.* Leaning back again, he crosses one leg over the other. "So ask. You have my word that no harm will come to you."

I think it over for a second, while Zara gives me a subtle shake of her head. She knows as well as I do that asking the question could be seen as making an accusation, and we're not here to do that. We're just here to gather information. "I don't need to ask. I know you didn't have anything to do with it."

"Why is that?"

"Because the Luna's don't initiate. They only act in retribution."

He smiles. "I'm impressed. Most people would have jumped on that chance. But you're right, of course. We have no need to go after any of the smaller organizations. They are inconsequential. They know it would be suicide to challenge us, and so we all remain one big, happy family."

Just another version of what Jun told us. And Damian. They all seem fine with the status quo as it is, so why is someone going around killing members of each gang. "You don't believe you're targets?" I ask.

"Look around, Emily," he says, motioning to the houses around us. "This is no small operation. We're not exactly hurting for resources here. If someone were to attack the Lunas, they would be bringing the wrath of God back down on themselves. Everyone knows you don't go after the guys with the biggest arsenal at their disposal. Why do you think the United States hasn't been invaded since the Mexican-American war?

"Because it's all about might, and power," he says, closing his fist. "No one will ever touch us, because we are the strongest. Not to mention, our special *arrangement* with your government."

I try not to show my surprise, instead pretend like I know what he's talking about. "Right, of course. But you must have your suspicions then about who could be involved."

Javier picks up his lemonade again, taking another sip. "We believe it's infighting among the smaller groups. There has been talk about a new player in town, though we haven't heard anything substantial."

"Anything you could provide would be helpful," I say.

He leans forward again. "My father wouldn't want me telling you this, but there's a new group from eastern Russia, bringing in goods from the Baltic."

"Who are they with?" I ask.

"No idea. We figured you might know."

I nod. "Thanks for the tip."

He tilts his glass in his father's direction. "It's more than *he'll* ever give you. He's a very...paranoid person. Doesn't believe in trusting people."

"But you do?" I ask.

"What can I say? I'm part of a new generation." Javier continues to engage us in small talk until Cervantes finally stands. We take note and head back in her direction.

"You're welcome here any time, Gemma," Felix says, though he barely looks in our direction. "Next time, don't feel like you need the attack dogs. I think you and I can be civil on our own."

"I appreciate you taking the time," Cervantes says, then turns to Armaz. As we're heading out, I catch Javier offering us a friendly wave and a smile, but I see something else behind it, and I don't wave back. He only grins and goes back to his drink.

In no time, we're back in the drizzle and are escorted to the Tahoe again. We wait until we're outside the gates before anyone says anything. "Well," Cervantes says, giving us a genuine smile. "I think that went about as well as could be expected."

Chapter Twenty

THE ENTIRE WAY BACK, Cervantes tells us about her discussion with Felix, which amounted to a big, fat nothing after it was all said and done. He engaged in a lot of double-speak and veiled innuendos, but never came right out and gave her anything concrete. Not that she expected him to. "I'm much more interested to hear what Javier had to say."

"You never expected Felix to talk," I say.

"I've known Javier since he was in his teens," she replies, "back when I was a young agent, still becoming familiar with the landscape. But I could see Javier wasn't like his father, he had a different philosophy."

"Much like Santino did after Marco."

She nods. "Back then, Felix wasn't head of the Lunas, but he was headed in that direction. And it was clear what kind of man he already was. Unfortunately, it was my involvement with Felix which eventually helped him get where he is."

"Through an agreement with our government?" I ask.

I catch her eyes in the rearview. "He told you about that, huh?"

"He mentioned it," Zara says. "Kind of a big piece of the puzzle to leave out."

"I didn't want you going in there with any expectations," Cervantes says. "I knew Felix would cockblock me at every turn, but I was hoping one or both of his sons would be present. They're a little more...flexible than their father."

"That's why you were so adamant about all of us going together." I can already feel my face burning.

"Look, you two are young, and you're pretty. I don't care if you want to hear it or not. Men like Felix and his family, they like beautiful things. You always had a much better chance of getting information out of them than I did."

While I'm not blind to pretty privilege, I don't like exploiting it. And I really don't like *being* exploited without my knowledge. "You used us."

"You're damn right I did," she replies. "We're on the brink of a local war. I don't know if you've opened your eyes lately, Agent Slate, but it's getting hostile out there. Each group is convinced one of the other gangs is responsible, and they're not too discerning about who they go after. No one is stupid enough to touch the Lunas, but they'll go after each other. And once that powder keg is ignited, it will be hell to get it under control again."

"Even if we find who is responsible, will the White Hand and the Kings and everyone else believe us?"

"It's hard to say, but it's a start. And if they do, we can prevent a lot of retaliation. In fact, I wouldn't mind using this opportunity to obliterate the White Hand altogether." She turns in her seat, taking her eyes off the road for a moment. "But that depends on if Javier gave you anything helpful."

"They suspect a new faction coming out of Russia, moving goods here from the Baltic," I tell her. "I don't think they have any hard proof—"

"But it's something," she says, turning back around. "Good work. I'll work with my contacts in the CIA. At least this gives us a direction to focus our efforts."

"What about Toscani?" I ask.

"He's still of interest. Interrogate him if you can find him. Until then, I'm going to focus on this angle. We'll need to start monitoring local Russian expat movements. They may be working with people who are already here."

"Is that smart?" Zara asks. "They may just be refugees looking to escape a dictatorship—"

"Or they could be forward agents," Cervantes interrupts. "It's possible this group might have their government's backing like the Dragons do. Either way, we can't be too careful. If this new group *is* responsible, the killer is already here. We'll make this our new priority one."

I sit back, not feeling great about this turn of events. I find it suspicious how our witness fingered Toscani *and* that he's seemingly disappeared, then all of a sudden there is a new organized crime unit coming into the field from Russia? None of this lines up.

"I'll need to pull some of your personnel to help us work this new angle," Cervantes says. "So, you two will be on your own looking for Toscani. If we manage to get this Russian angle covered, I can dedicate the resources back to you. But until then, we have to act like this new group is already here and making waves."

"Understood." Though I don't say what I'm really thinking—that Zara and I just got sidelined for a shiny new toy.

THE REST OF THE WEEK IS MOSTLY UNEVENTFUL. THANKFULLY, there are no more strange cars stalking us, and no more killings, at least none that match the MO of the previous deaths. Whoever was out there targeting the local gangs seems to have quieted down. I don't know if that's because of Cervantes's efforts or not, though from what we know from Nadia and Elliott, the search for the Russians hasn't been going well. According to them, the team hasn't found any evidence to back up Javier's claims. Cervantes isn't willing to give up, she just doesn't believe they're looking in the right places.

Zara and I spend the rest of the week continuing our search for Toscani, which includes going over the surveillance footage. The nights are late, and by the time I get home, I'm so tired all I want to do is sleep and not think anymore. But then I remember this is my last week in this apartment, and part of me is sad about letting it go.

Finally, Saturday morning rolls around and Liam shows up first thing in the morning with the moving truck. Thanks to Zara and Nadia's help, everything in the house is already packed up and we get started loading everything. Timber is both excited and confused to see his house being packed up and stored, but thankfully he doesn't get in the way and instead just watches with interest as Liam and I nearly throw our backs out getting all the furniture in the truck.

When I moved into this apartment, I just had some movers bring what little I'd kept from my house with Matt. I didn't bring a lot with me because I knew I couldn't stand the constant reminder of all "our" things all the time. And over the following months, I developed a style all my own, though I didn't realize just how much I accumulated over the past year and a half. Now that I have to move it all myself, I'm starting to question what would happen if I just left half of it here for the landlord to deal with.

"Helloooo lovelies," Zara says, poking her head in the door as Liam and I are wrestling with my mattress.

"Perfect timing," Liam says, dropping his side. "Tagging you in."

"Hey!" I yell. "She's my relief, not yours."

"Sorry, you snooze you lose." He grabs his water bottle and takes a long swig.

Zara sets a small container of pastries on the counter. "A

little fuel to keep you going," she says. "But I'm just here to observe."

"Don't tell me you can't lift anything," I say. "I've seen you at the gym."

"Oh, I can. I just don't want to," she says, grinning and taking a doughnut out of the box.

"Just what I needed," Liam says, taking something covered in powdered sugar out of the container and taking a huge bite, sending white fluff everywhere.

I chuckle and join them at the island, wiping the side of Liam's mouth before I snag a bite of the pastry myself. Timber is right under my feet looking up at all of us, his eyes wide and his tongue barely sticking out of his mouth. "Don't even think about it," I say when I see Zara reaching into the box.

"I wasn't, just getting seconds for me," she says a little too innocently.

"Uh-huh." I pat Timber's head and grab a snack out of the baggie of his treats I haven't packed. He scarfs it down without even smelling it. "Did you even chew?" I ask.

"He knows he can trust you," Liam says. "He'll literally eat anything you give him. Some dogs aren't like that. They have to inspect it first."

"He's never been that kind of dog," I say. "Half the time I think he swallows his dinner whole."

"That's cause he's a growing boy, yes he is," Zara says, getting down on the ground and rubbing his face.

"Okay, well the adults in the room have work to do," I say and grab Liam by the collar before he can snatch another pastry.

"Have fun, Timber and I will supervise," Zara replies, sitting down on the floor with him.

Liam and I head back over to the mattress and start wrestling with it again. But before we can move it very far, I feel Zara on the far side, helping to guide us. "You get one freebie."

"Thanks," I say and the three of us manage to get it out to the moving van and secured in the side. "Box springs next."

"Ugh," Zara says, as her phone rings. "Hold on, important call. This is Foley." Her eyes go wide, and she motions for me to grab my phone, but I left it somewhere inside. "Hang on one second, Emily is right here. I'll put you on speaker." She switches over, and I hear the harried voice on the other end. It's Cervantes.

"Where are you two right now?" she asks.

"At my place," I tell her. "I'm moving today."

"I need you both to meet me at the Amtrak Maintenance Facility off Ninth. You'll see the lights."

"What's going on?" I ask.

"The Lunas just got hit."

Chapter Twenty-One

ZARA and I didn't bother changing, instead figured it was best for us to get down there right away. Liam assured us he could take care of moving everything without me. I hate to leave him high and dry like this, but this case keeps popping up at the most inopportune times.

After almost a week of silence, the killers have struck again. I don't even need to see it for myself to know how bad it's going to be. The whole way there, I can't help my feeling of dread, knowing the Lunas will respond to this attack, and they won't be quiet about it.

"Who would be crazy enough to go after the Lunas?" Zara asks as we speed our way down there. We figured it would be easier to take her car since mine was already full of stuff from the apartment.

"Someone who wants a war," I say. "And I'm not convinced it's the Russians."

"Especially since there hasn't been any evidence pointing to them," she says. "Other than…" She trails off as the scene comes into view. The maintenance building that services all the Amtrak train cars is to our right, a massive structure of steel and aluminum. Beyond it, close to a large parking lot near the tracks, are about ten police cruisers, all of them with their lights flashing. A couple of other cars are parked nearby, including Cervantes's Tahoe. As we pull up, I'm surprised to see not only Cervantes on the scene, but SAC Wallace as well.

"Sir," I say as Zara and I circle the car, headed for what I assume is the scene of the crime.

"Slate, Foley," he says, his arms crossed, examining the scene. Cervantes comes over, her face flushed.

"I'm sorry to call you on your day off—"

"Slate doesn't know the meaning of the word, you don't have to worry," Wallace interjects.

Cervantes doesn't seem to notice, instead she motions for us to follow her. "As far as I know, Felix isn't aware of this yet. But it's only a matter of time. I hope the two of you made some progress on Toscani, because we haven't found a thing about these supposed Russians."

"We went through everything we have," I tell her, trying to keep up with her fast pace. "Best we can figure is he left on February twenty-eighth and hasn't been back to the city since. We checked all the flight records and couldn't find a scan of his passport anywhere. We assume he's still in the country but don't know for sure."

"Who is in charge in the interim?" she asks.

"No one," Zara replies. "At least, no one seems to be looking out for the whole organization. There's a manager at his factory, but that's about it."

"I don't like it," Cervantes says. "They are the last ones that haven't been hit—everything points to them. And their boss is conveniently missing." She brings us to where I can see three shapes on the ground, each covered by a blue blanket.

"Any idea of what vehicle they were driving?" I ask.

"We don't have any information at this point," she replies. I want to get as much from this as—" She trails off as we see two large black SUVs pull up. The officers taping off the area try to block them out, but the SUVs drive through the tape, stopping just short of where the three of us are standing.

Two of the same men I saw at Felix's compound get out of the first SUV, followed by Felix and two more in the second SUV. He breezes past us like he doesn't even see us, and heads for the bodies.

"He can't——" I begin, about to say he's going to contaminate the crime scene, but Cervantes holds me back. I push her hand away and stomp after Felix, determined to stop him. "Sir, you can't be here, this is an active crime scene."

"I don't care what it is, I'm seeing this for myself," he says. I know it's probably not smart, but I grab him by the arm to stop him from going any further. He stills immediately, looking down at my hand on his arm.

"Emily," Cervantes yells. I turn to see the men who were with Felix reach into their coats.

"You want a bloodbath here today, agent?" Felix growls. "Because I'll give you one."

Against my better judgement, I let go of his arm and the men relax, which causes all the other officers around us to relax as well. Felix must know his men are outnumbered ten to one here and still, he'd open fire and take the risk, probably dying in the process.

He doesn't look back, only heads to the first body where he throws off the blanket. It's Armaz. And from what I can see, the bullet pattern is the same. Two or three to the chest, and one right between the eyes. Felix steps over the former employee and heads to the next man, whom I don't know. He looks like just another grunt. But when Felix reaches the third body, I can't help but gasp.

Felix collapses to his knees in front of Javier's body. The man I drank a lemonade with only a few days ago lays before us, dead. I walk up behind Felix to get a better look, but it's the same story as the other two. The man before me quietly sobs, and I feel like I can hear him uttering a prayer of sorts.

He takes one of his son's arms and lays it across his body, then does the same to the other arm.

My analytical mind is telling me he's contaminating the scene. That every move he's making is potentially destroying evidence we might be able to use to find Javier's killer. But my emotional brain tells me this is a father grieving for the loss of his son. A grown man who was cut down in the prime of his life. I want to ask Felix the details of everything that happened here. Of who they were supposed to be meeting with, and who might have done this.

I stand behind the man for what seems like an hour until he finally gets up. I don't notice any other activity around us; it's like the whole world has stopped and it's just me and this man, this…criminal. And yet I *feel* for him.

When he turns to me, his eyes are red-rimmed, but his face is stoic. "Agent Slate, my son was obviously mistaken the other day when he told you of a Russian faction. This is the work of that lying toad Santino."

"How can you be sure?" I ask.

He grits his teeth and I see a couple have gold replacements. "I know a double cross when I see it. And mark my words, he will not live to see the day he regrets his actions."

"How—"

"Despite all his protestations and promises, it seems he is the same lying weasel as his uncle. Well, if he wants a war, he's got one." He brushes past me again, headed back for the SUVs.

"Wait," I say. "Was Javier supposed to meet with the Toscanis? Is that how you know it's them?"

"I know it is them because they remain whole, while the rest of us suffer our losses," he says. "Javier and Armaz were making a simple exchange with one of our well-known suppliers. That is all. But I received a call from the suppliers early this morning, their vehicles had been sabotaged and they never made the meeting."

He walks past Cervantes and Zara, the other officers and finally, Wallace. "Mark my words, I will burn this city to the ground to flush him out. You can count on that, *Gemma*." He glares right at Cervantes before he closes the door. The rest of his crew return to their vehicles and peel away, leaving nothing but tire tracks in their wake.

"This is exactly what I didn't want," Cervantes says.

"He said Javier was wrong about the Russians," I tell her.

"Dammit, I *knew* it," Zara says. "There hasn't been any unusual activity out of Russia in months. That never made sense."

"Why would he even suggest it then?" Wallace asks, having come up to join our group. His arms are still crossed and he's glaring at the ground, but I feel like the question is directed at me.

"My guess is Felix didn't think Toscani had the balls to go after him. Javier said he thought the Russians would be the only ones who would make such a move."

"So then Toscani is behind all this after all," Zara says.

"Felix seems to think so. Either way, we need to find him. Now."

Cervantes turns to Wallace. "Call your people. Get everyone on the search. I don't care how many field offices we need to involve. Santino Toscani is out there somewhere, presumably still in the country. We need to find him and take him into protective custody until we can figure out what's going on."

"Protective custody?" I shout. "He doesn't deserve protection."

"If we don't, Felix will kill him before we can find out what his endgame is," she replies. "This city is on the brink. The other gangs may have been willing to hold off for the time being, but as soon as the Lunas get involved, it will be every man for himself. And given the amount of territory those four organizations hold, there will be a lot of innocent people killed by Felix's bloodlust."

"Protecting Toscani is only going to make things worse," I say. "Felix will see it as betrayal. You want to talk about a war? What happens when the Cartel challenges the US Government out in the open?"

"I'd say the odds are pretty good on that one," Wallace quips.

"And how much of that death are you willing to take responsibility for?" I demand. "Because you sure as hell only seem to want to take the wins."

"Careful, Agent Slate," he says. "I'm not your personal punching bag."

"No? Because it feels like I'm yours sometimes."

"Okay," Zara takes my arm and leads me away as Wallace scowls at me. "You're not going to get anywhere antagonizing Wallace, especially not in front of other agents," she whispers as we get out of earshot. "I know he's an asshole, but don't make right now the moment for that battle."

"I just…did you see who that is over there? It's Javier. We were *just* with him."

"I saw," she says softly until we're on the far side of the sets of train tracks. People begin moving around the scene again, starting the gruesome work of cataloging all the evidence and looking for anything that the killer might have left behind. "Look, we need to find Santino. *Someone* knows where he is. Who haven't we talked to yet?"

I rub my forehead, trying to think. "I don't know. I feel like we exhausted all the possibilities."

"There's something we're missing," she replies. "We're just not seeing it."

"If this is Toscani, then what's he doing all this for?" Zara asks. "Why risk a war like this? What's he gaining?"

"Respect? Not to mention he's been able to steal all the goods from each one of his rivals," I say.

"True, but I'm not sure a couple of trucks full of goods are enough to invite this kind of heat down on his organization. He has to know all his drivers are at risk, his warehouse, everything." She screws up her face, thinking. "If we can figure out what he wants, I think we can find him."

"What do they all want?" I ask, plopping down on the pavement. "Power and influence. And don't forget money. They love money."

She squats down beside me, one arm on my shoulder. "I know this isn't great timing, and I know you're burnt out."

I look up at her, and even as the words come out of my mouth, I know they're a lie. "I'm not burnt out."

"Instead of what should have been a relaxing week with your boyfriend and his family, you were galivanting all over the state looking for a killer. Then you come back, only to have to return to Ohio and get grilled by an underqualified, pompous detective about something you had no involvement in. *Then* you come back home only to find you've been thrown into the middle of what's effectively about to be a turf war in the capital city of the United States, and you're being asked to solve all of it. Not to mention, you are making the biggest move of your personal life ever since you lost your husband."

I let out a long breath and my shoulders slump. "Well, when you put it like that…"

"Not to mention your boss won't get off your case. Even *I* can't figure that one out." She pauses. "When was the last time you talked to Doctor Frost?"

"Umm…" I make a face trying to remember.

"Time for another appointment then," she says.

"Wait a second, I was the one who recommended him to you, shouldn't I be the one—"

"Nope," she says. "You shouldn't. As much as you want to be, you're not superwoman."

I lean forward and wrap my arms around my legs. "I just was hoping today would be a new start for Liam and me.

We've all been through so much the past few months; it just seems like it's been nonstop. I thought maybe once we came back from Stillwater, we'd have some time to just...live our lives." I look across the railyard at the men and women going about their jobs, setting up evidence markers. Then I look over to Wallace and Cervantes, who seem to be having a terse conversation. I love my job, I really do, but I can't keep going like this forever. Zara's right, I am burned out.

"Let's get you back to your boyfriend," she says. "If Felix decides to ignite the powder keg tonight, there's not a lot we can do about it. Unless Santino Toscani just miraculously happens to pop up out of nowhere."

"Unlikely," I say. I smile as Zara helps me up. "You forgot to mention my crazy aunt who may or may not be stalking..."

My eyes go wide as I realize we may have missed something after all. Something big.

"Em? What is it? What's wrong?"

"I think I might know how to find Santino."

Chapter Twenty-Two

"YES, I realize it's the weekend, but this is something of an emergency," I say into the receiver as Zara drives.

"I'm sorry Agent Slate, but we have protocol here. You'll have to wait until tomorrow," the woman on the other end of the phone tells me.

"You don't understand," I say. "If I don't speak with Marco Toscani tonight, Washington DC may be on *fire* tomorrow."

She pauses on the other end. "Let me put you through to the district attorney. He handles all our inmate requests of this nature." There's a click before I can protest, and soft music begins. I roll my eyes and make a gagging face at Zara.

"Not being very cooperative?"

"Bureaucratic bullshit it is what it is. They have a policy that inmates can't be seen after noon on a Sunday without a prior appointment. For an FBI agent! They just don't want to go to the trouble of rounding him up so we can speak with him. And why is a DA even involved in this? Shouldn't his job be done once the criminals are in prison?"

She wrinkles her forehead. "They want you to talk to the DA?"

The phone clicks again. "This is DA Hodges, who am I speaking with?"

I huff. "This is Special Agent Emily Slate with the FBI, Violent Crimes. I'm calling because I need to get in to see Marco Toscani, and it's urgent."

"I'm sorry Agent Slate, you'll have to wait until tomorrow. From what I understand the prison doesn't—"

"I've already been fed that line and I know it's bullshit," I tell him. "Look, we need to find Santino Toscani, and we think his uncle might have a good idea where he is."

"And you need to do this right now?" he asks.

"I wouldn't be calling if it wasn't urgent."

He pauses. "Where are you?"

I exchange a quick glance with Zara as that was not the question I was expecting. I check the GPS. "Headed to JCI, on I-95 right now. About forty-five minutes away."

"Turn around, we need to meet in person first," he says.

"Why? That will only delay—"

"Agent Slate, if you want to get in to see Marco Toscani today, you will turn around. There's something we need to discuss, but I'd prefer it be face to face. Meet me at my office." He rattles off the address, and I put it into the GPS. Zara gets over in the right lane so she can take the next exit.

"Okay, I got it but I don't understand—"

"You will when we meet," he replies, and I hear something in his voice. It's not panic, more like apprehension. But why would he be apprehensive about Marco Toscani? "I'm here now, just let the security guard downstairs know who you are, I'll clear you to come up."

I check the GPS's estimated time. "Okay, we should be there in about twenty minutes."

"Good. See you then." He hangs up.

"Well, that was weird," I say, staring at my phone a moment. "Guess I better call Liam to let him know we won't be back anytime soon to help."

"I'm sure he'll understand. He knows this job is unpredictable," she says.

"I'm just not sure *I* understand. What's going on with Marco Toscani?"

She glances down at the GPS. "I guess we'll find out in about twenty minutes."

~

WE PULL INTO THE PARKING LOT OF THE DA'S BUILDING, which is a stone and marble eyesore and doesn't seem to match a lot of the other historical buildings in DC. This one is about five blocks from the mall, though, so we're able to avoid the Sunday traffic.

We have to show our credentials to even park in the underground lot, and the car has to undergo a security check by officers with dogs. I'm already chomping at the bit, and it's taking a lot longer than I'd like to even get up to see Hodges. Finally, we're able to park and go through security in the lobby before being directed to the elevators. We get off on the fifth floor and follow the signage directing us to DA Hodges's office. The door is already cracked, but I knock anyway.

"Come in."

We enter to find DA Hodges behind his desk, wearing a loose brown suit that's been undone at the collar. His tie sits on the desk next to him. He looks up, removes a pair of delicate spectacles from his nose, and stands. "Agent Slate, I assume?"

I reach out and shake his hand. "Sir. This is Agent Zara Foley."

Hodges shakes Zara's hand as well. "Have a seat, please."

His office is what I would expect for a US District Attorney. Most of the shelves are lined with volumes upon volumes of law books while a portion of the shelves have been reserved for photos with notable government representatives or celebrities. Hodges looks to be in his late fifties, which means he's probably been in this job a while. His hair is thinning, though there's still enough left that I can see it was once a rich brown.

We take our seats across from him in plush, leather chairs. His desk looks to be solid oak, complete with a small green banker's lamp on the side. It's also full of papers and folders from what I assume are current cases he's working. "We don't mean to take up a lot of your time," I say as we sit. "But it's imperative that we see Marco Toscani as soon as possible."

"What's your interest in him?" Hodges asks. It's not exactly a friendly question, but I sense the genuine curiosity behind it.

"His nephew, Santino Toscani is the primary suspect in a series of murders that have been happening all over the city. Perhaps you've caught wind of them?"

He shakes his head. "Can't say I have."

"Gang violence," Zara says. "Someone is targeting the local criminal enterprises, looking to make a statement."

"And you think Santino Toscani is responsible?" Hodges asks.

"The Toscanis are the only ones who haven't been hit yet," I say.

"Makes it kind of too obvious then, doesn't it?" He tents his fingers, and leans forward, lost in thought. "If Toscani is behind it, he's just painted a major target on his back," Hodges says.

"Exactly why we need to find him," Zara says. "Some of these gangs are ready to go to war if the culprit isn't found."

Hodges leans back into his own chair, rocking it back and forth slightly as he appraises us. I can tell he's trying to decide if he can trust us with something, but I have no idea what that could be. "What are we missing?"

He lets out a long breath, taps the arm of his chair a few times, then sits back up. "You're probably wondering why, when you called to schedule a meeting with Marco Toscani, you were transferred to me. That's because for the past six weeks, I have been in contact with Marco Toscani on a regular basis."

"For what purpose?" I ask.

"He's acting as an informant for the DA's office in exchange for a lighter sentence."

"An informant of what?" Zara asks.

"For his nephew's activities," Hodges says. "Obviously this is all being kept hush, hush, as I don't want word of it getting out. Marco Toscani was a big score, and we're not about to let him off easy. But we figured if we could pump him for some useful information, maybe we could move him to a…less intense facility."

"Has he been able to give you anything solid?" I ask.

"A few things," Hodges says. "We've managed to pick up a couple of Santino's drivers for transporting illegal goods, but all of them have confessed to working on their own, *without* Santino's involvement. Apparently, he's keeping his hands clean. Or so they say." He rolls his eyes. "Not that I believe it for a second." He picks up a pen and taps it on the top folder of his desk absently, like he's thinking. "When did these events begin?"

I exchange a glance with Zara. "About three weeks ago. The White Hand was hit first. Then the Steel Dragons. And just this past week the Jefferson Kings and La Luna Roja."

"Shit," he says. "That's serious."

"Tell us something we don't know," Zara replies.

"Has Marco given you any indication of where Santino is right now?" I ask. "We need to find him and…" I hesitate. "… bring him in for his own protection."

"So far, Marco has provided no information on the where-abouts of Santino Toscani," he says matter-of-factly. "But most of our conversations have revolved around the organization as a whole. Not the man himself. Marco isn't the most… outgoing of people. Normally I'd wouldn't give two shits about you talking to the man, but I can't have you disrupting a potentially useful relationship which could lead to a lot more arrests and even the dissolution of the Toscani Family Organization."

"Why would Marco agree to that? I thought the family was his primary concern," I ask.

"We feel like prison has changed his attitude. A year inside will do that to someone, especially with as much solitary as Marco has been forced to endure."

"Forced?" Zara asks.

"He kept starting fights, antagonizing the other prisoners. JCI didn't have a choice. He's been on his own probably three-fourths of his entire sentence."

I shoot a look at Zara. *Antagonizing the other prisoners.* "Are you saying we can't get in to see him?"

Hodges taps his pen a few more times. "It's taken months for us to build a rapport. I'm afraid if we let you two loose on him, he'd just clam back up. And right now, the information he's providing has been useful. I'm sorry, but I just don't think it's a good idea. However, I have a meeting with him on Tuesday. I'll ask about finding Santino. Though from what I understand, the two men despise each other—another primary reason Marco is helping us. He'd rather burn the organization down than let Santino run it."

"We don't have until Tuesday," I tell him. "Both the Hand and the Lunas are ready to go to war. If we don't figure out who is behind this before—"

"I'm sorry," he says. "It's the best I can do. I wish I could be more helpful, but if we lose this thread, we may never get it back."

"Is taking down a relatively small criminal organization worth all those lives?" Zara asks, anger in her voice. She has a right to be angry; I am too. And she asks a valid question.

"Honestly, Agent Foley, I don't really care what one gang does to another. The more they kill each other, the less paperwork I have to deal with, and the better off we all are."

"And what about the innocent civilians caught in the crossfire?" I ask. "This war won't stay localized to just members of the gangs. Everyone will suffer."

He sets his pen down. "I don't know what you want me to say. You've asked the question, and I've given you your answer. Toscani is off-limits for the time being."

"You can't be serious," I say.

He picks up his glasses, replaces them on the bridge of his nose, and opens up his laptop off to the side. "Have a good rest of your weekend, agents."

I stare at him a moment longer only to realize he's not going to budge before I finally get up. Zara, who is usually right behind me, stares at him even longer, but Hodges doesn't seem to care. Finally, she stands, and we head back out.

"What an asshole," she says while we're still within earshot of his office. There's no way he didn't hear it.

"We can't wait for Hodges to have his meeting on Tuesday," I say as we reach the elevators.

"So, what do you suggest?" Zara asks. "It's not like we can go behind his back."

"Can't we?" I ask.

"Em, if Hodges finds out—"

"We're no worse off. He's not going to ask about Santino, he's focused on his own investigation." It doesn't surprise me someone like Hodges isn't willing to look at the bigger picture. He's probably been working these criminals so long all he can see anymore is his own immediate goal.

"So, what do we do?" she asks.

"Find someone who can get us into JCI. *Unofficially.*"

Chapter Twenty-Three

It took exactly one phone call to get us back on track. Though, it wasn't a phone call I ever wanted to make. I hate asking for help, especially when I should be able to take care of something myself, but this situation is close to spiraling out of control. I don't have time to wallow in self-pity or doubt, and I sure as hell don't have time to protect my pride.

We needed help, so I pulled our ace in the hole. I just hope it was worth it.

As we pull up to the main gates of JCI, a guard comes out to meet us from the small booth on this side of the massive gates. We show him our identification and our badges, which gets us into the parking lot at least. Thankfully the gate guard isn't about to question two FBI agents coming into the prison. The real test of whether my phone call worked will be once we get inside.

We're stopped just inside the main doors by another set of guards, and we're required to leave our weapons and anything sharp before going through the metal detectors. Once through, we approach a small window where a man sits on the other side, playing on his phone. Given it's almost eight p.m. on a Sunday night, I guess not a lot goes on at this hour.

"Agents Slate and Foley," I say, showing him our badges through the bullet-proof glass window that separates us. "We're here to see Marco Toscani."

He glances up, skepticism in his eyes. "Deposit your IDs in the drawer," he says through a small microphone below the window. A small metal drawer extends to our right. We do as we're told, and the drawer retracts. He scans our IDs into the system, giving us the side-eye as he does. I'm sure he's been instructed that no one but Hodges and those approved by the DA are to see Toscani. Especially if he's still in solitary.

He pulls his lips between his teeth as he removes the IDs from the scanner and puts them back in the drawer, which opens on our side again. We remove them as a loud buzzer sounds. For a second, I think it's an alarm of some sort, and we're to be escorted out of here for attempting to circumvent the system. But instead, he speaks into a microphone again, but this time it sounds through the whole room. "Escort two." He picks up a phone and speaks something into it that we can't hear through the glass. After he hangs up, he presses the microphone on his side so we can hear him again.

"You're going to go with Officer Danvers, who will meet you at those doors over there." He points to a large metal door to our right, just past a small room which looks to hold snack and drink machines. "He will take you to a holding area where the prisoner will be brought to you. Do not touch the prisoner, and do not hand the prisoner anything. Your visit will be supervised at all times."

"We know the drill," I say, but I feel like he's cut off his side of the mic before I can say it. He's already gone back to his phone when the metal door opens, and we're met by a large guard with biceps the size of my head. He nods and holds the door for us before shutting it back behind him. A small green light beside the door turns to red as soon as he does, and he calls in his position over his radio.

"Here to see the big cheese, huh? Man don't get many

visitors," Danvers says, leading the way. We head down a long hallway before we're taken to a room with only two tables and some chairs. The lights are off when we enter and Danvers switches them on, causing the bright fluorescents to flicker a moment and bathe the room in a harsh, white light. The room doesn't have any windows, but there is another door at the far end of the room.

"Take a seat. I'll be back in about ten minutes."

As soon as he's gone, I take the chance to examine the room. There are video cameras in all four corners, each of them clearly on. I'm sure the place is wired to pick up sound as well. If he doesn't hear about this tonight, Hodges will be aware of our little visit first thing in the morning. And I'm sure the very first person he'll call is Wallace.

"We'll try to keep this as brief as we can," I tell Zara. She nods in agreement, and we wait in silence for Danvers to return.

After only about five minutes, the other door to the room opens and Danvers appears, this time with Marco Toscani.

He's wearing the standard prison-orange and beige slip-on shoes. His hands have also been bound, though his feet remain free. Looking at him, I can see the resemblance to Santino. They have similar facial features, and Marco is a similar height to his nephew. But this man is much more imposing in person. He wears a full beard and moustache, which have been trimmed and are speckled with gray. His curly hair has also turned gray, but it only makes him look more distinguished. He's a man who holds himself not like a prisoner, but like he's still running a massive criminal organization. I'm fascinated by his confidence.

If he's surprised to see us, he doesn't show it. He only gives each of us one look before walking over and taking a seat at one of the tables. Danvers closes the door behind him and stands guard, keeping his eyes on Toscani.

I stare at Toscani a moment, trying to get a read on him,

but he's not giving up anything. The man is like a statue, staring straight ahead. Finally, he turns and looks up at us. "Well? Let's get on with it." His voice is rough, and it sounds like he might be a smoker. Zara and I take a seat across from him, and I notice what looks like a cut that has freshly healed over his right eye. It's not immediately apparent, but it seems Hodges's warning about Toscani starting fights wasn't an exaggeration.

"That looks like it hurt," I say, nodding to the cut.

"Are we here to talk about my injuries?" he asks. He has something of an accent which makes me think he's probably at least bilingual.

"No. We're here to talk about your nephew."

He narrows his gaze. "Hodges didn't send you."

"No," I say. "We're here for something else. We need to find Santino. He's gone missing."

He thinks about it for a minute, and I wonder if he might not be willing to speak to anyone *but* Hodges. But then he surprises me. "How would I know where that little shit is hiding?" he asks.

"You must have some idea," I say, glad he's at least willing to talk. Otherwise, all of this would have been for nothing. "He worked under you for years. You're family. You know things about him no one else does."

"You mean he undermined me for years, sold me out to the feds." Marco looks down, scanning for our badges, but we purposely put them away when we came in here. I don't need him more antagonistic than he already is.

"We want to bring him in," I say.

"Maybe he's already dead. Did you think of that?" Marco asks. He says it without emotion. Like it wouldn't matter to him one bit if Santino had been killed or not.

I actually hadn't considered he could be dead already, considering we're looking at him as the architect of all these killings. "We don't believe that's the case. We think he is operating remotely, pulling strings from somewhere else."

"What strings?" Marco asks, screwing up his face.

"We believe he's behind some high-profile deaths that have occurred recently," Zara says.

"Deaths?"

"Enemies of the Toscanis," I say. "We think he's been orchestrating the deaths of rival operations."

Marco sneers. "Himself?"

I shoot Zara a look. "We don't think he's doing it himself. More than likely he's hired—"

Marco scoffs. "Of course he has. Why get his hands dirty when he can pay someone to do it for him?" He leans forward his hand outstretched to us. He closes it in a fist. "If my nephew had any vision, he *would* do it himself. That's what a respectable leader does, they show how it's done instead of passing it off for someone else to do the job for him." He says it with such disgust I'm surprised he doesn't spit right on the table.

"Is that how you would do it?" I ask.

"I wouldn't be stupid enough to start killing my rivals," he says. "But it sounds like something my nephew might try. *If* he's desperate enough." He grins, looking away from us for a moment. "Maybe he's feeling the pressure. He knows he doesn't have long at the top. Maybe he decided to do something drastic. A…what do you call it? Hail Mary?"

I think back to Hodge's remarks about the deal he has with Marco. Marco himself could be the reason for some of that pressure. That might have been his plan all along. "Are you saying Santino is in danger of losing control of the Toscanis?"

Marco gives us a sly smile and shrugs. "Who can say? Maybe he's finding the job is too difficult for him. But instead of facing the consequences of his actions like a *man*, he's decided to go into hiding until everything dies down."

He taps on the table with his index finger as he looks off into the distance. "Yes, I can see it. He builds this elaborate plan. But on the eve of its execution, he gets stage fright. Decides to cower until it's all over. He's *paura delle conseguenze.*" He glares at us. "Afraid of the blowback." Marco shoves a finger into the table. "*That* is my nephew. A coward."

Has this been Marco's plan all along? Undermine his nephew as Santino had undermined him? It would certainly make sense, given the nature of the family and what little I know about Marco Toscani. I wonder if Santino suspects his uncle is the one who has boxed him into a corner.

"You're saying perhaps things aren't going very well for Santino, and he's feeling pressure? And as a consequence, he's decided to what…start a turf war?"

Marco narrows his gaze. "It takes the spotlight off him, no? If his men are busy fending off rival gangs, they won't be so focused on his ineffective leadership. He might even be smart enough to leverage it into gaining more power. Though…against the Lunas…" He *tsks,* shaking his head. "*That* is a stupid move. That is suicide."

I'm surprised with how open he's being. Then again, he *really* dislikes his nephew. Maybe Marco just likes seeing the results of his weeks of work with Hodges finally coming to fruition.

"You wouldn't be upset if Santino was ousted, would you? Even killed?"

"He's my sister's son. My blood. I would mourn for him, but I would also say he got what he deserved. Santino should have stayed where he was."

"Except he turned on you," Zara says.

"He turned on the *family*," Marco says. "He turned on everything he grew up knowing. Maybe if he'd actually had the guts to kill me, I might have given him some respect. But he went behind my back, made a deal with you people. Took the coward's way out."

"Isn't that what you're doing now?" I ask. "By working with Hodges?"

"What I have done with Hodges is insignificant compared to what that boy did to me. I have merely slowed operations. Made things inefficient enough to become a problem. I have not stuck my knife in his back when he wasn't looking and twisted." He pauses, drumming his fingers on the table again. "He has brought this upon himself. When I was arrested, I gave up everything I had. I thought that was the worst that could happen. But to see what he has done to our family's organization…to know that he has corrupted it into a shadow of what it once was? That was a fate worse than any I could have imagined." He smiles. "I will be glad to see it crumble."

"Then help us find him," I say. "The sooner we have him in custody, the sooner he can no longer control the organization."

"No," Marco says, the word coming out as a whisper. "He does not deserve to be in here. He deserves to watch everything he loves die. And he deserves to die with it."

"But that won't happen," Zara says. "Not if he stays in hiding. And what if this gamble works, and the other gangs end up wiping each other out, or at least hurting each other so much that they're powerless against the Toscanis? That will only make him more powerful. That will put him in the exact position you don't want him in."

He considers her words for a moment before leaning forward again. I see Danvers stiffen, but he relaxes when it's clear Marco isn't going much further than the table. "You will arrest him?"

"We will interrogate him," I say. "And as soon as we can connect him to these killings, then yes, we will arrest him."

He takes a deep breath. "As much as I want my nephew to suffer, I can't ignore that you could be right. Things now are…unpredictable." He smiles at us again, though there's more to it. A satisfaction. "He should be out in the open."

"Does that mean you know where he is?" I ask.

"I can provide you with a list of addresses. Places known only to the Toscanis. Safehouses, if you will."

"We would very much appreciate that," I say. "What do you want in return?"

"You can't give me what I want," he says. "But I think I might just get it anyway." He turns to Danvers. "I need a pen and a piece of paper."

Chapter Twenty-Four

"I DON'T LIKE any of what just happened in there," Zara says as we're headed back into the city. In my pocket is a small piece of paper with three addresses written on it, provided by Marco Toscani.

"Neither did I. He's got a huge chip on his shoulder."

"Sounds like he's just butthurt his nephew got the better of him," she says.

"And he's willing to destroy his own legacy to return the favor." Marco was *more* than cooperative, and it wasn't until we were almost done that I figured out why. Marco knows if we find Santino and bring him in, that news will travel quickly. *Everyone* will know how to get to him. And Marco is probably betting the Lunas or someone else might be willing to kill a few feds if they can get to Santino as well.

By capturing and bringing Santino in, we'll be painting a target on our own backs too.

"Maybe at least now we have a chance to find Santino and get a handle on this situation."

"I hope so. Are you going to call Cervantes?"

After all the security checks, getting in and out of the prison, and our little meeting with Marco, it's almost ten-thirty. But Cervantes doesn't strike me as the kind of person who cares about being bothered late at night. Especially considering how important this might be.

"Yeah, I will, I just…" I lean my head back and rub my temples.

"I still don't get Hodges," she says. "He acted like us going in there was going to disrupt years of work. But, if anything, I think we just made his job easier for him."

"You know how some guys are," I say, my eyes closed. "They want all the glory for themselves. I can't wait for Wallace to get that phone call in the morning."

"What do you think he'll do?"

"The same thing he always does. He'll probably threaten to ship me off to Montana again. It's obvious he doesn't want me around. I thought maybe after the whole fiasco with Cochrane that we'd come to an understanding—"

"You mean when Janice nearly threatened to fire him after we handed the FBI its biggest mole in history?"

"Yeah…he calmed down after that. Got off my back. But it's like ever since the whole thing with Magus and the bombings, he's been back to his dickish self. I don't know what changed."

"Other than the fact you weren't supposed to be on that case?" Zara asks.

"Hey," I say, turning to look at her. "It was *you*. There was no way I *wasn't* going to be on that case."

"I'm just glad you were," she says.

I am too. I can't afford to think about Wallace right now. Instead, I watch the lights of the city as they go by. There really isn't any separation between DC and Baltimore anymore; they form almost one large megacity where the lights at night stretch for miles. They're hypnotic to watch. I don't get to just sit here and look very often; usually I'm the one driving. But I'm finding I don't mind the passenger seat these days nearly as much as I used to.

I let out a long breath. "Okay, time to call Cervantes. We'll need to set up an operation at all three locations. I don't want Santino somehow getting word that we raided one of his safehouses and he flees another."

"That's going to be a big op," Zara says. "At least thirty people. And we'll probably have to partner with the locals for each one."

She's right. Each safehouse, while close to the DC area, they're all in completely different areas. There's no way we could cover all three at once.

I pull out my phone to begin dialing when there's a bright flash of orange off to our left. "Em," Zara says, her voice full of apprehension.

I look to the source of the light and see what looks like a dark cloud rising in the night. "What was that? An explosion?"

"I think so," she says.

"Where was it?"

"That's…uh, that's over in the warehouse district. Not far from where we found Javier this morning."

"The warehouse district?" I watch as the cloud continues to billow and rise in the air, and I can see the glow of flames as something big burns. "Take the next ramp; that's no small fire."

She nods and takes the exit. Because it's Sunday night, traffic is light, and we're able to navigate the surface streets, bringing us closer and closer to the source of the fire. Along the way, I get a pit in my stomach as I begin to recognize the area.

We've been here before. On more than one occasion.

As Zara turns the corner, a fire truck goes blazing by us, sirens and lights blaring. We follow it all the way and are joined by another truck as the massive building on fire comes into view. We hang back, allowing the fire trucks to be the first on the scene. Other sirens wail in the distance.

Zara stops the car, and we both get out to look at the blaze before us.

"Em, that's—"

"I know," I say. "It's Toscani's warehouse."

$\sim$

I CALL CERVANTES FROM THE CAR, INFORMING HER OF THE warehouse fire and what we learned from Toscani while the whole place erupts in organized chaos. The primary concern seems to be preventing the fire from spreading to any of the neighboring buildings, and given how hot it's burning, the fire department is having a difficult time getting close enough to extinguish the blaze.

By the time Cervantes arrives on site, it's burning even hotter than it was when we arrived.

"Folks, you need to move back!" the same fire chief who assisted us with the raid on Drummond's club yells. "We don't have this thing nearly under control yet."

We get back into the car and drive two blocks away where we meet Cervantes just pulling up in her Tahoe. The police have cordoned off a five-block radius around the fire. Thankfully, it happened at night on a weekend, not in the middle of a Wednesday during business hours.

"Lunas or Aryans?" Cervantes asks as she gets out of her car, wrapping a coat tightly around her. The wind has picked up, which is only making the fire fighters' job harder.

"My bet is Felix," I say. "He's not going to waste any time, not after what happened this morning. The Aryans have had all week and still haven't made a move."

"Aw, that was going to be my answer," Zara says.

"You're probably right. It also doesn't hurt that the White Hand has been hurting since they lost their shipment. They aren't as well-funded as the other organizations, and despite all their posturing, I think they're probably just trying to keep things from falling apart at the moment."

"Good, let them," I say.

"They'll just reform somewhere else," Cervantes says. "They always do. Someone's bigoted daddy will give them a fresh influx of cash, and they'll be off to the races." She stares up at the warehouse, which is partially hidden by another building from our vantage point. "Looking at a total loss?"

"I think they must have used napalm or something," I say. "We caught the initial explosion as we were coming back from JCI after a very interesting conversation with Marco Toscani." I hold up the piece of paper with the three addresses on it.

"How reliable is the intel?"

"He hates his nephew, that much is for certain," Zara says. "I wanted to do a check on each of the properties first, make sure we weren't being led on a wild goose chase."

"A check?" Cervantes asks.

"Property records search along with looking at any surveillance cameras in the area. Someone had to buy those properties. I just want to make sure they lead back to the Toscanis. We've already been given one red herring already."

Cervantes curses. "I can't believe Felix did that." She looks up into the night sky. "Strike that. I can. Because he can be a vengeful son of a bitch. He doesn't know when someone is trying to help him."

"Is that what we were doing the other day?" I ask.

"Agent Slate, you have a very good reason for being salty with me. I played a hand, and it didn't work out. But that's life; most of everything we try will fail. I had to give it a shot. And now…" She stares up at the warehouse again. "Now it's too late."

"We can still find Santino," I say.

"You don't know Felix's bloodlust like I do. Once he gets started, he won't stop. Not until he's burned everything the

Toscanis are to the ground. Do we know if there were any people in there?"

"No clue," I tell her.

"I guess Santino's plan really backfired," Zara says.

"He should have known better than to go after the Lunas," Cervantes says. "Talk about an over-inflated ego."

"I don't like it," I say, wrapping my arms around myself. It really is growing colder out here by the minute. "I get Santino may have been under a lot a pressure, and yeah, maybe going after some of his rivals was a desperate plan. But he had to know how the Lunas were going to respond, right? Especially with killing Felix's son."

"Not all criminals are smart people, Agent Slate," Cervantes says, preparing to head back to her car. "Don't overthink it. Let's get back to the office so Agent Foley can do her due diligence and you and I can start working on prepping teams for those addresses."

I look back at the building continuing to burn. "Shouldn't we…stay and investigate?"

"What's there to investigate? It was retaliation. Pure and simple. I'd bet you a year's salary the Luna's are behind it. Not that you'll find any evidence in there. If they did use a type of napalm, it will have burned any evidence away."

I hate to admit it, but she's probably right. It's not like we'll be able to get in there anytime soon, anyway. Even if they manage to get the fire under control, it's going to take a few hours to fully put everything out. And then we'd at least have to wait until daylight. The clock is ticking. There's no telling what else Felix has planned.

I nod. "We'll meet you there." Cervantes heads back to the car, while Zara stays by my side. "Can you give me a second. I need to make a phone call."

"Sure," she says. "Take your time." She heads back to the car, and I duck into a small alleyway between two of the buildings to get out of the wind. I pull my phone out and call the only person I really wanted to see today.

"Hey, where are you?" he asks after picking up on the first ring.

"I'm close to downtown. Toscani's warehouse just went up in flames."

"You're kidding," Liam says.

"I wish. Listen, I just wanted to apologize again for today. I know I left you high and dry."

"It's no problem," he says. "I managed to wrangle Elliott and Nadia away from their desks for a few hours. They helped me finish up at your place before tackling mine. The truck is all packed up and ready to be unloaded at our new place."

I smile but can't help a few tears from falling. "This is not how I wanted this day to go. I wanted it to be a fresh start for us…just one day without all this…bullshit."

"It's okay, Em. Don't worry, I won't unpack the truck without you. Even if I have to keep it for an extra day."

"Might be a few extra days," I say, telling him about Toscani's addresses.

"Yeah, that's true. Well, worst case scenario I'll just hire some guys to unload it. Then we can just head in and enjoy our new place together."

"Is Timber still at my place?" I ask.

"No, he's here with me. I didn't want to leave him there alone. We're enjoying some guy time. He's exhausted from all the excitement today." The image of the two of them huddling on the floor brings a smile to my face. His phone cuts out for a second before he's back. "Uh-oh. I'm getting a call from Wallace. I'm assuming this is related to what you just told me?"

"Probably," I say. "Sorry to get you called in on your day off."

"It's no trouble," he says. "I better take this. See you back in the office?"

"Headed there now," I say, trying to keep my energy up.

"I'll grab you a coffee on the way," he says.

I smile and wipe my cheeks. "Thanks, but you don't have to do that."

"I know," he says, "but you're getting one anyway."

After we hang up, I head back to Zara's car, feeling like I've been drained of all energy. Usually, I would be revitalized by this kind of break, but I think because it's happened on today of all days, I'm just not feeling it.

"Hey," Zara says as I slide into the passenger seat. "Everything okay?"

"No," I tell her. "Let's just get there."

Chapter Twenty-Five

I'm squatting in front of a row of bushes in front of what looks like a normal suburban DC house. All the lights are off, and the streetlight at the end of the driveway is the only thing providing any illumination to the area. Just as I stand up to order the rest of my team in, a deafening explosion destroys the house from the inside, sending shards of glass, wood and shrapnel flying everywhere.

I duck down, covering my ears and shaking violently.

"Em," Zara says.

My eyes snap open to realize she's gently rocking me. I'm in a dark room on someone's couch. The only light is streaming in from the nearby door. I try to move, but my body feels so heavy it's like I've awoken from a ten-year sleep.

"Wha—"

"C'mon, they're just about ready," she says, flipping on the light in the room. I shield my eyes from the bright light and remember I'm in one of the offices adjacent to Cervantes's department. I sit up, rubbing my eyes for a second while I get my bearings.

"Did you get any sleep?"

"Maybe thirty minutes," she says. "I wanted to spend as much time on those addresses as possible."

"What time is it?" I ask, fumbling for my phone. It's plugged in on the small side table beside the couch.

"Almost four. Cervantes is getting everyone ready for the debrief."

Four a.m., which means I got exactly an hour and fifteen minutes of sleep. Cervantes is determined not to wait on Santino any longer and figures the best time to go after him is at night. I'm inclined to agree, but after the Sunday I had, I would have preferred a full night's sleep. Thankfully, I always keep a spare set of clothes at the office, so I'm not still in the same jeans I was wearing all day yesterday.

When I follow Zara out into the VGF's bullpen, I'm not surprised to see Liam, Nadia and Elliott are already there along with about ten other agents. I sidle up beside Liam. "When did you get here?"

He wraps one arm around me and pulls me in. "About forty-five minutes ago. Wallace brought all of us in on it. I think he's anxious to get this over with so we can all get back to our other cases."

"Sounds about right," I tell him. "You should have come woken me up."

"You needed the sleep," he says. "Plus, I knew you were much less likely to attack Zara if she was the one who got you."

"You mean I would be much more likely to fight back if she came out swinging," Zara says, looking over her shoulder as we take a set of seats near the middle of the bullpen. Cervantes and Wallace are at the front, but Wallace just stands off to the side. This is clearly Cervantes's operation.

"That too," Liam says. He hands me a cup of coffee. "As promised."

Cervantes clears her throat, getting everyone's attention. "I know it's early, so thanks for being here." Behind her on the screen is a map of DC, with each of the addresses we provided her marked in red. "If you aren't aware, the Toscani Warehouse was hit late last night. According to Captain Billups, it's a total loss. Though, the fire department was able to prevent the fire from spreading. We believe this was a retaliatory act on the Toscani Crime Family by La Luna Roja, but no evidence has been found at the scene yet."

She turns and taps on each of the three dots on the screen. "Instead, our goal is to try and find and capture Santino Toscani at one of these three locations. Thanks to the efforts of Agents Slate and Foley, we believe he's hiding out in one of these targets. Our mission is to raid all three at once. Hopefully one team will get lucky."

Immediately, my dream comes back to me, the house exploding before we can even get in. I tap Zara on the shoulder. "You didn't find anything strange about those houses, did you?"

"Strange?" she asks.

"Yeah, like…I dunno."

"No, not really. They're all owned by different entities, not people, so that's something. But I wasn't able to trace them back to the Toscanis."

As Cervantes continues to talk, I can't help my mind from going to the worst possible place.

"Em, what is it?" Liam asks.

"What if this is all a trap of some kind?" I ask. "What if Marco and Santino are in on it together, somehow? And we're headed right into the middle of a massacre?"

"I dunno, Em, Marco *really* doesn't like his nephew. You think they would do that?"

"No, I guess…I just had a…"

"A what?" Liam asks.

I'm being an idiot. It was nothing more than a bad dream, brought on by stress and lack of sleep. The raid will go fine. I just hope Santino is actually in one of these houses. "Nothing. It was nothing."

We finish listening to Cervantes's presentation before she lays out who is doing what. Zara will be leading the team that will take the first house. Thankfully Elliott ends up on her team. Agent Robles, another agent I don't know, will be taking on the second location while I head up the third. Unfortunately, Liam and Nadia are assigned to Agent Robles's team. My team is made up mostly of agents I don't know from Cervantes's team, along with Alexandria Police, which we'll meet a few blocks from the site. We're scheduled to hit all three houses at exactly five-fifteen a.m.

"Okay people," Cervantes says. "Expect resistance. We don't know what kind of backup Toscani might have in those houses, so be on alert. With any luck, one of you will come back with our man in tow."

We don't waste any time getting our vests and other equipment. While we're not officially *arresting* Toscani, we are taking him into custody for both questioning and for his own protection. We all receive copies of the warrants that have been signed, though I'm sure Cervantes had to work a little magic to make that happen so quickly.

We head out, and I elect to drive my team in one of our unmarked SUVs. Agent Craig Osborne is in the seat next to me, a hard-faced man who doesn't look like he does a lot of smiling. Behind me are Agents Collins and Vega. Collins looks young, like he can't be more than a few months out of training while Agent Vega seems to have years of experience under her belt, at least in how she moves and handles herself. There's another SUV of agents behind us, plus the local officers we'll meet on the scene.

The odds of us finding Santino in that house are one in three, but we can't take any chances. And it's been a while since I've been part of a raid. They're always gut-churning because you never know what you're going to run into behind those doors. It could be a sleeping family, or it could be a guy with a shotgun, ready to blow your head off.

I can't quit thinking about my dream, but I shove it to the back of my mind. Now is not the time to get distracted. We need to find Santino, bring him in and get to the bottom of this. I only hope he can provide some answers for us, otherwise Cervantes will have nothing to stop the Luna's wrath. I know she's hoping she can appeal to Felix's humanity, especially if she can get Toscani to admit to the crimes, but I'm not so sure. Felix doesn't strike me as the kind of person who quits until he has accomplished his goal. And if his goal is to kill Santino, we all need to be very, very careful.

We pull up to the preset meeting point with Alexandria Police, having taken a wordless trip from headquarters. Either it's too early in the morning or everyone is too focused for small talk, which is perfectly fine with me.

We pull up, and I get out to meet Sergeant Phelps, who is in charge of the SWAT team accompanying us. I'm not a fan of SWAT, but in some cases they're necessary, so I make a quick round of introductions, then we go over the plan. Me, Collins and Osborne will be at the front with half the team while Vega, Phelps, and the rest of the agents will be part of the back half of the team. We'll start by covering all the exits then waiting for the appropriate time before we head in.

As soon as everyone is on board with the plan, we don our night-vision goggles. The sun won't be up for another two hours and given the relative level of low light, they'll be more helpful once we're in the house.

Vega leads her team off and around the corner while Osborne and I lead the front team along side streets until we come to the road in question. Vega has the easier job, staying out of the light in the back. But there are streetlights, making it difficult to move everyone at once and not draw any attention to ourselves.

We do our best to keep everyone low and moving, and

finally reach the home. It's not exactly like the one in my dream, which makes me feel better. It's a two-story colonial, though it's probably not more than sixteen hundred square feet inside. There's a small garage on the front and Osborne takes a group of SWAT with him over to the garage entrance on the side of the home.

I motion for Collins and the rest to follow me as we get up under the window closest to the front door. A cursory inspection reveals no cameras of any kind, which strikes me a little odd, but I don't have time to question it. We're less than five minutes from the deadline.

Agent Collins and I slowly move up to the door, staying out of the way of the windows. There doesn't seem to be any movement inside or around the house. I check my phone as Cervantes's voice crackles in the headset in my ear.

"All teams, prepare to move in. Team C, rear positions."

That's Zara's team. I hope she and Elliott have things under control over there. She's about fifteen miles away from me. Liam and Nadia are about twenty miles south on the other side of the river. It feels like they're all so far away.

Ready? I mouth to Collins. He nods, checking his weapon but keeping it pointed at the ground. My weapon is in the same position, and two of Phelps's men creep closer, holding a two-person battering ram. It will make short work of the door.

Cervantes counts down in five-second increments. Finally, it's go time, and the men ram the door.

"FBI!" I yell out. "Hands where we can see them!" I check inside the door but see no one, nodding for Collins, who enters and covers the foyer. I follow behind him, checking all the blind corners. The two men with the ram have dropped it outside and are in after us, running up the stairs. "This is the FBI," I call out again. "Anyone in this house, remain where you are with your hands up." I hear commotion from my right but realize it's probably only Osborne in the garage. Everyone moves with quick, precise actions. We're on high alert and I'm relieved the rest of my team seems as efficient as I am.

Collins nods again and I head into the living room, keeping my back to the wall. It's empty, as expected, and Collins shoots past me, checking the kitchen.

"Clear in the back," Vega calls out.

"Front is clear," I reply, then Collins and I head upstairs as Vega and her people begin appearing in the different rooms.

"Garage is empty," Osborne says, coming up the stairs behind me.

Upstairs, the two officers are already searching the bedrooms.

"Clear!"

"Clear here!"

It's already looking like this isn't the place. Collins and I head into the third bedroom, but it's empty save for some old furniture. Nothing in the house looks like it's been used in a while. I try the light switches, but as soon as the overhead light comes on, the bulb bursts.

"This place have a basement?" I ask and Collins just shrugs.

We all make our way back downstairs to find Vega and her people going through each room. "Nothing," she says. "Anyone home upstairs?"

"Negative," Osborne says, brushing past me. He's already unfastening his vest.

I tap the Bluetooth in my ear. "This is Team B. House is clear, no sign of him."

"Team C is clear," Zara says. "He's not here either."

"Team A?" Cervantes asks. There's no response. "Where are we Team A?" But the line is dead. That's Liam and Nadia's team. "All units, converge on Team A, and someone get comms back up."

We leave Phelps's team to finish up on the scene while the rest of us dash back down to where we parked the SUVs and jump in. I don't even think to wait for the others before I pull away from the curb, but thankfully, they're already in the vehicle.

"Jesus, Slate, slow down. You're gonna kill us before we even get there," Osborne says, but it just has the effect of making me drive faster.

"Is she serious?" Collins asks.

"Slate," Vega says. "We can't get there in time to be any good. Slow down."

"I disagree," I say, all my focus on the road. Early morning traffic has already started, but I weave around all of it, not even bothering to honk my horn.

"This is how I'm going to die," Collins says from the backseat.

Osborne reaches for the steering wheel, and I catch his arm without looking away. "Touch it and I'll go faster."

He retracts in his seat and responds by putting on his seatbelt. I also see him brace himself against the dash. Honestly, I don't care what any of them think. Something has happened to Liam's team, and I wasn't there. The dream immediately comes back into my mind. Could Toscani have really rigged the house to blow? And if so, how close were Liam and Nadia when it happened?

Cervantes continues to speak on the radio, but there seems to be a lot of cross traffic, so much that I just shut it out, focusing on getting to Liam's location as quickly as possible. It takes all the willpower in my being not to go to that dark, dark place. I can't help but think about the unpacked moving van, full of our stuff. Of the new home, still sitting empty.

I grip the wheel tighter, and floor it.

FIFTEEN MINUTES LATER, WE'RE APPROACHING THE SCENE. IT'S a trip that should have taken twice the time, but I didn't exactly follow local traffic laws to get here. Two local cruisers are blocking the road, and there's an officer waving us down. For a brief, infinitesimal second, I consider crashing right through them, but I step on the brake and stop the SUV just a few feet from the cruisers, causing the officer to jump back.

"Goddammit, Slate!" Osborne yells, but the car is in park and I'm out of the door, running for the house before I hear anything else. My heart is thumping in time with my feet as I race forward, determined to get to the house as fast as possible.

I'm passing more SWAT from other teams and even a few other agents, but I pay them no mind. All that's in my focus is…the house.

When it comes into view, I'm surprised to see it's still standing. There are at least four bodies, all splayed out on the lawn in front of the home. At first, I'm afraid one of them is Liam until I realize that none of them are wearing uniforms and instead, they're all men in various states of undress, shouting and squirming. I look up to see Liam coming out of the house with Nadia right beside him. And between them, his arms clamped behind his back, is Santino Toscani.

Chapter Twenty-Six

"WHAT THE HELL is wrong with me?" I ask as we head back into HQ. Liam is by my side as we go through the normal security checks.

"You are under an enormous amount of stress right now," he says as the agents in security hand us back our weapons. "And you haven't gotten a lot of sleep."

"That's no excuse, I could have gotten someone killed," I say. "All because I was convinced you had been blown up."

"It was just a small communications blackout," he says. "When we knew Toscani was there, we had to go radio silent until we had a handle on how many people we were dealing with. Normal procedure."

"I know, which is why I'm kicking myself." I should have known better. We head back down through the double doors into our department. We're due to speak with Santino, but not until after he's been through processing. Apparently, he took a shot at Nadia, though he claims he thought he was shooting at a burglar. The story isn't holding up well and now he *really is* under arrest.

"You just need time to reset," he says. "Let's head back to my place. My bed is in the van already, but I've got a couple of sleeping bags I can pull out. You've been running full throttle for almost twenty-four hours straight."

I'm about ready to suggest we just find a cheap hotel so we at least don't have to sleep on the floor when I spot Wallace coming out of his office, his face already flushed.

Ah, shit. I guess I knew this was coming.

"Slate, in my office, right now," he says.

I take a deep breath, gathering myself for what I know is about to be another round as Liam comes up beside me. "Not you, Coll."

"Sir, if this is about the incident this morning—"

"It is," Wallace says. "And apparently another one last night. Your girlfriend is doing an excellent job of disregarding everyone's judgement but her own."

"I'm sorry, *his girlfriend?*" I say, stopping in my tracks.

"Bring it in here, Slate," Wallace says, indicating his office.

I know I should go in there, but it's like my body won't move. I feel like I've taken about as much as I can from SAC Wallace. And right now, I'm not sure I care about *what* happens. "No, sir. I'm done. We're done with this."

"Excuse me?" he asks.

"Whatever game it is you think you're playing; I'm done being a part of it. Reprimand me, fire me, do whatever you think is best for the Bureau. But I'm not going to sit in that office and listen to you try to explain why me going over Hodges head was a bad thing. I'm also not going to listen to you sanction me for violating just about every traffic law imaginable. I know I did that. I made a mistake, and it was wrong. And if you think that's a fireable offense, be my guest. Hell, *charge me* if that's what you think it will take."

He seems dumbfounded. And for whatever reason, I can't seem to stop myself now that I've started. "Because that's what it's always been about, hasn't it? When you first started in this office, you made it very clear that you did not want me here, and you were prepared to transfer me to be someone else's problem, isn't that right?"

"Slate, I'm warning you—"

"But then my old boss became your new boss, and you couldn't do that anymore. You *had* to work with me. And yet, despite the fact I have done everything I could to try and improve our working relationship, you still seem hell bent on seeing that I fail. I mean, what sense does it make to send me down to Louisiana to work what seems like an impossible case, but then when I bring you an *actual request* from a local LEO, you deny it?"

He begins to stammer, removing his hornrims and attempting to wipe them with his tie. "Those aren't— you're—"

"I remember that one vividly," Liam says. "My old department in Virginia specifically requested FBI assistance, and you denied it. Because it was *her*, wasn't it?"

"Did you put *that* in your report? Or did you just sweep it under the rug?" I ask him. "Because you seem more than happy to ship me off somewhere else. But when I actually need your help with something, you're nowhere to be found."

"You are mischaracterizing things, as usual," he says. "This department has certain fiscal goals it needs to meet, and there's only so much budget to work with. My decisions were based purely in the numbers as I saw them," he says. "You standing here, accusing me of prejudice, isn't doing you any favors."

"That's bullshit and you know it. There isn't a *budgetary* concern when there's a killer on the loose. Not in the FBI. We don't trade money for people's lives."

His entire body posture changed. Where before he was deflecting, trying to avoid my gaze, he's now locked on to me, body stiffening. "You want to talk about favoritism?" he spits. "The leeway this department has shown you has been *immeasurable*. I've never seen anything like it. You seem to think you can come and go as you please, that the rules don't apply to you. Deputy Director Simmons has no idea how much you get away with. And every time I prepare my reports, I have to amend them to remove your...outlandish activities. All because you were the one who brought down Deputy Director Cochrane."

"No one asked you to do that," I say.

"Trust me, nothing would please me more than to remove you from this office. Thankfully, you have finally given me everything I need to see that happen. I was going to run you through the ringer a little first, but you've saved me the trouble." He smiles. "Deputy Director Simmons won't be able to overlook or explain this away. By this time tomorrow, you'll be on a train to Nebraska."

"As much as I know you'd love that," I tell him, "who do you think authorized my access to see Marco Toscani in the first place?"

The realization dawns on his face.

"More like I went around it. I knew you wouldn't have my back. You never have. Ever since the Magus case, you've made your feelings about me crystal clear." He seems completely thrown by the fact that Janice was the one who authorized us to speak with Toscani in the first place. It hadn't been a call I wanted to make, but I was desperate, and after explaining the situation, she agreed it was imperative, no matter what DA Hodges said.

"I don't have time for this," I say, heading for my desk. "I have a suspect to interview."

"The hell you do," he says. "You're on leave, as of this moment. And you can believe I'll be taking this up with one of the other directors."

"Be my guest," I say, mostly in anger because I'm not even sure how he plans on doing that. Is he thinking about going around Janice now? This is why I hate politics. I just want to be able to do my job without all the baggage. Yes, I went overboard this morning. *That* I can understand. But Hodges? Wallace is just doing it to be spiteful.

"Wait a second," Liam says. "You're putting her on leave for a few traffic violations? It was early morning—there was barely anyone on the road."

"Don't you start, Agent Coll," Wallace says, pointing in his direction. "I've never approved of this little office romance as it has obviously compromised your judgement. Your feelings for your coworker are exactly part of the—"

Before he can finish, I rush up to him, fully intending to deck him. Wallace's eyes go wide and he shies away, holding his hands up to protect himself, and I can't do it. When he's actually confronted, it seems he doesn't have a backbone to hold him up. It's probably better anyway. Decking my boss wouldn't look good for my case and isn't something I'd be able to explain away. But looking at him there, instinctually shying away from me, feels like a victory. "Just…heading back to my desk to gather my stuff."

He straightens his jacket and clears his throat, trying to pretend nothing happened. "The formal reprimand will go into my report this afternoon."

"Whatever you feel is necessary," I tell him, gathering a few things from my desk, including my old clothes I changed out of this morning.

"Feel free to put me on leave as well," Liam says. "I think it's probably best we're not around each other for the time being."

Wallace narrows his eyes, and I can see his mind working, trying to figure out the financial ramifications of letting two agents go at the same time. "As much as I'd love to do that, I can't. You captured the suspect, you're due down in the interview room in an hour. But your concern for your colleague is…alarming. You'd be willing to throw away your career for nothing. You weren't the one to violate protocol."

"Neither was she," he says.

"Liam, save it," I say, softly. I don't want him putting his career on the line for me. Not when he's up against someone who won't listen to reason. "It's fine."

"Glad you and I finally agree on something, Agent Slate. I'm sure IA will be contacting you soon regarding this incident. I'll let Cervantes know you're no longer available for the case."

God, he just likes to keep pushing my buttons. It's like now that he knows I won't hit him, he's ready to say everything that's been on his mind for the past three months.

I head out of the office without another word, forgetting I don't have a vehicle to go home in and nothing but an empty apartment to return to. I'm not quite sure what I'm supposed to do with myself.

"Hey, wait up," Liam says, trotting after me.

"Why? I basically just got fired," I reply, heading for the elevators, my stuff under one arm.

"Once Janice—"

"I don't want her to," I say. "I made this mess myself. I should have been thinking clearer this morning. All I've done is give Wallace exactly what he wants: a reason to get rid of me."

"C'mon, Em," Liam says as the elevator opens. "Public endangerment? It's never going to hold water. We do that kind of stuff all the time because it's *necessary*."

He's probably right. But Wallace is going to drag this out as long as he can, no matter what. And I'm just going to have to stand there and take it. I'm only now realizing how much of a hostile work environment he's created for me ever since he took the job.

Liam holds open the elevator door, keeping it from closing. "You should go," I say. "Interview Santino with Zara. He'll talk to her. Probably."

"I don't want to leave you alone. What are you going to do?"

"I dunno," I say. "I'll figure something out." The look on his face just about breaks my heart. He moves to get into the elevator with me, but I stop him. "No. The best thing you can do for me right now is not lose your job."

"I'll call you once the interview is over. Then maybe we can head back and unpack the van at the new place."

"Yeah, sounds great," I say, but even I don't believe the words coming out my mouth. He finally lets go, and the elevator doors close, sealing me off from the world. I have to take a few deep breaths, otherwise I'm going to lose it right here. I don't know what kind of influence or power Wallace really has, or what he can actually do, but I know he can make things as hard for me as possible. I think I would be happy never seeing his face and those stupid glasses of his ever again.

All I really want to do right now is take a long, hot bath. My apartment may be empty, but I haven't turned in the keys yet and technically I still have a few days left on my lease. Who cares if there's any furniture in there or not?

As soon as I'm back outside in the morning sun, I pull out my phone and call myself a cab.

Chapter Twenty-Seven

YOU NEVER REALIZE how much stuff you use until it's all packed away in boxes where you can't get to it. Even though I have some clothes still in the back of my car and an overnight bag with my essentials, all of my towels are in a box in the back of the moving van. After the cab drops me off, I have to head back out and grab some cheap ones from the local big-box store before heading back home and drawing myself a bath.

It's weird being in a practically empty apartment. Even weirder, Timber isn't here. He's still over at Liam's place, which makes the apartment feel like a ghost of its former self. Where before it was a home, now it's nothing more than a lump of walls, devoid of any purpose. I wasn't here long enough for the paint to fade or the carpet to develop divots from our routines. I've left no permanent mark.

I can't help but feel a profound sense of sadness as I walk around the empty unit, looking in all the rooms and seeing nothing of my life here anymore. It's like I've been untethered from this world, and I'm stuck somewhere in limbo.

Instead of a bath, I take a quick shower, preferring not to be here longer than necessary. I thought it would be relaxing to come back one last time and soak it all in, but now that I'm here, all I want to do is leave. It isn't anything other than a space waiting for someone new to call it home.

I'm not out of the shower ten minutes before I hear the doorbell ring. Normally that sound is followed by the clicking of Timber's toenails on the floor as he rushes to the door, but the absence of the sound is deafening to me, and I almost have to take a minute and gather myself. My hair is still damp, but I head for the door anyway. It's possible I could have ordered something online and forgotten to forward it to the new address. Though as I reach for the door handle, a thought strikes me and I pull back. What if it's another letter? Can I really handle that right now given everything else that's going on?

I pause a moment longer, waiting to see if whoever is there will go away. But instead of ringing the bell again, a heavy knock slams against the door instead. "Slate, I know you're in there. Your car is outside."

*What the...*I open the door to find Janice Simmons standing in front of me, sporting a long, black trench coat over her suit. In her hand is her signature vape pen, which she stows in her pocket as soon as she sees me.

"Janice?" I ask. She takes one look at my hair, and I feel I have to explain before she asks. "I...just got out of the shower."

She arches an eyebrow at me, and I move aside to let her in. "What are you doing here?"

She steps into the apartment, looking around. "It doesn't look much bigger empty, does it?"

"I guess not."

She walks over, inspecting the mantle, another wall where my bookcase once stood, then walks into the kitchen. "Strange...isn't it?"

"What's that?"

"How we can relate so closely to a place, we feel we

become part of it. Where we live. Where we work. Sometimes our places define us." Something is wrong; I've never known Janice to wax poetic about anything. She's as strait-laced as they come.

"What's going on?" I finally ask.

"What are you doing here, Emily?" she asks, turning to face me.

"I...well I was going to take a bath, but I—"

"That's not what I mean." She clasps her hands behind her back and walks around the island in my direction. "I mean why are you here instead of back at the office, interrogating Santino Toscani?"

"You haven't heard from Wallace yet," I say.

"On the contrary. Agent Cervantes asked me to speak to SAC Wallace to find *you*."

I draw down my brow. "Why would Agent Cervantes contact you?"

"Because apparently, like a lot of people, she can't stand dealing with Wallace. She finds him to be a pompous, self-important ass who thinks numbers are more important than people." It takes considerable effort for me not to smile. She shoots me a knowing glance and continues. "What I don't understand is why you have let him get under your skin."

"I almost hit him, if that helps," I say. Janice's mouth upturns the slightest tic at that, but it disappears immediately. "But I didn't think openly violating his orders was a good idea."

"Wallace never would have been my choice for your SAC," she says. "The decision was made when it looked like I was on my way out. And by the time I'd been appointed Deputy Director, the entire Bureau was in the middle of an upheaval. It was decided that minimizing the disruption would be best for everyone involved, which meant Wallace stayed where he was. There was also no chance of him being part of the Organization. A bonus, given the circumstances. However, that doesn't mean he is a good SAC."

"Definitely not," I reply.

"I owe you an apology, Emily. I should have been paying closer attention, but being Deputy Director comes with a number of additional responsibilities and my time is…stretched."

"I can't even imagine."

"Regardless, don't focus on Wallace. Let me worry about him. For the time being, continue to report to Cervantes for as long as you're on this case. We'll figure out the rest later."

I'm dumbstruck. "What does that mean?" I ask.

"The details aren't important right now," she says. "What *is* important is you getting back to work." She checks her watch. "Santino has been in custody for almost six hours now, and so far, he's refused to speak even one word."

"But Zara—"

"Can only get so far with a man like that," she says. "Agent Foley is a capable agent, of that there is no doubt. But in some cases, we need someone more…intimidating."

I smile. Trying to imagine Zara intimidating is like trying to imagine a very pissed off squirrel. They could still tear you apart, but they're gonna look really cute right up until the moment they attack. And I'm betting they're not letting her attack Santino, not in the way she needs to.

"What about my record?" I ask.

"It's ludicrous to think such a small charge would result in the dismissal or even suspension of an agent, especially considering you were acting within the parameters of your duties," she replies.

"But I—"

"Emily," she says. "Take the win. Your compulsion to agonize over your mistakes is probably your biggest flaw. Cervantes wants you back at the office to speak with Santino so we can try and get this situation sorted out."

"Yes, ma'am," I reply.

"Good. I have—"

Before she can finish there is a bright flash outside the windows of my apartment, followed by a deafening boom. Janice and I don't waste any time finding cover. Her weapon is out, but mine is still in the bathroom with everything else. Janice motions that she's heading outside, and I nod. For the second time in a day, I find myself covering a blind corner, unsure what might be on the other side.

She heads out first. I wait a beat, the follow her out, staying low. Before I'm even out of the door I can feel the heat on my skin.

And then I see it. A vehicle right in front of my building, fire coming out all the windows. It's the same Ford Granada Zara and I saw earlier, though the brown color is quickly burning away to show the metal underneath. As Janice and I stand there watching it, the windshield explodes from the heat, and flames lick the edges of the metal frame.

"That's not your car," Janice says, her weapon still out, but pointed at the ground.

"No, ma'am," I say.

"I can see the outline of a body in the driver's seat." She pulls out her phone. "This is Simmons. We need fire and emergency units to 161 Tradestone Drive. Vehicle fire. At least one casualty."

"What—" I say, my voice going hoarse. Is that her? Is that Emily, burning to a crisp with the rest of the car?

"Slate, keep it together," Janice says. "Who does this vehicle belong to?"

"I—don't know," I admit. "I believe it's been stalking me for the past week. There was a BOLO out on it a few days…" I trail off. "I think that might be my aunt in the driver's seat."

"Suicide?" she asks. The car continues to burn, but the flames are beginning to abate as the fire runs out of fuel.

"Possibly," I say, my mind going back to the letters. If she was behind them, I can't say she was the most stable person. And considering she almost ran into us the other night, something that might have killed all of us if her car had struck mine, I can't discount the possibility. She was looking for a way to get my attention. Maybe she finally decided she'd found the ultimate answer.

"I have to admit, you don't make things easy," Janice says.

"Seems to be my specialty," I reply.

My old boss takes a deep breath. "Regardless, you still have a suspect to interview. I'll stay here and take care of this. You can make a statement later. Right now, I want you on Toscani."

"But…" I protest, watching the fire burn.

"No arguments," she says. "Go, do your job. You can deal with this later."

I nod, though I'm still somewhat shell-shocked. I begin to head back into the house to gather my things.

"Emily," Janice says, causing me to turn back. "Good luck."

Chapter Twenty-Eight

"WHAT DO we call the shortest suspension in history?" Zara asks as she catches sight of me, heading into the interrogation area. "I didn't even get a chance to come over and hit you on the head for being such a dummy." But when she sees my face her entire demeanor changes. "What's wrong?"

I tell her about the car and the fire. "Janice is still at my apartment, taking care of things there."

"Jeez, Em, are you okay?" she asks.

"I...I don't know. What if that is her in the car?"

She gives my arm a supportive rub. "Maybe it isn't her. Maybe it's just some crazy person."

She's right. There will be an autopsy on the remains, and DNA tests. We'll have answers eventually. And I can't focus on that right now, not when Toscani is less than five hundred feet from me.

Giving Zara an appreciative nod, I straighten my blazer. I had to pull another suit out of my car and unfortunately, it's somewhat wrinkled from being packed up for the better part of a week, but it will have to do.

She lowers her voice. "I heard you almost hit Wallace."

I shoot a look at Liam, standing nearby with a Styrofoam

cup in his hand. He immediately averts his gaze, staring up at the ceiling and whistling. "I see nothing is sacred around here."

"Not between us, it's not," she says. "I'm just glad Janice kicked some sense into you."

"It *was* nice speaking with her again. I don't know why I've been so hesitant to reach out to her in the past."

"Because you're a hardhead, that's why," Zara replies. "Speaking of which…" She points to the interrogation room where Santino is being held.

"No dice, huh?"

"No dice, no balls, no crackerjacks," she replies. "He's sealed shut, waiting for his lawyer."

I look around. "And where—"

"We're still waiting," Cervantes says, coming over from one of the other interrogation rooms. "I have all our agents that were part of the raid this morning working on interrogations with everyone we found in that house, but no one is making much progress. We had to physically restrain Osborne from going after one of the more combative men, but other than that, they've all been radio silent. I'm sure on Santino's orders."

"I can't believe none of them are willing to crack," I say. "One of them must have some leverage we can use against them."

"I've been looking for the past half hour after my initial round with Santino didn't get us anywhere," Zara says. "My guess is he was keeping his most loyal soldiers close to him."

"Did you tell him about Felix? And his warehouse?" I ask.

She nods. "Still nothing."

I swallow hard. Despite their expectations, I'm not sure what else I can do here. If Santino isn't willing to budge, we don't have many options. "How long until the lawyer arrives?"

"Could be between now and Labor Day for all we know," Cervantes says.

I sigh. "Okay. I'll see what I can do." I look over at Zara, but she holds up her hands.

"I've already given it a shot. He's all yours."

I turn to Cervantes, who just gives me an expectant look. Though, when my gaze catches Liam's, he just lifts his cup to me in something of a salute, giving me a supportive smile. I'm sure Zara will give him the rundown on the car fire while I'm in with Toscani.

Setting my gaze, I head for the interrogation room. I don't have a plan; I'm just going to give this my best shot. Maybe he'll continue to clam up until his lawyer gets here. Then again, maybe his animosity for me is so strong he'll finally break. There's only one way to find out.

I open the door to the bare room, and I'm immediately reminded of my apartment. The two spaces are near-identical to each other. Santino Toscani sits on the far side of a metal table, his arms crossed as he stares at the ceiling. I catch the look of surprise on his face when he sees me, though he doesn't say anything.

"Long time no see," I say, though it's only been a few months since our last crossing. "I bet you were wondering if you'd see me today, weren't you?"

"Figured when that little friend of yours was in here earlier you wouldn't be far behind," he spits.

Yep, he's still pissed.

"We've got a lot to talk about Santino," I say, pulling out the other chair and sitting down. "First and foremost, the reason you're here."

"I already told the other one, I want to see my lawyer."

"Okay," I say. "Then you just sit there and listen. I'm happy to lay it all out for you. And then maybe you can decide if you want to respond or not. Sound good?"

He just glares at me like he's hoping he can melt my brain with his gaze.

"Great, let's get started. First off, your uncle says hi."

This causes him to raise his brows. He opens his mouth like he wants to respond, but shuts it again, crossing his arms.

"Let me see, you've already been told about the warehouse fire," I say, gauging his reaction as I go through the list. "The fact that every criminal organization in the city wants your head, including one very upset Mexican drug lord who I had the chance to meet personally." I give him a placating smile. "I really didn't think you had the balls to go off and kill his kid, though."

"You don't know what you're talking about," he says, sitting up. "I—" He shuts his mouth again before he can say anything further.

I just give him a sweet smile. "Let's see, what else. Oh right, your uncle told us he was undermining you, selling information to a federal DA in exchange for a lighter sentence. That may be why you've been having so many supply and personnel problems lately."

"Marco," he says, slamming his fist down on the table. "God damn snake in the grass. Can't handle the fact that I was running the family better than he was. Decided he'd rather see the whole thing go up rather than let someone else take it for him."

I'm assuming this is the most he's talked so far, which I'll take as a win. "So you knew Marco's been sabotaging you for the past few weeks."

He only grits his teeth at me.

"What I want to know is, why go after the other gangs in the first place? You had to have known that unless you'd managed to cripple them, they'd be coming after you. And no offense, but I've seen your house. It doesn't hold a candle to what the Lunas have."

Santino is starting to go red in the face. Whatever is going on in that head of his, I'm close. But he's proving tougher to break than I'd expected. My hope had been that I could get him hot enough he'd crack without being able to help it, but it seems he has more self-control than I've given him credit for.

"Okay, you don't want to talk, that's fine. We'll have you moved to another facility where you can wait for your lawyer, since he seems to be running a little bit late."

"You mean, move me from here?" he asks.

"Sure. We have other holding facilities around the city. I'm sure you'll be more comfortable in one of those." I'm betting he also knows that none of those will be as secure as the J. Edgar Hoover building. Even the act of moving him gives any one of his enemies an opportunity to take him out. Though it would also put other officers in the crosshairs. By now, word has to be getting around that he's shown up.

I stand and head for the door.

"You can be a real bitch when you want to be, you know that?" he asks. "I want immunity."

"I'm sorry?"

"Immunity. Drop the bullshit attempted murder charges. Anyone comes running into my room in the middle of the night, they're gonna get a gun to the face. How was I supposed to know it was an 'officer of the law'?" He uses air quotes when he speaks. "You drop that charge and give me immunity, and I'll talk to you. *Without* my lawyer."

"I can't give you immunity if you orchestrated the murders of those men," I say. "I'd hope you wouldn't think I was *that* stupid."

"I didn't have anything to do with those," he says, but I don't budge. "Okay, okay. How about immunity on…let's say local trafficking charges. After all, I wouldn't want to need to use my fifth amendment rights."

I consider it. I still have full authority, assuming Cervantes's original order still stands. But I feel like this needs to be a group decision. "Give me one moment." I exit back out and head into the room next door where Cervantes, Liam, and Zara are all watching along with a few other agents and techs. "Well?"

"I feel like this is a trap," Cervantes says. "He's obviously taken a page from his uncle's book."

"I don't care about him moving counterfeit goods," I say. "I want to know what he knows about these murders. Let's face it, Toscani is never going down for the same crimes that took his uncle down. He's too smart for that."

"We're not giving him carte blanche," Cervantes says. "The last thing we need is another criminal thinking they can get away with whatever they want."

"Then constrain it to past activities only," Liam suggests. "Make him feel like he's getting a reset."

"I dunno. I wish we hadn't lost our witness," Cervantes says. "Unreliable as he was."

That gives me an idea. "Do we have a photo of Conrad Garza?" I ask.

"There's one in the record somewhere from where he came in, why?" she replies.

"Shoot it to my phone. I want to try something."

"Here, I got it," Zara says, sitting down at one of the terminals in the room and typing away. "It should be in your inbox."

"That was fast," Cervantes says.

"It's her specialty." I motion to Cervantes. "Can you accompany me back in there?"

"Of course, but I don't—"

"Let me just try this," I say. "I have a feeling we might be able to offer Santino immunity after all without the moral questioning."

She gives me a *go ahead* motion and we head back into the interrogation room. "Santino, this is Special Agent Cervantes, head of the Violent Gang Force. She brought me on to help find you when all of this began."

"I don't give a flying fuck," he says. "Do we have a deal or not?"

I pull out my phone and open the file Zara sent me, showing him the picture. "Do you know this man?"

He squints, but I catch the recognition immediately. There's something else there too, but it's so brief I'm not sure what to make of it. "Why? What's it to you?" he asks.

"Let's just say this might help us trust you," I tell him. "Who is he?"

"A lowlife named Dominic Russo. He used to work for my uncle, but I haven't seen him ever since Marco went to prison. I figured he'd kicked the bucket."

"That's very interesting," I say. "This man came to us not more than a week ago and fingered your people for the deaths of the two Steel Dragons."

Santino twists his face. "That's a fucking lie. I didn't—" He trails off.

"Why did you go into hiding, Santino?" Cervantes asks.

He seems to reset himself. "Do we have a deal? Immunity in exchange for information?"

She exchanges a look with me, and I give her a nod. "We have a tentative deal. Immunity for any past trafficking crimes. But it doesn't cover murder or attempted murder of any kind."

Santino points to the glass wall. "I want it in writing. And I want my lawyer to have a copy. *Then* I'll talk. I know how you feds like to conveniently *lose* things."

"We're not going to stab you in the back," I say. "We're not your uncle."

"No deal until I see the paper," he says.

Cervantes grumbles and heads back out of the room while I stare at Santino. He seems to relish in it, knowing he's holding the cards we need. I don't like making deals like this, but sometimes we don't have a choice.

Fifteen minutes later, Cervantes returns with an agreement and one of our notaries, who watches as Santino signs both copies. I hope we're not making a mistake here; but Santino, while an asshole, has always tried to run a cleaner business than his uncle. He's not a mobster, at least not in the traditional sense.

"There, you have your copy," Cervantes says, handing the other one to the notary who leaves. "Now talk."

"Not until my lawyer gets his hands on this," he replies.

"Dammit, we don't have time for this," I say. "We can't wait another hour for your lawyer to show up when and if he wants to. Text him a picture and let's get on with it."

He gives me another one of those smarmy smiles, taking his time with the picture and being deliberately slow as he does. He then folds the piece of paper and puts it in his back pocket. Finally, he knits his hands together, staring at us.

"I figured something was wrong once all these shipments started getting picked up," he says. "Did I want to start illegally importing goods into the country again? No." He taps his jacket pocket as he sees both me and Cervantes stiffen at this admission of guilt. "This is a tough business, and it's impossible not to...pad the profits a little. Not to mention we were losing the respect of everyone around us. I knew if we didn't start moving goods again and soon, we'd be too easy of a target."

"So despite everything you told me and Zara during our last meeting, you decided to get back into the world of illegal imports and exports," I say.

"What can I say? I have to make difficult choices." He shoots a glance at Cervantes, relishing the fact we can't touch him for this. "But not more than a few weeks after we began 'normal' operations again, my trucks start getting yanked. And only the ones carrying anything...*unique*. I knew it wasn't my drivers because they didn't implicate me, always took responsibility for it themselves. But it meant I had a mole in the organization, and I couldn't figure out who."

"Someone was feeding information to your uncle, who was then feeding it to the DA," I say.

"I knew someone was working against me but had no way of flushing them out. As soon as I started to interrogate my own men, someone took out the Aryans."

"The White Hand," I say.

"Call them whatever you want, they're a racist cult that my family has tussled with for years. After Marco got snagged, I had to go in front of those bastards and negotiate a truce with them so I could get the family back on its feet. Do you know how humiliating it is to have to ask for mercy from someone who doesn't believe in your right to exist?" He sits back in his chair. "My uncle, he would have just kept on killing them. And they would have kept killing us until the end of time, that much I can assure you of. Did I like doing it? No, but I knew that the family wasn't strong enough to keep it up, not after what happened to Marco. It was all I could do to hold things together."

"So, you brokered a peace to give yourself time to rebuild."

"You're damn right I did. I wasn't about to let them get away with it. But I didn't have the ability to fight back. Not against any of them. After Marco when to prison, I went to each of the four organizations, and pledged I wasn't like my uncle. And that the Toscanis would stay out of everyone else's business."

"That's quite the feat," Cervantes says.

He turns to her. "Isn't it? Most people in my position would have been too short-sighted to see the big picture. But I knew if we didn't do something drastic, the family would be wiped out in a matter of months."

"So that's what Damian Drummond meant when he said you each minded your own business."

"No one wanted a full-out war," Santino replies. "Maybe there were some that did, but it wasn't the majority. And with

Marco gone, they were willing to give us…a blank slate, so to say." He glares at me. "Especially when I said we wouldn't be encroaching on any of their businesses. The Dragons have the weapons, the Kings the personal goods and drugs, the Aryans the opioids…I didn't want to get into that. At least not until we were strong enough to defend ourselves."

"And yet, every organization but yours was hit. That's kind of convenient, don't you think?"

"Agent, how *stupid* would I have to be to go after every other gang in the city and not stage a hit on myself? How does that look?"

"You're saying you were set up?" I ask. "By who?" He points to the phone in my hand. "Dominic?"

"Marco."

"We know he was setting you up," I say. "The DA confirmed as much."

He shakes his head. "As soon as you showed me that picture I knew. Marco has been running two schemes this entire time. Squeezing me from both sides in an attempt to destroy what is left of the family."

"You're saying he orchestrated the hits on the other gangs in order to make them come after you?" Cervantes asks.

"After me, my business, my assets, everything. As soon as the Aryans were hit, I knew something was going on, which is why I went into hiding. I knew the killer would probably expect me to be stupid enough to try and say it wasn't us, but instead, I just sat back and watched what happened. And one by one, the dominoes fell, leading straight to me. I suspect the hit on the Aryans was designed to be the only one, but when they didn't get the job done, the others were taken out one at a time until finally, he had no choice but to go after the Lunas."

Santino smiles. "Apparently, Felix was the only one crazy enough to go to war."

"But how would Marco even orchestrate such a thing?" I ask.

He shrugs. "I don't know, but it doesn't surprise me. He's a resourceful son of a bitch."

I turn to Cervantes, motioning for her to follow me out. "Do you believe him?" she asks as soon as we're back out in the hallway.

I knock on the door to the next room and Zara pops her head out. "Remind me what DA Hodges said about Marco's reward for cooperation."

"I believe he said Marco received lighter security and more privileges," she says.

"Which might have included relaxed phone conversations or he could have even gotten his hands on a cell phone," I say.

"And you think he orchestrated all this from prison?" Cervantes asks.

"It makes sense, doesn't it? While he's feeding information to Hodges on one end, he's preparing a second campaign against his nephew on the other. A much more deadly campaign, something he never would have been able to achieve with the DA."

"I just can't believe he'd be willing to destroy everything he created with the Toscanis," Cervantes says.

"We need to search all the prison's phone records. Figure out if Marco really could have pulled this off," I say.

"I can get right on that," Zara replies.

Liam appears in the doorway. "Do you believe him?"

"I'm not sure I do," I say. "Santino has always been a slippery one. We need evidence to back up his claims. Someone needs to find Conrad Garza or…Dominic as Santino calls him."

"Let me check with Nadia and Elliott," Liam says, heading off. "They might be able to track him down."

"We need to have another discussion with Marco," Cervantes says. "Not that he'll admit to anything. But we need to move quickly. There's no telling what else Felix has planned."

"I'm pretty sure he's planning on killing Santino," I say.

"It's no good," Zara says, coming back in from the other room. "I can't get anything on Marco's activity at the prison. Everything has been sealed under order from DA Hodges."

I throw Cervantes a glance. "Then I guess we need to pay Mr. Hodges a visit."

"What about him?" Zara asks, indicating Santino.

"We can hold him for a few more hours, but once his lawyer gets hold of the attempted murder charge he'll tear right through it." She curses under her breath again. "Let's just hope we can get our answers before we have to cut him loose."

I pull out my phone, already dialing the number for Hodges. "In the meantime, I think it will be best if our DA in question meets us at JCI. We need to get all this sorted out, the sooner the better."

Chapter Twenty-Nine

"THIS IS LUDICROUS," Hodges says, his arms folded as he leans up against the wall of the same meeting room Zara and I first encountered Marco Toscani. He's barely said a word to Cervantes, instead focusing all of his ire on me.

"I wouldn't be so cocky," I tell him. "Considering your *cooperation* with him might have just ignited a gang war in the middle of Washington DC."

He only rolls his eyes while Cervantes paces the room, waiting on Toscani. She's been a bundle of nerves ever since we left headquarters, and the few hours it's taken to get here and through security haven't helped matters. It's almost two p.m., and as the three of us stand there, my stomach grumbles. Having barely eaten anything since yesterday, I need something if I'm going to keep going.

"Anyone want something from the vending machines?" I ask. I know heading back out to the common area means I'll have to go through security again, but right now a candy bar or a bag of chips sounds as good as a ribeye.

"Knock yourself out," Hodges replies. He's been antagonistic ever since we arrived and met him here, first accusing me of breaking protocol and then when that argument fell apart, blaming me for tampering with his informant. He's convinced this whole operation will destroy any leverage he has with Toscani and any chance of bringing down the rest of the crime family has gone down the drain. Not only that, but there's a weird energy in the room. Hodges and Cervantes seem to be purposely avoiding each other.

"I could use a coffee," Cervantes says.

Looking at her, her palms sweaty, I conclude the *last* thing she needs is a coffee. I'll get her a bottle of water and say the machine was broken. But as I'm heading for the door, the door opposite us opens and Officer Danvers leads Marco Toscani in once again. Given with how flustered he seems—being shuffled about, not walking in here confidently like before—I have to wonder if maybe Santino was right. Marco didn't expect to have to go through this again. But then, what *did* he expect by giving us Santino's location?

Hodges is off the wall and approaching Marco before either Cervantes or I can move. "Mr. Toscani," he says, presenting himself as if he's the one who requested this meeting. He offers for him to sit down at one of the two tables in front of us.

"What is all this about?" Toscani says, looking at each of us. "Why am I back here?"

Hodges leans forward, a placating look on his face. "There seems to have been some confusion—"

"Santino fingered you for setting the gangs against him," I say, cutting Hodges off. We're not going to sit here and beat around the bush.

Marco furrows his brow. "You found him?"

I nod. "Right where you said he'd be. In one of the three safe houses. Picked him up early this morning. And the first thing he said when we started talking was that you had been orchestrating the attacks on the other gangs to frame him."

"That is preposterous," Marco says. "How would I even

do that? My every move is watched, I am kept in solitary a majority of the time—"

"Because you enjoy picking fights with the other inmates," I say.

He vehemently shakes his head. "No. They enjoy picking fights with *me*. I was the head of the Toscani Crime Family. Don't you think that made me more than a few enemies? The guards…" He looks back at Danvers with disgust. "…they do not care what goes on here. They can barely be counted on to stop a fight, much less fill out a report correctly."

I narrow my gaze and turn to Danvers. "Is that true?"

He gives me a noncommittal shrug. "Everyone here is overworked. We do the best we can."

Marco mimes spitting at his feet. "You do *nothing* to protect us."

Danvers reaches for his baton, but I hold up a hand, stopping him.

"Regardless, you already have a motive to undermine your nephew. Is it so hard to believe that you would attempt to set him up? Wouldn't that be poetic justice?"

"No," he replies. "Justice would be having the little shit in here and me back out there. Which is why I even agreed to work with this…this brownnose." He motions to Hodges.

"Wait," I say, directing my attention at Hodges. "You came to *him*? I thought it was the other way around."

Hodges winces. "I believe Mr. Toscani is incorrect."

"Don't you pull that with me, not now, not after I've given you everything I've had," Marco yells.

"And what have you given me?" Hodges yells back, real anger in his voice. "A couple of shipping routes? A few drivers who refuse to flip on their boss? Do you know how much time—"

"Don't you talk to me about *time*," Marco growls. "I have had *all* my time stolen from me. You gave me assurances that if I cooperated, I would be given privileges." He looks back at

Danvers. "So far, the only privilege I've seen is more of the inside of my cell. When do I get my due?"

"When you give me something *concrete*," Hodges replies. "Why didn't you tell me where Santino was hiding? You told her!" He points to me without actually looking at me.

"Because I didn't actually think he'd be stupid enough to be there," Marco says. "I don't know who is behind these attacks you speak of, but I know it is not me. When am I supposed to arrange something like that? When I'm on the shitter?"

"Cool it, Toscani," Danvers says.

I get the guard's attention. "How often is his cell searched?"

"Every few days," he replies. "We toss everything to make sure no contraband is getting in the prison."

"No way a cell phone could make its way into someone's hands?" I ask.

"It's happened before, but usually in gen pop. Toscani is isolated so much of the time he doesn't have the opportunity. Even if he did, we got signal killers all over this place. Cell phones don't work except in the yard and outside the security areas."

I look down at my own phone and realize I don't have service here. "How long have you been blocking cell signals?" I ask.

"'Bout six months or so. Just got the new tech in last year. Warden's pretty happy with it."

"You see?" Marco says. "How else would I orchestrate such attacks?"

I don't like how this is going. Despite not being able to get a signal, I do still have access to all my photos. I bring up the picture of Conrad Garza and show it to Marco. "Who is this?"

He squints at the picture a moment. "I know this face… but I do not know his name. He is a friend of my nephew's.

Used to run around together as teens. Mother died when he was little, I believe. Drugs...or some such."

"He's a friend of Santino's?" I ask.

Marco nods. "I haven't seen him in years, but I never forget a face. He and Santino went to school together. I don't know where he is now. How did you get that picture?"

"He came to us," I say. "Fingered your nephew's organization for the murders. But..." I glance over at Cervantes. "He's disappeared since."

Marco finally sits down, his head tilted back. A smile forms on his face. "*Nipote...cos'hai fatto?*"

"What does that mean?" Cervantes asks.

He fully smiles now. "My nephew, he has pulled one over on you. Me as well."

"How do you mean?" I ask. "What's going on?"

"Do you not see?" Marco asks, jamming his index finger into the table. "He has made a very calculated risk...one that would cement him in the legacy of our family forever if he managed to pull it off. But...the chance of success is so low... why would he...?" He sits back. "Ah. I see."

I sit down in front of him. "What do you mean? What has Santino done?"

He leans around me, looking at Hodges. "You will transfer me to a lower-security prison. And I want protection. A guard at all times."

"This isn't a negotiation," Hodges says. "You tell us what you know, and we'll see about getting you more privileges."

He holds up both hands. "Then I admit, we are at a standstill." He crosses his arms, looking not at the table, but past it, shaking his head and smiling, like he can't quite believe what he's realized.

"Here's a deal," I say, getting his attention again. "Right now, Santino has pointed the finger at *you*. Which means he may be willing to testify that you are behind all of these murders. And without any corroborating evidence and the fact you're already a convicted criminal, that's what we have to go with. *Someone* has to answer for what's happening out there. Now I'd rather know the truth and get the right person, but I'll take you if I have to."

"You cannot convict me. Not without evidence," he says.

I stare right into his soul. "Wanna bet?"

He must see the conviction in my eyes because he shies away for a moment, before coming to himself and attempts to reestablish his former posture. "I will not give away what I know for nothing."

"If that's how you want to play it," I say, standing. "But I have ten murders on my desk and I'm just itching to pin them to someone. You don't like solitary? Get ready for a lot more."

"*Pezzo di merda!*" he yells. "One day I will be out of this place. And on that day, I will remember you, Agent Slate."

"Mr. Toscani, there is no way you are *ever* leaving this prison unless you tell me what I want to know."

"There is an old saying in my family," he says, his teeth on full display. "It's always the one with the dirty hands pointing the fingers."

"What the hell does that mean?" Hodges asks.

"You're saying...Santino set himself up?" I ask.

"Do not underestimate my nephew, agent," Marco says. "I was in control of my family business for twenty years. I am not someone who is bested easily. But he was sly enough to send me to this Godforsaken place...and I never saw it coming. If I wasn't so disgusted, I would be impressed."

"Wait, so Santino is behind the killings?" Cervantes asks.

I try to work through the scenario in my head, but the lack of food is making it more difficult than usual. "He knew how it would look if everyone was attacked but him..." I say. "But instead of covering his tracks, he placed the blame on you." I point to Marco. "Why? It would have been much easier to just kill a couple of his guys, and no one would have been the wiser."

"It is because of him," Marco points to Hodges.

"Me?" Hodges asks, looking like a deer caught in the headlights.

"You started a line of communication with Marco," I say, "looking for a way to take the Toscanis down for good." I motion to Cervantes. "And you bought into it. Didn't you?" Cervantes's face flushes. "I was told this could be a prime opportunity." She doesn't look at Hodges as she says it. "We had a chance we might not get again."

"You were both working together," I say. *That* explains a lot. This whole thing has been a setup from the beginning, and Santino played all of us.

I turn back to Marco. "Santino got wind of it somehow. And he knew if you made a deal with the DA, you could do to him what he did to you. He needed a way to keep you in prison...for good."

"Very good, agent," Marco says. "You see now the duplicitousness with which he works."

"*That's* why he went into hiding," I say. "Not because he was running scared, but because he knew there would be fallout from his actions, and he needed to stay out of the limelight until everyone figured out Marco was behind it all."

"But he was the one who told us it was Marco," Cervantes says. "How was he planning on blaming him if he never intended to get caught?"

"*That* was the risk," Marco says. "He would have been counting on *you* to make the connection. He wanted to make it look too obvious that it could have been him."

Santino was planning on giving up his uncle *when* he got caught, not if. He must have figured it was a matter of time. "It's a nice story," I say. "But we need to find proof. We need Conrad Garza."

"If it were me," Marco says. "I would have made sure he's out of the country already." He holds both his hands up as if he's offering a suggestion. "Just a thought."

"He might be right," Cervantes says. "We need to check the airports. See if anyone matching his description has flown out since last week. It would explain why we can't find him."

I turn back to Marco. "You said you didn't expect us to find him. Then why give us the addresses?"

"I had nothing else to lose," he says, pointing to Hodges. "My work with this man had resulted in nothing for me. I hoped a fresh round of cooperation might buy me a little more freedom."

"We'll see about that," I say. "One of you is lying. And whoever it is can expect to find themselves here for a very long time."

Marco grins. "My nephew is clever, but he is not God. He also doesn't remember faces like I do." He nods to the phone in my hand. "Remember that when you question him again."

I motion to Danvers that we're done. Marco only stares at me as he's taken from the room. Once he's gone, I turn back to Cervantes. "It would have been helpful to know you two were working together."

"It wasn't exactly a formal arrangement," Hodges says. "I saw a potential benefit, and Agent Cervantes wanted another win."

"It was a chance to finish what we started with him," Cervantes says, motioning to the door. "To finally begin cleaning up this city."

"But you said yourself, no matter how much you do, someone else will always be there to fill the void." I sigh, unable to believe we have two potential suspects now. "We need to see if his story holds water. I'm not sure I'm ready to believe Santino would paint that large of a target on his back for a *gamble*."

"At least we still have him in custody," she says as we head out and back through security. Once we're back outside and I have service again, I dial Zara.

"Z, this is a lot more complicated than we thought. We

need to prep Santino for another round of questioning. And we need to find Conrad Garza, he's the key to this whole thing. Start checking the nearby airports. He might have picked up a flight somewhere."

"I'll get right on it," she says. "But Em, we're not going to be able to prep Santino."

"Why not?" I ask.

"Because his lawyer finally showed up. They just walked out of here about fifteen minutes ago."

Chapter Thirty

As MUCH AS I hate to admit it, I think we are royally screwed. Santino is in the wind, having expertly positioned himself to face no consequences for the raid this morning. And without Conrad Garza to back up one story or the other, we're at a standstill with Marco, who has been remanded back to his regular cell.

Cervantes and I make our way back to the office, but all I can think about is how both these men are attempting to manipulate us. And right now, either one of them could be behind these killings. Or hell, both of them for that matter. And I am getting tired of being used.

"Em, I had no idea…" Zara says as we head back into the office. Her face is a mess of anguish. "We didn't have a defense. The lawyer and the immunity papers—"

"I know, it's okay," I say. "There's nothing anyone could have done. We were in the middle of a communications blackout in the prison."

"I couldn't find any evidence that Marco has spoken to anyone other than few monitored calls he's made over the past few months. I checked the transcripts myself. No coded messages as far as I could find."

I slump down in a chair as Cervantes heads back to her office, not saying a word to anyone. "And I think we established making a call from a cell phone in the prison would have been...difficult." I nod in Cervantes's direction once she's out of earshot. "She and Hodges know each other. They were working together to take out the Toscanis once and for all."

Liam spots me as he comes through the common area, though he's already got his jacket on. "Hey, I was just...are you okay?"

I give him a weak smile. "Just...tired. And hungry."

"I was about to go back to check on Timber for a few minutes. Do you want me to pick anything up for you?"

"A cheeseburger would be wonderful," I say. "With a helping of fries *this* big." I hold my hands a good twelve inches apart.

"Make that two," Zara tells him.

He nods, giving us a quick salute. "Will do. I'll be back in an hour." He comes over and plants a quick kiss on the top of my head.

After he's gone, Zara slumps down beside me. "So now what?"

"No luck on finding Conrad Garza?"

She pinches her lips. "I'll have to check with Nadia. I had her and Elliott start working on that while I went over the phone calls. Buuuut...if they found something, I'm sure we'd know."

I lean my head back so it's up against the wall. "Yeah, probably. Santino says it's Marco. Marco says it's Santino. And the crazy thing is—either one of them could be right." I sit a little straighter. "Santino didn't happen to say where he was going, did he?"

"He wasn't in a talkative mood after his lawyer showed up," she replies.

"Now that we know the location of his safehouses it's

unlikely he'll head back there. With such a large target still on him, he wouldn't be stupid enough to go back to his regular home. So, where's he going to hide out until all this dies down?"

"*Will* it die down?" Zara asks. "Felix is convinced Santino is responsible for his son's death."

I have to admit, if all this *has* been a ploy by Santino, he may have seriously miscalculated the Lunas' response. By trying to implicate Marco, he might have inadvertently made himself a much bigger target.

"Even if we had a tag on him, it isn't like we could interrogate him again. With that immunity trick, he essentially gave himself a get out of jail free card." I sigh. "I should have pressed him harder when he was here."

"He manipulated us all," she says. "Plus, he's probably trying to get out of town as quickly as possible. At least, I would be if I knew I was being hunted by a maniac."

"Santino may have gambled, but whatever his original plan was, he's out in the world now." I lean forward, my elbows on my knees. "What do we know about Santino? What is he thinking?"

She gives me *the eyebrow.* "You seriously want to profile him right now?"

I shrug. "Got anything better to do?"

She takes a deep breath. "Okay. He's arrogant."

"Selfish."

"Misogynistic."

"A prick."

"Practical."

I point at her. "Yes. He's practical. A numbers man." I can't help but think about Wallace. "Why is it that all guys who deal in numbers tend to be assholes?"

"Because they can't relate to other people?" she suggests.

"Hey, ouch." I give her a smirk.

"You're different. You're not all judgy and dickish. I mean, we're all a little screwed up in our own way, right?" I see her eyes go distant for a second. "But that doesn't mean you're a bad person."

"Where did you go just now?" I ask. "Is everything okay?" She waves me off. "We're getting off-topic. The point is, he's analytical."

"Which means he probably has some elaborate backup plan for this contingency," I say, reserving the rest of that conversation for later.

"Or…" she says, thinking. "Maybe not."

"What do you mean?"

"His warehouse burned down, right? Wouldn't you be just the least bit curious if your place of business was destroyed? Wouldn't you at least want to look at it once?"

I frown. "Santino doesn't strike me as the sentimental type."

She shakes her head. "No. He'll be thinking about the insurance proceeds. But there's still something about seeing all your hard work…everything he's done. We know he's egotistical—"

"Definitely," I say.

"He might want to take one look. To see what this gamble has cost him."

"That's a big risk."

She shrugs. "People don't always do what's best for them." She's right. I stand, heading for Cervantes's office.

"Ma'am?"

She looks up from her desk. Gone is the nervous energy from before; it's as if the woman has completely deflated. In fact, she looks absolutely miserable. "We only wanted to get a win for once," she says before I can start. She's already making excuses for her actions. "Do you know how hard it is to fight back against these criminal enterprises? Exploiting every loophole, using every inch of the system to their advantage." She holds out one hand. "See? Already he's out and free in the world again. All because he knows how to work the system."

Even though I feel for her, especially since I was the one who convinced her she should drop the charges against Santino, we can't get bogged down by guilt. That's one thing I've learned about this job. "We've all made mistakes," I say. "But we're doing the best we can. We think we might know where Santino is headed."

"Where?" she asks.

"His old place of business," I say. "But we don't have long. It may be our last chance to nab him before he disappears forever."

Her eyes go wide. "*Shit.*" She gets up, grabbing her jacket. "I'll get a team together while we're on the way. Let's move."

"C'mon," I tell Zara as I follow Cervantes out. "We don't have a lot of time."

She stands, following along. "But what about the cheese-burgers?"

ZARA AND I ARE IN THE BACK OF CERVANTES'S TAHOE, calling in the operation and getting local law enforcement on site before we can. If Santino really is going back to his old warehouse, I don't want to lose him. Meanwhile, Cervantes is pushing the pedal to metal, getting us there as quickly as possible. The odds we'll catch up with Santino before he disappears are small, but I believe Zara is correct. I think the desire to look would be too strong for anyone as egotistical as him to ignore.

I just hope we're not too late.

Coordinating with the LEOs, they get a couple of black and white's close to the warehouse, but I tell them to keep their distance. I don't want Santino seeing the police and flee-ing…*if* our theory is correct. I want to make sure they cut off any escape paths. It only takes us about fifteen minutes to get to the warehouse district from downtown, and Cervantes gives an acknowledging wave to an officer as we pass about two blocks out from Santino's warehouse.

My hope is that if he's there, we can make this quick. I've decided the best way to go about this is to bring him in on the charges based on the information we obtained from Marco. Then I'll let their lawyers fight it out. But I'd much rather know where Santino Toscani is at all times than let him loose in the world again. If he really is behind this, he's done an immense amount of damage.

The lot that once housed Santino's warehouse is still mostly blocked by police barriers from last night. The building's skeleton is still there, but the roof is completely gone, and there are massive scorch marks on the sides of the aluminum frame. I can see the steel trusses are still in place, though a few have collapsed. The back half of the building has completely caved in. A building I was just in not more than a week ago.

However, some of the police barriers around the front gate have been knocked to the side, making a hole large enough for a vehicle to pass. Cervantes takes it slow, driving into the parking lot that last night had been full of fire trucks and emergency vehicles.

"Hey," Zara says, elbowing me. "Look."

Parked off to the west side of the building, just barely visible from our vantage point, is what looks like a brand-new Mercedes. "Was his lawyer driving a Mercedes?"

"Probably," Zara says. "It fits."

Cervantes pulls the vehicle to a stop and kills the engine. "No surprises. We get him back into custody, and that's it."

Both Zara and I nod. "If he's in there, we're going to have to be extremely careful," I say. "The structure has been compromised. I'd rather not go inside if we don't have to."

"We can't possibly cover all the escape routes," Zara says.

Looking at the building, she's right. "We'll check the car first, then head in if we have to."

The three of us exit the vehicle, careful to not slam our doors. Despite being in the middle of the city, it's eerily quiet out here. It's as if the aftermath of the fire has sucked all the sound out of the area, and there's nothing left but silence.

We make our way over to the Mercedes to find it unlocked but without anyone inside. While I can understand Santino may have wanted to come to see the damage for himself, I can't believe he would actually want to go *inside*.

Unless there was something in there he wanted. Something he was sure wasn't destroyed in the fire. He's here for more than just a look.

"Stay here," I tell Cervantes.

"I'm the senior officer," she says, "and it's my screw up. I should be the one going in."

"Zara and I have been in here more than a few times. We know our way around," I tell her. "It makes more sense for us to go."

She winces, but finally nods. I motion to Zara. "Let's just take it slow. No sudden moves and keep an exit in view at all times. If something looks like it's unstable or about to fall, we get out."

"No sweat. Just navigate a maze of sharp and deadly objects without triggering a collapse. Got it."

"And yell if you find him," I say.

"Are you crazy?" she asks. "Haven't you ever seen an avalanche movie?"

"Good point. Maybe just…"

"Call you?" she suggests.

I smile. "Yeah, that'll work." She shoots me a signature Zara look before heading to the main entrance where the offices were located. They're in a smaller section of the warehouse near the front with a lower ceiling. Meanwhile, I make my way over to the loading dock where all the trucks would park their trailers for loading and unloading. All the trailers have been removed by the police, at least those that weren't caught in the fire, and most are sitting about twenty to fifty feet away, still open and awaiting their goods.

The rolling garage doors to the loading dock have either been destroyed or removed in the fire-fighting process, so it's easy to get inside. But once I'm in, it very much is a maze. The floor of the loading dock is full of soaked equipment that's either half burned already or completely destroyed. Light floods in from the open ceiling, giving the area a spooky, abandoned sort of vibe. I'm reminded of an abandoned church, with its high ceilings and light that reaches into places it hasn't been allowed for a very long time.

At the far end of the warehouse, where a lot of the machinery and equipment for assembling Toscani's HVAC systems was located, the back wall has collapsed, creating what looks to be an impassable section of the building.

I sure hope he didn't go back there.

Making my way around the equipment, I listen for any sounds of life or movement, but there's nothing. When I reach an area where a stack of crates has collapsed on its side, I'm forced to climb over or go back. I decide climbing over is the quicker option as I'm getting antsy. Where is Toscani? More than likely he's on the far east side of the building, where his office used to be. But getting there is easier said than done.

As I get to the top of the crates, I get a better view of the entire building. Strangely, out past the collapsed back wall I spot a black SUV. It's too far away to make out clearly, but it looks like Cervantes might have pulled her car around the back of the building, though I don't know why. Just as I'm about to send her a text, I catch the sound of movement ahead of me.

I slowly climb down the stack of crates, then creep forward, inching toward the metal stairs that lead to the office overlooking the production floor. I'm not thrilled about needing to climb the stairs, but it makes sense Toscani would be up here. If he needed something out of this place, this is where it would be.

As soon as I reach the top, I catch movement directly ahead of me in the charred office portion. The walls are completely black, and all the wooden components have splintered and burned.

And there, in the middle of the room beside a ruined desk, is Toscani, shoving a crowbar into one of the walls.

"Santino," I say, sighting him with my weapon. "Put it down."

Chapter Thirty-One

SANTINO LOOKS UP, amusement on his face. "You *have* to be kidding me," he says, though he hasn't dropped the crowbar.

"You heard me," I tell him. "Put it down. And let me see your hands."

He chuckles, shaking his head. "You know what, Agent Slate? You are a real pain in my ass."

"Good," I tell him. "Crowbar. Now. I won't ask again."

He sighs, and deliberately puts the crowbar to the side, raising his hands. "Fine. I'll go quietly. But I'd really like to know, what exactly are you doing here?"

"Santino Toscani, you are under arrest for suspicion of conspiracy and murder," I tell him. "Your uncle—"

He laughs before I can finish. "You believe anything that crazy old man has to say? I thought we already went through this. In fact, I remember signing an immunity agreement. I believe my lawyer has a copy."

"Immunity from trafficking illegal goods. Not conspiracy to carry out the murders of rivals from other criminal enterprises," I say.

"Agent Slate, you can't be this stupid," he says. "My uncle—"

"Remembers you and Conrad…or *Dominic* were old high school friends. That you two were always getting into trouble together. That he's never worked with that man in his life. And that you sent him to us in an attempt to frame him."

Something crosses Santino's face. "Frame him? By what? Telling Garza to blame me? How does that work?"

"Considering you told us Garza worked for your uncle under another name, then it would only lend credence to the theory he was the one who set you up," I tell him. "But let's try a different theory, shall we? You found out your uncle was working with the feds to disrupt your operation. You knew eventually he'd make enough deals to get a reduced sentence or get out entirely. And you couldn't have that—after all, where would that leave you? You figured the best way to keep him in prison was to make it look like he orchestrated all these hits, for him to shoulder the blame. But the only way to make it convincing was to leave yourself off the hit list. That way everyone would assume someone else set you up." I glare at him. "It's like you said, who would think you're *stupid enough* not to go after yourself?"

He grits his teeth. "That's a big risk."

I nod. "One that if it paid off, would get Marco out of your hair forever while at the same time hurting and obtaining a large amount of goods from your enemies. The same enemies you had to go crawling to, asking for leniency when you were trying to save the Toscanis from destruction. Something that would have been humiliating—and you would want revenge for."

"It's a fine theory, Agent Slate. Too bad you don't have any evidence to prove it," he says.

I smile. "Once we find Conrad Garza—"

"*If* you find him."

"—then we'll know who was really behind this."

He sighs but keeps his hands up. "My lawyer is right downstairs. I'm sure he'll have these charges cleared before you can even get me in the back of your vehicle. All you're doing is wasting your time."

"Let's find out," I say and motion for him to turn around. He does and I approach cautiously, cuffing one hand and then the other behind his back. It doesn't escape my notice how badly the floor creaks under me as I walk through the place. There's no way the floor is stable.

"Careful, agent. Hope you haven't been binge eating in between your harassments."

"Shut up and stay still." I holster my gun and turn him around, leading him to the door. The floorboards continue to crack and creak and each one sounds like a gunshot going off. I try not to think about it as I lead him along. "What were you looking for here anyway? What's worth risking your life over?"

"You wouldn't understand," Santino says.

"Try me."

"An old watch, my father's. It's still in the fireproof safe back there. Piece of crap, really. But it was the last thing he gave me before he died. I wanted——" He stops short, and I almost run into him, until I peer around him and my eyes go wide.

In front of us stands Felix, a large pistol in his hand, and his face raging like fire. He's in the doorway, blocking our exit. "*Hijo de la fregada*," the man spits.

"Felix," I say, slowly moving around Santino. I need to get in front of him, but Felix turns the gun on me, and I stop roughly right beside Santino. "Don't do this."

He turns his attention back on Santino. "You come to us in peace…a truce, you say. And all the while you were nothing but a snake in the grass. Just like your uncle."

"No!" Santino says, though he can't exactly put his hands up considering they're cuffed. "My uncle did this! He did this to all of you. He deliberately made it look like I was the only one that wasn't hurt. If I attacked all of you, I'd be smart enough to attack myself too."

Felix furrows his brow, but I can see the resolve on his face. He came here to kill Santino, and he's not leaving until he does. "It matters not," he says. "You are alike. My son is dead and Toscanis are responsible." His face twists into a rage, and I see it all happen in slow motion. I shove Santino to the side just as Felix pulls the trigger. The shot is like a cannon. In an instant I have my weapon out and I fire twice at Felix, both are good hits. His face goes blank for a second before he stumbles, toppling and falling backward down the stairs.

I look over at Santino who is on the floor, bleeding from the shoulder. I bend down to try and help him, only to hear the floor crack one more time. Santino's impact from his fall might have—

Before I know it, I'm weightless. The world flying up around me until I land, hard, on a carpeted floor. My gun is somewhere, but at the moment I'm more concerned with making sure I didn't impale myself on something. Thankfully, the area under the upstairs office was little more than additional offices that didn't seem to catch the brunt of the fire.

I look over to see Santino has landed on someone's desk and I rush over to him, checking him for additional injuries. He's moaning as blood continues to gush from his shoulder.

"Dammit," I say, and fumble for the key to his cuffs, getting them unlocked so I can get a better look at the wound. It looks to me like the bullet might have gone through. If I hadn't pushed him away, it probably would have pierced his heart.

Santino screams out as I put pressure on the wound.

"I'm no doctor, but I don't think this is fatal," I say.

"Why—why didn't he understand?" Santino says, though I think he's a little loopy. "I never would have made it that...obvious."

"That's the problem when you craft an elaborate and overcomplicated plan," I tell him. "Someone might not get it." I look over as Zara comes rushing into the office.

"I heard the shots," she says. "Are you okay?"

I nod. "But he's not. Bullet to the shoulder."

"Paramedics are on the way. Cervantes called them in. His lawyer was up front, I left him with her. We can technically charge him with trespassing."

I pull off my blazer and fold it over Santino's wound, then grab his hand and press it down. He cries out again. "Hold it there, hard."

"Did he confess?" Zara asks.

"Not really," I say. I'm reasonably sure Santino's frustration at Felix's response was genuine. He seemed more upset that Felix thought he could actually be behind the killings than being shot. "Here, stay with him a second." I spot my gun beside an overturned water cooler and I grab it, heading out of the office area. I round what debris is out in the floor until I come to the stairs again, finding Felix crumpled up at the bottom. His eyes are open, but his neck is at the wrong angle. There's a look of surprise on his face, as if he can't believe these were his last moments. I check for a pulse, but there is none.

If my bullets didn't kill him, the fall most certainly did.

"Everything okay?" Zara asks when I come back in. She's helping Santino keep pressure on the wound. In the distance I hear the approaching sirens.

"Let's just get him help before he bleeds out."

WE STAY WITH SANTINO UNTIL THE PARAMEDICS ARRIVE, BUT even as they're about to escort him away, I don't let the man out of my sight. He's not pulling another Houdini on me, especially now that I finally think I know who is behind all of this.

The other reason I want to stay with him is because if Felix was able to find him, it's possible the Dragons, the Kings, or the Aryans will be able to as well. And we don't need any more attempts on his life, not until I can get him in an interrogation room again.

We manage to get him safely to the hospital, and I end up posting a full-time guard of two agents outside his doors at all times. They are not to let him out of their sights.

As we're leaving, we pass Santino's lawyer, who looks somewhat shaken at the events. Zara told me on the way over that she found him going through some of the desks in the front offices, though she has no idea what he was looking for. Whatever it was, he seemed guilty when she caught him. The trespassing charge is pretty weak and probably won't hold up, so we ended up dropping it in favor of sticking with Santino. But to see his lawyer now, I'm not sure he's realized the extent to what he's gotten himself into. His client is in for it.

As soon as Zara and I make it back to the office, Liam greets me with a hug and—more importantly—what looks like a ton of food.

"Oh, you are a saint," I tell him, going straight for the first burger I see in the box. It's gone in under a minute and I look up to see a slightly horrified look on Liam's face. "Don't pretend like you haven't seen it before."

"I'm just glad I didn't hand it to you," he says, grinning. "I might not have gotten all my fingers back."

"Very funny." I'm so famished I don't even care. I'm just glad to have Santino back in custody. And knowing we'll have another go at him before he can disappear has eased my conscience. Thankfully Zara was right, and Santino was a bit more sentimental than I'd given him credit for.

"I spoke with the fire chief," Liam says. "He told me that, when they were fighting the fire last night, they found what looked like melted gold bars running down one of the walls. Apparently, the fire had broken through that safe Santino was trying to get in and melted everything inside. He said they removed them from the scene and added them to the evidence locker."

I can't help but shake my head. "A liar to the end," I say.

"Makes sense," Zara says, her mouth full of fries. "Why else risk going in there?"

Before I can answer my phone buzzes in my pocket. I fish it out, getting salt all over the front. "Slate."

"Agent Slate, this is Doctor Jameson from down at the medical examiner's building. Do you remember me?"

"I do," I say. I worked with him on the Jaden Peters case. "How are you?"

"Good. I have a note here to call you when we're done with the preliminary autopsy on Felix Moscada? Is there anything in particular you're looking for?"

"Just looking for cause of death," I say.

"Oh, I can tell you now it will be the neck injury. He didn't have enough time to bleed out from the gunshot wounds."

"Oh, okay," I say. "Thank you."

"Is there anything else?" he asks.

"No, that's...that's all I needed."

"Have a good day, Agent Slate." He ends the call. I think about taking another bite of my burger, but I set it down.

"Who was that?" Liam asks.

"Medical examiner. Felix died from a neck fracture due to his fall."

"That's good news," Zara says.

"Yeah," I reply, though that does little to assuage my guilt. The fact is I still killed a man. Or...my actions led to his death. Self-defense or not, it's a big deal. And one way or the other, I'll have to turn in my weapon for the standard IA investigation. I really bet they're starting to love me down there.

"Hey, what else were you going to do, let him shoot you both?" Liam asks, rubbing my leg.

"No, it's just…it's never easy. There are some parts of this job I never get used to."

"I think that goes for all of us," Zara says, heaping more fries into her mouth.

She's right. We've all had to face the hard decisions.

Just as I'm about to pick up the burger again, determined this time to take a bite, Nadia comes running up. "You guys are going to *love* me. Oh, hey. Cheeseburgers."

"What?" I ask. "What's going on?"

She smiles, taking her focus off the food. "Guess who I found?"

Chapter Thirty-Two

"GARY BRYAN," I say slapping the file down on Cervantes's desk.

She looks up. "Who?"

Zara and I have come in to make our final report. Even though Agent Cervantes wasn't completely honest with us about her original intentions, this is still her case. "Otherwise known as Conrad Garza. One alias of several he's been using the last four years working odd jobs for Santino Toscani. Also known as Jesse Sims, Pete Jackson, and Dominic Russo."

She picks up the file, flipping through all the information Nadia and Elliott uncovered. Apparently when Nadia sets her mind to something, she doesn't give up until she's accomplished her goal. She ended up going through every face and record in not only the local airports, but also the municipal bus stations, the train depots and even the local car rental services. She found Garza—or Bryan, his real name, getting on a bus headed to St. Louis four days ago. Once she had him pinned, it was easy enough for the St. Louis police to pick him up and ship him back to us.

"You've already spoken with him?"

I nod. "Turns out he's not addicted, as we were led to

believe. That was apparently a ruse to throw us off and make us question it just enough." She looks up at me with concern. "From what Nadia gathered, he's a former theater major who has remained friends with Santino, while enjoying a lavish and lush lifestyle as a result of that friendship."

She continues flipping through the file. "He had me fooled. Is he willing to testify?"

"Considering he's never been to prison before, he flipped quickly. Confirmed that Santino had set the whole thing up. And he's willing to go before a grand jury."

She scoffs. "Hodges will be happy."

Zara sets another folder down on her desk. "We just finished another round with Santino. He's willing to sign a confession in exchange for leniency."

She looks up at us with surprise. "A *confession?*"

Zara grins. "Apparently Felix showing up made him realize his gamble hadn't paid off. The thought of more crime bosses hunting him down seemed to help motivate this new, more contrite Santino. He thinks he'll be safe in prison. That, and we told him about Gary Bryan." She gives me a satisfied look. "*And* he's identified his accomplices. Expats from Kazan, a pair of twins and their little sister. Apparently, the sister is the one who has been doing most of the killing. Trained by the SVR out of Moscow. He's willing to give them up, but he has a…request."

Really it was more of a demand, Zara is just being diplomatic.

She arches an eyebrow. "What?"

"That he's placed in a private security prison and is never transferred to JCI."

She leans back, smiling. "So he never has to see his uncle again. I'm sure we can work that out. I guess there was a threat from the Russians after all."

"Javier's intel wasn't wrong," I say. "He just didn't realize they were working for Toscani this whole time."

"I guess it's a good thing I brought you two in. Your reputations were deserved." she says, though she doesn't look as happy as I expected her to be.

"Did we miss something?" I ask.

"Toscani might be out of the picture, but everything else is in anarchy. His people are in the wind, the Lunas are on the brink of their own civil war over who will control the enterprise from here on, I've got two different agencies breathing down my neck because they relied on that relationship with Felix, not to mention all the other damage done to the other organizations. It's just turned everything into chaos. And chaos is impossible to predict."

"It's not an easy job to manage," I say.

"No, it's not. Even if Felix were still alive, he'd be impossible to manage any longer. The loss of his son…" she trails off, holding up her hands. "Regardless. You did the job I needed you to do. Thank you…for looking past some of my missteps."

"We all made them," I say. "None of us is perfect."

"I'll make sure to send my praise up the chain," she says. "Your new SAC will be pleased, I'm sure."

I furrow my brow, turning to Zara who looks as confused as I am. "We have a new SAC?"

"Oh, I don't know all the details," she replies. "I just know Wallace is—" she stops herself. "I've learned better than to make assumptions by this point. I'm sure you'll be informed shortly." She stands, shaking each of our hands in turn. "Excellent work. Thank you."

We thank her again, then leave the office, both of us still exchanging looks as we head out into the bullpen. It's late in the evening, and everything is quiet as most agents have gone home for the night.

"What did she mean by that?" Zara asks. "Is Wallace out for good? What did Janice say?"

As far as I know, she's still heading up the investigation

into the car fire outside my apartment. Everything is still in analysis, so I haven't spoken to her in a few days. "I—"

"Agents." I look over to see Janice approaching us, a stern look locked on her face.

"Ma'am," I say, still thrown by what Cervantes told us.

"Slate, follow me," she says. Zara ushers me on and I follow Janice to the elevator bank. We wait in silence until the doors open. She steps inside first and I follow, though I wait for the doors to close before saying anything.

"Is this about the car?" I ask. "Did you identify the body?"

"Not yet. DNA is taking a while due to the condition of the corpse. We don't have any ID on the owner of the vehicle yet, either."

"Then what exactly—"

"Patience." I know when to shut up, though that isn't often. The elevator stops on the second to top floor and we get off, headed down a corridor to my left. Large offices occupy this part of the building and Janice leads me into hers, which I've never seen since she was promoted.

It's much like her last office, just larger and with nicer amenities. Her desk looks like it could be the sister of the resolute desk, and her chairs are a dark green leather. There's also a couch on one side of the room across from a large bookshelf that takes up the majority of the wall space. A large picture window looks out on the city.

Janice rounds her desk and takes a seat, pulling a vape pen from one of her desk drawers. She gives it a puff or two as I take a seat across from her.

"I wanted to let you know, as of this morning, I've dismissed SAC Wallace."

My eyes go wide. She actually did it. "On what grounds?"

"We agreed to call it a difference in command structure," she says. "Your department is being reorganized. Something that should have happened three months ago, but given the upheaval, the Bureau was trying to keep the blowback to a minimum." She reaches into her desk and pulls out a file folder. "As I told you, I would handle it."

"What's that?"

"My workup. On Fletcher Wallace."

I look up. "No way he was dirty."

"Thankfully, no. But when I looked back at his behavior these past few months, I saw a pattern emerge. One which lined up with your activities."

"What do you mean?"

"You are, I'm sure, aware that Wallace wished to have you transferred before the events surrounding Deputy Director Cochrane."

"He made that much absolutely clear," I say, remembering just how antagonistic he was towards me when he first took up the position.

"Based on my research, it looks like that desire never quite disappeared. I went back through all his notes regarding your cases. Things were relatively calm until the bombings in Baltimore, Philadelphia, and New York. After you helped capture Simon Magus and expose his infiltration into the ATF unit, Wallace was humiliated. Your next assignment, the investigation into 'paranormal' activity in Louisiana, was a deliberate set-up. You were supposed to fail."

"What?" I ask.

"He had caught wind of the case through the grapevine and was looking for a way to humiliate you back. He figured such a ridiculous case could never be solved and that it would be a black mark on your record." She takes another puff, smiling. "I think he underestimated you."

"So when I called, asking for assistance in Stillwater a few weeks ago—"

"He denied you, knowing that it would only serve to prop up your status. He had hoped that by denying the request, you wouldn't have the resources to succeed."

I'm gob smacked, unable to speak for a moment. "How do you know all this?"

"Because he admitted it. When I confronted him about the erratic behavior, he had no valid excuse. And when I put the pressure on him, he finally cracked. He admitted to me that he had been afraid from day one that you would be the one to take his job. He had hoped that by tarnishing your star a bit, he'd be more likely to stay in the position longer."

"You have got to be shitting me," I say, thinking back all those months ago. I remember poor Detective Rodriguez suggesting he might be intimidated by me, and she'd never met the man. I just didn't realize he was that insecure.

"At any rate, he agreed to resign rather than face formal charges for discrimination in the workplace," she says. "He'll have a difficult time getting a job with a security clearance again."

Wow. Wallace gone, just like that. I take a deep breath, feeling the weight slip off my shoulders. "I think I'm going to need a session with Doctor Frost after this."

"I don't doubt it," she says. "In the meantime…reorganization. This means we're changing things up in Violent Crimes. The first order of business is setting up smaller units that will be able to handle specific types of cases. Since you've been on something of a roll lately and have more experience in this area than anyone, I'm promoting you to supervisory special agent and you'll have a team working under you. You'll be one of five new SSAs in the department, all of which will report to a new supervisor, who has yet to be named."

"Wait a second," I say. "I'm getting a *promotion?*"

"It comes with a pay increase, but you get more paperwork. So…" She shrugs. "Nature of the beast."

"What sorts of cases—"

"The kind you're already working. The hard nuts to crack. Cases that seem like they have no answer. Your instincts have already proven correct on more than one occasion. And I believe that you would do well as a supervisor."

"Do I get to pick my team?" I ask.

"I should say no," she replies. "But I know there are certain agents you work with better than others. As much as I don't want to admit it."

I can't believe this. It's almost too much to handle. "Thank you," I say after fumbling over my words for a moment. "Really, thank you."

"Don't thank me yet," she says, standing, and I stand as well. "The general feeling upstairs is that this is a better allocation of resources. I already know you will do well." She reaches out and I shake her hand, trying to contain my excitement. "And I will let you know the minute we have something on that body."

I leave her office, almost brimming with energy. I thought snagging a confession out of Santino had been a high, but it's nothing like this. For some odd reason I'd never really seen myself as anything else other than a special agent. I've never thought about a promotion beyond my current position, probably because I love doing the job so much already.

Wow, Zara is going to *freak out*. She's also going to be my first choice. Janice knows that; hell, everyone knows that. And Liam...oh, I need to call Liam. I dial his number while I'm in the elevator.

"Hey," he says. "How'd it go?"

"What? Oh! The interrogation...really great," I say, having already forgotten about it. "But I've got amazing news. I..." I pause.

"What is it?" he asks. "The car? They found something?"

"No," I say reconsidering. "I think it's better I tell you in person. I'm coming home right now. But get ready to celebrate. This is big."

"Like, how big?" he asks.

"*Big.*"

I can already hear the smile in his voice. "Alright Ms. Slate, you got it. I'll head out and grab something delicious. Considering the house is still empty." Unfortunately, the Santino case has taken most, if not all of everyone's time, including Liam's. We've been living out of our suitcases for the past few days in our new place. But Timber has already fallen in love with all the extra room. We agreed we'd finally unpack the truck once all this was over, and if I get my way, that will be first thing in the morning. I can't think of any better way to start our new life together.

"Okay, see you in a bit," I say. "Love you."

"I love you too."

I run by the office to see if Zara is still here, but it looks like she's already left for the night. I don't blame her, sometimes meetings with Janice can drag and she probably didn't want to wait around. I'll tell her first thing tomorrow. I'd love to get a little placard printed up to put on my desk before she gets into work. The look on her face will be priceless.

When I reach the basement where my car is parked, all my thoughts are on the possibilities. What kinds of cases will we work? Will they be cold cases, or ongoing unsolved mysteries? I wonder what our range will be and how much autonomy we'll have. I back out of my spot and leave the garage thinking Janice was probably right, it *is* going to be a lot of paperwork. But right now, I couldn't care less.

As I'm driving, my mind is alight with all the decisions I'll need to make. Who else can I put on my team? And would it be weird if Liam was working under me? I'll have to ask if that's even allowed. Already this feels like a challenge—the good kind. And I have to admit, I'm excited for what's to come.

Almost before I see her out of the corner of my eye, I *sense* her.

When I look, the figure appears to my right, running in my direction. I slam on the breaks and swerve, but it's not

Where did it all go wrong for Emily?

I HOPE YOU ENJOYED *TIES THAT BIND*. IF YOU'D LIKE TO LEARN more about Emily's backstory and what happened in the days following her husband's unfortunate death, including what almost got her kicked out of the FBI, then you're in luck! *Her Last Shot* introduces Emily and tells the story of the case that almost ended her career. Interested? CLICK HERE to get your free copy now!

Not Available Anywhere Else!

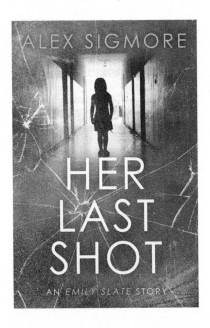

You'll also be the first to know when each book in the Emily Slate series is available!

CLICK HERE or scan the code below to download for FREE!

The Emily Slate FBI Mystery Series

Free Prequel - Her Last Shot (Emily Slate Bonus Story)

His Perfect Crime - (Emily Slate Series Book One)

The Collection Girls - (Emily Slate Series Book Two)

Smoke and Ashes - (Emily Slate Series Book Three)

Her Final Words - (Emily Slate Series Book Four)

Can't Miss Her - (Emily Slate Series Book Five)

The Lost Daughter - (Emily Slate Series Book Six)

The Secret Seven - (Emily Slate Series Book Seven)

A Liar's Grave - (Emily Slate Series Book Eight)

Oh What Fun - (Emily Slate Holiday Special)

The Girl in the Wall - (Emily Slate Series Book Nine)

His Final Act - (Emily Slate Series Book Ten)

The Vanishing Eyes - (Emily Slate Series Book Eleven)

Edge of the Woods - (Emily Slate Series Book Twelve)

Ties That Bind - (Emily Slate Series Book Thirteen)

Coming Soon!

The Missing Bones - (Emily Slate Series Book Fourteen)

The Ivy Bishop Mystery Thriller Series

Free Prequel - Bishop's Edge (Ivy Bishop Bonus Story)

Her Dark Secret - (Ivy Bishop Series Book One)

A Note from Alex

Hi there!

I hope you enjoyed diving into the seedy underworld of drugs, guns and money along with Emily and Zara! One of the best parts about writing books like these is the ability to explore worlds I'd never be able to venture into in real life! Though I'm sure if Emily was by my side, I'd be able to drum up the courage.

There's only one more book left in "season two" of Emily's story, so make sure you don't miss out on the next chapter! All the answers you've been dying for will be revealed soon!

In the meantime, keep an eye out for a brand new series I'm writing about a down-on-her-luck cop who lives in Western Oregon. It's called the Ivy Bishop Mystery Thriller series and I hope you'll love Ivy just as much as you have Emily and the gang.

And as always, if you haven't already, please take a moment to leave a review or recommend this series to a fellow book lover. It really helps me as a writer and is the best way to make sure there are plenty more *Emily Slate* books in the future.

As always, thank you for being a loyal reader,

Alex

Made in the USA
Middletown, DE
02 May 2024